ONE MAN /

# INTO THE ALTER

ONE MAN / TWO WORLDS

# INTO THE ALTER

MATTHEW J. SEATON

ALTERBOOKS.COM

ISBN: 978-1-7357358-1-8

Editor: Tim Marquitz

Cover design, illustration & interior formatting:
Mark Thomas / Coverness.com

*For Elektra*

# PART 1

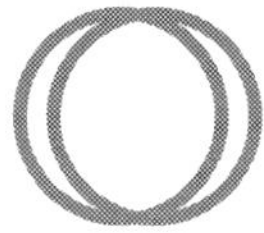

# PROLOGUE

"Sweet dreams, Mr. Grady."

The chamber door screeches as the rubber seals interlock, entombing my naked body.

The man in charge of the lab coats has a rather enigmatic look. He could have been transported out of an old 1970s sitcom. Brown curly hair sits on top of his head in a perfect globe-like sphere. His almond eyes, which open mere millimeters, still manage to pierce through me. He reaches down, grabs ahold of the chamber latch, turns it, and with a loud mechanical *click*, it locks.

The voice in the corner of my mind chastises, *what have you done?* And with that, I question everything. Is this my chance for a new beginning or the day of reckoning? Some would say I have the perfect life and perhaps a few weeks ago, I would have agreed. Life is all about choices. The choices you make bring you closer to things or further away. All you have in life are your choices. I chose this, but did I choose wisely, or did I simply react to my grief again?

I lie here naked and afraid. Doubt slithers in, and I realize my life will never be the same again, but more importantly, *their* lives will never be the same again. My heart pounds, and my breath shallows when I think about all that has led me here.

I hear running water, and I'm bounced back into the moment. I peer down at my feet and observe the chamber filling with liquid. It is a clear, water-like substance, however more viscous, and I note it's nearly a gel-like consistency as a glop runs down the side of my foot. In a matter of seconds, my shoulders submerge and, ironically, it isn't warm, nor is it cold for that matter. It is exactly 98.7 degrees Fahrenheit, matching the human body temperature and infused with small bubbles, like carbonation, that tickle me as they explode on my bare skin.

The liquid covers my abdomen, which sits before me like a bowl of jelly, independent of the rest of my body. I have really let myself go. I have a tendency to eat myself through my depression which, in the end, only creates more depression, a deadly cycle of abuse and self-pity.

It fills past my ears, and I panic. My eyes dart back and forth, and I try to make eye contact with one of the lab coats, but that damn Brillo pad has his back turned to me, slamming away at his keyboard.

"Hey! Hey! help!" I shout, but my attempts are useless.

I recall reading that the chambers are soundproofed to prevent external noise contamination until the unit registers I have woken. I wish I had read that damn pamphlet more thoroughly. Perhaps then I would know what to expect next.

The liquid covers my eyes, and I lift my chin higher, trying to take as many breaths as I can manage. Did they forget to turn it off? I'm going to drown in here! When the liquid reaches my lips, I extend a few millimeters more and take in one final, penetrating breath.

I hold it so long I feel my face turn red. My eyes pop open and bulge from their sockets. I kick and stomp at the hatch to get their attention when a woman with a broad smile hangs over me and signals for me to breathe. Unable to hold my breath any longer, anyway, I gasp and feel the liquid rush into my mouth.

I choke as it runs down my throat. It rushes into my chest, and I feel it coat my lungs. With a gulp, a large bubble releases to the top of the chamber. I can breathe! Not only can I breathe, but it feels like the bubbles are breathing for me. I feel weightless. I'm floating.

Just as I am adapting to my ability to breathe in this substance, a rush, like cold metal, pours into my veins, and I notice they are now closely monitoring my vitals. I wonder why, but only for a moment. I see a nurse injecting a green liquid into my IV.

It hurts! It burns! I can feel every micrometer as it branches out through my vascular system. My ears unexpectedly pop as if descending from a mountain. My hearing intensifies, sending the EKG machine's continuous *beep* bouncing through my skull as though it's a pinball machine.

A shockwave pushes through my body. My muscles flex in pairs, and up and down my body it travels. Muscles I didn't even know I had, contract and release, sending electricity, jolting up and down my spinal cord. I presume this may be the Aqua-tens I was warned about and it is remarkably uncomfortable.

Suddenly, with extreme clarity, I realize this is all wrong! My anxiety soars, and I watch my heart rate and blood pressure climb. The alarms sound, and their attention is now drawn to their machines, and the Brillo pad slams away at his keyboard ferociously.

The speaker inside of my chamber activates with a loud, piercing squeal, "Everything is alright, Dylan. Mr. Grady, please try to relax! It will all be over soon."

I holler, "I've changed my mind," but my lips don't move. My voice can only be heard, echoing regret within my head. The man's face remains above me with a look of distress, and I understand there is no turning back now. My choice is forever solidified a mistake. They don't deserve this.

My chest tightens. The lights outside my chamber, like those seen in an operating suite, intensify, blinding me and sending my eyes to the back of my skull. In flashes, I am launched into glimpses of the world that lies ahead, but first, I am forced to revisit the horrific drama that led me here. Vivid pictures dart across my eyes, and the pain, both physical and emotional, shudder through me.

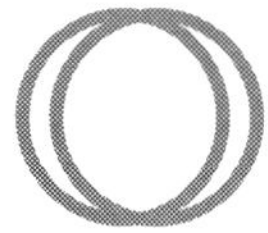

# CHAPTER 1

Life will extend you its hand and, at times, it will reach out and smack you across your face. As we age, we live several lives, and the vision of who you once were blurs and, in some cases, we appear to be another person entirely, another life viewed through a looking glass.

Through love, achievement, death, and divorce, we morph, and each contribute or take away from who we once were. I have often wondered if we are molded like clay or a rock chipped away until nothing is left because the darkest moments in our lives often affect the outcome most, sending our lives into a spiral.

"Hey, Daddy?"

"What's up, Annabel Bear?" I say.

Although she nears thirteen, I still call her by the pet name I knew she adored as a toddler. After all, she will always be Annabel Bear to me. I still miss her little voice calling me Daddy. I hear it whispering in the wind or in my dreams, tickling my eardrums when I walk in the park. My children have always been my favorite pastime. They are my stress ball. They have a profound effect on me and, in many ways, my happiness is reliant on theirs.

"Mom… Well, Mom says you cheated on her and hit her, and that's why you got a divorce."

I couldn't abstain from rolling my eyes and, with a snicker, I bury my head into my hands. Corina has always been in our children's ears, marking me the villain, attempting to alienate me from them every chance she gets. She has claimed many things over the years.

She accused me of adultery, and one would think that would explain her scorn but, the truth is, I never cheated on her. Well, perhaps I *did*, although not in the traditional sense. I often daydreamed of a life with a woman who would treat me as I deserved to be treated. Corina was a miserable person to be around. I became distant and short-tempered. She suffocated me with her negativity.

I often imagined what life would have been like if I had never married her. I thought back to the man I used to be. I wasn't the negative person I became under Corina's rule. I used to be a free spirit with so much love and ambition, fearless and stress free, but after I married her, I slowly shed into a shell of my former self. Sadly, I resent her. I understood returning to the man of my youth was not possible so long as she remained in control.

I lift my head from my hands and drag my hands down my face, pulling my eyelids down and exposing the underside of my eyes.

"I'm sorry, Daddy," Annabel says, looking away to the corner of the room where only awkward eyes wander.

"No, no, don't be sorry, sweetie." I sigh, thinking about what to say next. "But that's simply not true. Listen, I moved on quickly, and perhaps that may have been suspicious to your mother but understand that she and I had problems for years before we separated. Trust me when I tell you everyone is better off that Mommy and Daddy didn't remain married."

If Corina and I remained together, the stress would have killed me far before my time. She put an enormous amount of pressure on me. Nothing was ever good enough for her, and I would have continued down a path of misery and malcontent. The long hours I put in at work were for our family. I worked my ass off for our future to provide the life I knew she and I both wanted for our children.

Divorce was not in the plan, but perhaps it should have been long before there was a plan at all. I loved Corina, but not as a man should love his wife. I was her puppet, and when she didn't get her way, her wrath was unyielding.

I take a deep breath and consider the best way to tackle the second accusation. "I never hit your mother, nor was I ever violent towards her. As much as Mommy drove me nuts, I still loved her, just not the way a husband and wife should love each other. I always wanted the best for her before the divorce. Our arguments could get ugly, but the idea I was abusive is absurd."

"Not after?" Annabel asks, peering up from her hands with big blue eyes.

"Not after what, sweetie?"

Her mood shirt shifts to yellow, "You said you always wanted the best for Mommy before the divorce, not after?"

I should have been more careful with my words. She is getting older and is much more aware than she used to be. The fact is, Corina has been horrible to me since the divorce, even more so than in marriage. I always wished we could evolve and be civil for the sake of the children, but every olive branch I extend is returned broken. My children's love for their mother has always trumped my repugnance for her.

Of course, if they were removed from the picture, I would relish the chance to give her a taste of what she has put me through all these years. I am forever in a battle to correct my children's idea of who their father is. Corina delineates me, a ruthless, womanizing, abusive asshole who needed anger management. She painted me as everything she knew I have always loathed and continues to maintain this front even today to steer her self-loathing misery.

"I didn't quite mean it that way, Sweets. It's complicated, but I know how much you and sister love your mother, and I only wish the best for her because she is your mother. After all, there would be no Annabel or Haley without her. Do you understand?" I say quietly. "Please, know I love you and your sister more than any animosity I have for Mommy. Life is a lot shorter than you realize, and it's not worth wasting it angry."

She looks down at the table, her hands crossed and closed off, and her shirt shifts to a cool green signaling mixed emotions. "Then why would she tell me you hit her? Because, Daddy, Mommy said..."

I reach across the table for her hands and caress them as I arrange my thoughts, "Baby, we had one argument, and perhaps it went too far, and I'm not proud of it, but even in that madness, I controlled myself. I regret that night more than I can tell you, but it was a two-way street. Your mother and I were married for ten years, sweetheart. A lot happens in ten years and, well... relationships change. We grew apart. We resented each other, but as far as I'm concerned, I was nothing but a loving and faithful husband and father. Your mother brought out the worst in me and, to be fair, perhaps I brought out the worst in her, but regardless of whatever has gone on between me and Mom, it has nothing to do with you or Haley."

I desperately want to unload on Annabel. I wish she could see her mother for who she really is, a controlling, manipulative, monstrosity who has wounded everyone in her path to win her imaginary strife. Corina had turned all our friends against me and continues to play the role of a victim. My heart pleads within me to tell her that her mother was the unfaithful one and is, and forever will be, pathological, but all that would do is bring me down to her level.

Corina had been unfaithful for eight out of our ten years of our marriage and had the audacity to accuse me. It was the proverbial pot calling the kettle black. She branded me while inoculating herself. She is special. A special kind of narcissist, and she has forever put her indignation towards me before everything, including our children's mental health. In the end, I would rather my girls have some resentment towards me than live in a world loaded with uncertainty and distrust.

Corina has mutated my relationship with my children, and that is something I've always had to circumvent. If I had it my way, my children would never have any idea there was any animosity between their mother and me. The more they think we get along, and that Mommy and Daddy just didn't love each other anymore, the more mentally stable they would be, and the less harm would come to them. No child should have to grow up hearing their parents trash each other or use their children as weapons in their selfish war.

"Were you and Mommy together after I was born?"

"We separated when you were only a year old, so you probably don't remember me being there…in the house," I say.

I watch her digest, reaching into the depths of her mind. "Oh, OK."

"Your sister was five, almost six, actually. I'm sure you don't remember, but Haley does. It was very difficult for her…it was very difficult for all of us. I, uh…"

I resist the urge to continue. I recall how Corina poisoned Haley's young mind. She was afraid to come with me, terrified of leaving her mother alone. What was once a beautiful relationship with me was severely strained. Haley had become Corina's weapon, and she fired it often.

Annabel clears her throat, hesitates, but then blurts out, "Haley and Mom haven't been getting along lately. I mean, like, they argue all the time. Mom wants her to go to church every Sunday and, like, spend more time with the church kids like Johnny and Cheryl, but Haley usually sneaks out of the house in the morning to go hang out with her loser friends." She ends her rant with a long, exaggerated eye roll.

I was afraid this may happen. However, I expected it all the same. Haley is seventeen now. She's beginning to rebel against her mother's control, and sensing she is coming of the age, I've been growing concerned. I've seen the new group of kids she has been hanging around, and Annabel's right, they are losers. I don't approve. I was hoping this was a pit stop, but it appears to have shunted her in a new direction.

Admittedly, I've never approved of the influence of that church, either. I feel like it is more of a cult than a religion. Exorcisms are performed at least once a month, and people speak in tongues at every mass. Furthermore, the pastor presents himself as a man of the people, a man of God who lives in poverty among them.

However, the reality is that Pastor Giuseppe is a bonafide imposter. He drives an old broken-down Chevy Suburban to the church but has three self-driving BMWs in the driveway of his five-bedroom, 4,500 square foot home in one of the best neighborhoods within an earshot of the church. God has certainly blessed him at his congregation's expense.

I have always expected that, when my girls would come of age, they would be keen enough to see the church's hypocritical bullshit. Despite that, I admittedly would prefer the church and gladly sacrifice myself to it in return for my children's safety.

Haley's new crowd, I'm convinced, smoke a lot of weed, but I suspect worse. After all, it's true what they say, marijuana is often a gateway drug. I met her boyfriend, Jared, about a month ago, and I took him and Haley to dinner. That punk had the audacity to show up wearing a T-shirt branded with a marijuana leaf.

I'm not a stranger to drugs. They're an unfortunate byproduct of suburbia. Kids are bored, and they have suburban problems with suburban things to do, so they get high to explore the world around them through glassy eyes. Notwithstanding, however, it shows a real lack of respect, and it highlights the values of this punk. I would have never shown up to my girlfriend's parents' house wearing something that advertises me as a deviant.

When I was a teenager, I smoked weed, among other things, although I viewed myself as a good kid from a good family, simply enjoying my youth. I was merely attempting to create my own tales of teenage rebellion, but it was always important to me that the adults I had respected or wanted the respect of, to see me how I saw myself; a good young man with a bright future. I wanted them to know their daughter was safe with me because trust is crucial when a boy is spending time with your daughter.

Haley hasn't been herself lately, and my eyes, once closed, now remain open and watchful. The last time I had taken the girls to dinner, I suspect she was high. She was late, lethargic, and stared off into space, and she jumped down my throat every time I asked her a question. I was just making conversation, but she was paranoid, anti-social, and her eyes were glazed over. That isn't my Haley.

Corina has always locked them away like caged animals, and I feared the day would come when they would break free of her chains and slingshot to a life of rebellion. I was afraid for my children. I've been afraid for them for as long as I can remember.

Their mother taught them to lie throughout their adolescence, and at the sinless age of five, Haley's innocence fled her. She was taught the skill of deceit. It wasn't her fault. She trusted her mother, and Corina had instructed her to lie to keep me out of their lives. Haley was terrified of disappointing her mother.

I understand now these are the things she had to do to survive. To keep peace in her home and to protect me from her mother. Haley had trusted her more than anyone in the world, and she commanded her to lie to her father about everything, even insignificant things. Corina has abused these children, but her ignorance permits her to believe she is justified.

"I'm getting worried about her. It's late, she was supposed to be home hours ago. I only get to see you girls every other weekend, and I miss you. I really look forward to our time together."

"I know, Daddy," Annabel says.

"Listen, you should go upstairs and get some sleep, sweetheart. I'm going to call her again and wait for her on the couch."

"Oh, alright, Daddy," Annabel says with a sigh.

As I reach for my cell phone, she skirts around the table and slams her weight into me. Her arms wrap around and pull me in tightly. A hug reminiscent of the ones she gave me as a little girl. I have missed them so much.

"I love you, Daddy," she says, and her mood shirt transforms into a vibrant red.

Somehow, this makes me feel validated as a father. Like all the pain I've had to endure to keep them in my life was suddenly, overwhelmingly, worth it.

"Daddy," she says, squeezing tighter, "I know you're worried about Haley, but it was really nice having you all to myself tonight."

"Aw, I love you, too, baby girl." I pull her in, return her hug with one of my own, lay a kiss her forehead, and savor the moment for as long as I can. She walks towards the stairs, and I can't help but notice how much she has grown. She has transformed into a beautiful young woman. Her gorgeous olive skin, blue eyes, and dirty blonde hair give her the perfect mix of Corina's Sicilian and my Scottish features. Our relationship may have been flawed, but we certainly made two beautiful children.

I sit at the kitchen table, staring with the force of the Jedi, willing my phone to ring. The nervous energy builds, and I feel more anxious with every passing minute. I can't stop the images of desolation and lewdness that flash through my mind like a horrifying comic strip.

Perhaps sending Annabel to bed was a little premature. After all, she occupied my mind, and she has a rather calming presence. Nevertheless, I sit, agonizing over where Haley could be, who she might be with, and what she might be doing.

I pick up my phone and stop to admire the holographic photo that sits atop the crystal screen. My beautiful family. We looked so perfect two Christmases ago. My beautiful girlfriend, Stella, Haley, Annabel, Ileana, and Jay, posing in front of the fireplace, every smile baring teeth.

Life is complicated, and mine has certainly had its fair share of challenges since the divorce. Albeit, until recently, Haley has always managed to stay on the straight and narrow. Now, I worry about the direction she's headed and hope the road paved by our choices isn't irreversible. I certainly don't think their lives would have been better if Corina and I had remained married, but the mental charade their mother has played on them was destined to do damage.

I try Haley again, but I suspect she is declining my calls because they are immediately directed to voicemail. I call again, again and again, but all my attempts yield the same result.

"Hiiyeeeee, it's Haley, leave a message." *Beeeeeeeep.*

"Haley, it's Dad. You need to come home. I asked you to be home by seven so we could all have dinner together. That was nearly five hours ago! It's 11:45! We only see each other every other week. It's late, now come home! If I don't hear from you soon, I'll have no option but to call the police! At the very least, call me and let me know you're alive!" I slam my phone down onto the table.

I love cellular technology. I can hardly remember how we managed without it, but I admit I miss the dramatic emphasis when slamming an old land-line phone down onto the receiver. If done correctly, the person on the receiving end could hear you do it. They could feel the anger as though it were electronically sent through the phone line like an old *Looney Toons* episode. A ball of furry passes through the line until it reaches the handset only to explode in your ear, leaving you motionless, covered in soot.

My father was an expert. He had the touch, and it was the perfect exclamation to the end of his rant. As soon as I heard that phone crash onto the receiver, I knew just how pissed he was. It was time to cut the shit and do as I was told. Parents know when you're up to shit, but it's a matter of how much shit we're willing to tolerate.

I sit on the couch in silence, staring out of the window and into the dark night. I'm losing my mind, struggling to fight the horrid images that enter. I consider waking Stella. She often falls asleep when putting Jay to bed. Jay is three, and he won't sleep unless Mommy cuddles with him and runs her fingers through his hair.

I sneak upstairs, place my thumb on the fingerprint scanner, activating the smart door and peer through the suddenly translucent doorway. They lie peacefully, snuggled in Jay's bed. No one is better than Stella at calming and focusing my thoughts, but I can't interrupt their moment.

I have always had the tendency to let my imagination get the best of me. Stella and I began dating shortly after Corina and I separated and, consequently, I had just been given graphic details of Corina's extramarital affairs. It was rather traumatizing. I thought back to all her inconsistencies. The little things that didn't add up.

At the time, I chose to overlook them, but now, they suddenly become clear. She was with him. She was always lying, and I came to the unhealthy conclusion the biggest mistake I made in our marriage was trusting her. I made a promise to myself I would never be that blind again. As you can imagine, my initial inability to trust put a lot of stress on Stella. I was traumatized by the tales of deceit spun by my mind. A wounded mind can be your worst enemy, and when it gets out of control, it can be awfully hard to reel in.

Stella is my girlfriend, but that title feels remarkably erroneous. I hate the term, and she is so much more than that. We have been together for twelve years and have two wonderful children. Ileana is eleven, and little Jay is three, although, if you ask him, he isn't three, he is six months less than four. Smart little guy but, undoubtedly, it is something he heard from one of his sisters.

I have always viewed Stella as my wife, and God knows, she has earned the right to be. We started dating casually only a month after I was separated from Corina. I moved on quickly, and that sparked a shit storm in Corina. Naturally, she accused me of being the unfaithful one. Perhaps Stella and I started dating too soon, but if I'm being honest, my relationship with Corina was over long before it ended.

Stella has been my rock, my lover, and my best friend, and she has never wavered through any of my life's trials. The difference between the two relationships is monumental. Stella makes me feel like a man while Corina broke me down every chance she got.

Corina claimed Stella and I had been lovers long before we had separated. She even went as far as to hire a private investigator to take photos of us together and presented them to the court as if they had been taken prior to our separation. It was all nonsense, but she wore her claims of abuse and infidelity across her chest like a banner and would tell her tale to anyone who would listen. She loves to play the victim, but the truth is, she plotted our divorce long before she executed it. This was merely another string in her web of lies.

I lie down on the couch in the conversation room, periodically peeking out of the window whenever headlights shine through the curtains and scrolling through old photographs and videos until I feel myself dozing off.

In and out of consciousness, I hear my phone's phantom ring, and it reminds me of when my children were babies. Periodically, I would hear them cry in my sleep and launch myself out of bed only to discover them fast asleep, adorably stuck in an awkward position.

Headlights pass over my eyes, and I spring up anxiously, gasping for breath. I clear the fog from my eyes, but as the car zooms past the house, I slam myself back into the couch with a *thud*. Unable to fall back asleep and still plagued by the possibilities. I pick up my phone, met again by a blank screen.

I'm too anxious to sleep and too neurotic to sit in silence, so I turn on the smart wall and activate the television to occupy my mind. It still amazes me every time I see the wall transform into a magnificent screen. The news has obsessed over a new controversial technology. It allows you to transport your consciousness into an alternate reality. I'm not clear on exactly how it works, but the media is creating their usual pandemonium and manufacturing hysteria.

They describe a world where people flock to relive their lives in this Alter-life, leaving the Earth abandoned, left to perish without humans to police it. The truth is, the Earth could use some time without human interference. Either way, I find it to be rather unlikely people would flee to a life in an alternate digital reality. Even if they wanted to, I understand the cost is incredibly steep that even most one-percenters cannot afford it.

They go on to explain the world is simulated, constructed any way you'd like. You can be young, old, look like yourself or a famous movie star. Hell, you could even live as a woman regardless if you were born a man.

Their slogan flashes atop the screen: *Alter-life, where your life is our dream.*

A do over? Do it all over again in a world of your mind's creation. Sounds to me like an overpriced video game. Anyway, I love my life, even with all its imperfections.

They flash to protestors in the street, picketing in front of the Alter-life facility. Signs shaped in the form of a cross that read: Live for Today, Not in Yesterday. Another says: Don't Falter, Don't Alter! But perhaps my favorite is an oldie but a goodie. The always effective: What would Jesus do? I hate religious fanatics.

I hear a car door open with a *squeak* and slam shut. I shut down the smart wall, jump up off the couch, and discreetly peek out of the window. Haley flails her arms around Jared and kisses him the way a girl does when he is the only thing she sees. My stomach knots, and my irritation builds.

"How dare this punk disrespect me," I mutter to myself, but I try and remind myself she is no longer my little girl. Whether I like it or not, she is a young woman now, but she will always be my little girl.

She walks backwards up the walkway, blows him kisses, and waves goodbye, and with a squeal of the tires, Jared peels away. As she nears the door, I position myself directly in front of it, standing tall in the darkness with my arms folded, stalking her as if she were my prey.

She attempts to sneak in quietly, twisting the knob, gradually applying pressure in an effort to pry open the large, heavy door and make as little noise as possible. She knows it will chirp if opened too quickly. The door opens, and I remain silent, glaring at her within the shadows. She slyly uses her knee to nudge the door closed while skillfully holding the doorknob open.

When she turns around, she is startled by my silhouette. She jumps backward and covers her mouth and gasps, "Oh, my God! Dad? What are you doing there? Creeper!"

My eyes widen. "What am I doing?" I say, blood pressure steadily on the rise. "What do you think I'm doing? You were supposed to be home by seven. It's 1 am! I've been calling you all night! You don't answer your phone? No courtesy text? Where in the hell have you been?"

"Nowhere. Just watching a movie with friends. What's the big deal?"

"Haley, you're seventeen! You shouldn't be out until one in the morning with your boyfriend. Does Mom let you stay out this late?" I say.

"Mom doesn't let me do anything! If it were up to her, I'd be locked in a damn cage," Haley says, refusing to meet my eyes.

"Oh! So, it's Dad's weekend, and you think you can take advantage of me and stay out all night?"

"No," she says. Her eyes roll into the back of her head.

"Certainly seems to be the case. You know, I don't ask for much, but I do demand your respect. I refuse to be your punching bag!"

"No, clearly that's Mom's job!" she says and, instantly, tears well up in her eyes, and she averts them to the corner of the room.

"What, Haley? What the hell is that supposed to mean?"

"Nothing. Forget it. I'm going to bed," she says, brushing past me.

I reach out and put my hand on her, "No, I'm not going to just let that go without an explanation. What is that supposed to mean, Haley?"

Tears trickle down her cheeks, and when I look into her eyes, I can see something is really gnawing at her. Haley has never spoken directly about the twisted relationship her mother and I share. Sadness plasters her face, and I decide scolding her can wait until morning.

"Oh, come here, Haley my love." I pull her in and hug her tightly, resting my chin on her forehead. "Please, come talk with me for a few minutes?" I say, guiding her over to the couch.

I leave the lights off because I have a feeling this is going to be a delicate conversation, and I've always found it to be easier to have difficult conversations in the dark. People become less inhibited when you don't have to look each other in the eyes. Eyes are powerful windows to the soul, and I want her to feel as though she can speak freely without seeing hurt or anger in my eyes.

We sit in dark silence for several minutes, and I use the time organize my thoughts.

"Talk to me, Haley. What's going on? You haven't been yourself lately, and I'm really starting to become concerned. Where is all this coming from? Why would you say I'm Mom's punching bag?"

"I don't want to talk about it," she says.

"Hayley, it's me, Dad. I hope you know I'm always here for you. I just want you to be happy. Tell me what's on your mind, baby. I promise, I won't be angry."

With that, like a bullet shot from a gun, she unloads, "I'm not blind, Dad! I've seen the way Mom treats you. She's been a total cunt!"

"What?" I say, my mouth a gasp. "Watch your damn mouth, Haley! For God's sake, that's your mother!"

I see the spark of ferocity in her eye, but she resists the urge to continue her attack. She takes in a hearty breath and looks to the corner of the room, shutting herself off once again.

"Trust me, honey, no one knows how difficult your mother can be more than me, but—"

"Yup, knew there was a *but*."

"But I also know you love her," I say.

I've never heard her speak that way about her mother, and I can't help but wonder what has sparked this sudden animosity.

"Dad, why the hell are you defending her?" She pauses, but then blurts out, "I found your book!"

"My book?" I ask. My eyes narrow, and I look down to the floor. "What book?"

Initially, I truly have no idea what she's talking about, but then, like a knife to the heart, it strikes me. There is only one book she could be referring to, but how? It's remained safely locked in my desk drawer since the day her mother and I were finally divorced.

"Just forget it," she says. "Dad, I'm going to bed."

"No, Haley. Whatever it is, you need to let it out. You can't keep this bottled up. It will eat away at you until all that's left is animosity and anger. I don't like seeing you hurt, and I don't want whatever this is to come between us."

I grab her shoulders and square her up to face me, delicately place my hands on her cheeks, and in my softest tone, I say, "Haley, please. Please, talk to me. Tell me what's on your mind. I know it isn't easy to talk to me about certain things, but you need to let it out, baby. I promise I won't be angry, and I won't judge."

Haley sighs deeply, reaches for my water on the coffee table, and takes a sip. A few more minutes of awkward silence pass.

"OK, Haley, if you're not ready to talk, let's go to bed, and we can talk in the…"

"The Cunt Log, Dad! The one with all the printouts of your emails with Mom and your lawyers," she says. The words rolled off her tongue like a missile, striking me dead in my tracks.

The infamous Cunt Log. It was just as I feared, and yes, that is what I titled it. It certainly seemed to be a fitting title at the time. I was young, and I was incredibly angry. I created it back in 2020, only two years following the finalization of our divorce. I bought a label maker with the sole purpose to title it CUNT LOG, and it was the only time I had ever used that device.

Corina's consistent attacks raised my blood pressure, not just figuratively but literally. As a result, it took a stern warning from my cardiologist, a prescription of Lopressor, and several years of therapy to no longer let her constant onslaughts affect me.

Don't get me wrong, she still makes my blood boil, but I do a far better job managing my emotions. I needed a place to unload my thoughts, and the Cunt Log gave me a safe place to release. At least I thought it was safe.

"Dad, she has been horrible to you! All these years, I've watched you try and be civil with Mom. You rarely ever said a bad word about her, and she slams you every chance she gets and—"

"Haley-bear, what's happened between your mother and I…it has nothing to do with you…or Annabel for that matter."

She glares back at me with a look of disgust. "It has everything to do with us! She has always made us feel guilty. Because why? Because we loved you? It was like I had a secret: I loved my dad." She throws her head into her hands and sobs.

"Haley?" I lay my hand on her shoulder.

"I should feel guilty for loving *her*!" Her voice cracks, and tears flood her face.

I feel her pain, and it twists like a knife as I watch her face prune and her eyes well up.

"Dad, I'm going to confront her! I'm going to let her know I know what she has been doing on all these years!"

"And all that is going to do is make matters between me and your mom worse. Please, Haley, go to sleep. We can talk about this in the morning. I'll tell you everything, but give me a chance to help you understand things before you do something you're going to regret. We both need to sleep on it. Let's discuss it with a clear head, OK?"

"I'm not going to regret anything, Dad. I can't just let this go like it's nothing. I have proof now that she is full of shit, and I'm going to shove it right in her face when she denies it!"

My voice deepens. "No! Haley, you're not. Please, go to bed. We will discuss it in the morning. OK?"

"Yup, sure," she says.

Teenagers! They perpetually think they know everything. I was guilty of it myself. So passionate about things I thought I knew. I recall my father saying, "Oh, yeah, sport? Talk to me in twenty years." He was right! I cringe at the thought of my youthful intellect. I couldn't even scratch my balls right.

They've loved once, they're a therapist, win a science fair, a physicist. When they pass their driver's test, instantly they're a goddamned Formula One driver. Whatever lies underneath the surface, there are always a hundred different channels that complicate the system. There are always multiple sides to every story, and rarely is anything exactly as it appears.

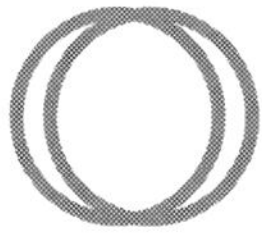

# CHAPTER 2

I spent the night tossing and turning, running over what I was going to say to Haley. I didn't cut our conversation short last night because I was tired, I cut it because I am mature enough to realize I need to prepare. How much of the log did she read, and how the hell did she get her hands on it?

The sun gleams through the blinds, but I remain lifeless in bed, gazing up at the ceiling. My eyes fixate on the fan, hypnotized by the blades as they spin like a typhoon. I allow myself to relish in the robins' morning melody. Their songs joyously serenade all who will listen. Life seems so simpler outside of my bedroom window, perched on the oak tree.

Many years ago, I may have been ecstatic at the idea of my daughters knowing the truth, *my* truth. All the strain and unnecessary stress Corina had layered upon us shouldn't go unpunished, should it? She chose to be my enemy, and it didn't have to be this way. We both love our children and, presumably, have wanted the same thing for them, their happiness.

We were young, and we weren't ready to get married. Neither of us understood what we wanted in a life mate yet. Was all this a result of my poor decisions made by my twenty-eight-year-old-self? After all, I asked her to marry me and, arguably, that was the worst decision of my life. If I could only go back in time, surely, I would spare everyone of this emotional mess.

I always thought that in time, things would resolve. Everyone would heal, and we could move on civilly, but perhaps time doesn't heal all wounds after all. The Lord knows I've tried to be reasonable. I've tried to extend olive branches, but she confuses my kindness for weakness, and it fed her desire to punish me.

I was kind because she is the mother of my children. I was kind because I love them, and their happiness and stability are far more important than our strife. All I have ever wanted was for our children to come away from our divorce unscathed. It was a choice and, believe me, it would have been far easier to return her wickedness with some of my own, but their mental health was in our hands, and I refused to take part in a selfish war.

I look over and admire Stella's long brown hair, fanned out over her pillow like a horse's mane. Very petite and graceful, she's like a tiny dancer, but don't let her appearance fool you. She's as feisty as a pit bull. She remains asleep, curled up in a ball, with a pillow tightly gripped between her legs. Even now, with her chiseled jaw slung open and a pool of drool puddled on her chin, her beauty mesmerizes me.

I reach over, wrap my arms around her, and pull her in tightly. She moans and nudges herself back into me until we are pressed together, spooning without space for an ant to pass between us.

I kiss her on the cheek and move to get up, but she pulls me back in and groans, "Nooooo, stay."

No one likes to cuddle quite like Stella. However, I often think she's an equal opportunity cuddler. She would cuddle with anything alive, regardless whether it wanted to be there or not. I jokingly call her Elmyra from the *Tiny Toons Adventures*. Elmyra was known to trap animals in the wild, only to smother them nearly to death whilst they attempted to free themselves from her loving death grip, "I'm going to love you, and kiss you, and hug you, and never let you go."

"I have to get up, love. I'm too restless," I say.

"Why, what's wrong?" she mutters, still half-asleep. Her voice is raspy, and her larynx begs her to remain in bed a bit longer.

"Haley didn't come home last night until after one. We had a talk but, unfortunately, she threw a curve ball at me. Shit got real, real quick, but now I think I know what's caused this radical change in her lately."

"Oh?" she says, suddenly more alert.

"She found the Cunt Log," I say.

"Ohhhhh, shit!" she says.

Seconds later, she abruptly springs upright in bed, eyes wide, and shifts her gaze out of the window.

"What? What is it?" I ask.

"When?"

"When what?" She remains silent and motionless. "Stella, what is it?" I demand.

"When did she find it? Was it about a month ago, maybe two?"

Stella asks, and by the look on her face, I can see she is recalling something significant.

"She didn't say. I didn't ask. Why, Stella?"

"Oh, boy, Dylan. Please, don't kill me," she pleads.

"What, babe?" My voice reduces to a growl, and I know I am not going to like what she is about to say.

"Well…I may have moved the log one of those weekends they were here and kind of…uh, well…"

"Stella! Kind of what? Stella, please, for God's sake, what?"

"I may have left it out on your desk," she blurts out.

I move to speak, but I'm paralyzed. All I can do is sit in silence with my mouth agape. The wind has been knocked out of me, but at least now I know how Haley got her hands on it. I bury my head into my hands and run them through my hair. How could Stella be so careless? Why did she take it out in the first place? She knows how incredibly delicate the contents of that book are.

"Dylan, I'm truly sorry, honey mou," she says, lips pouting and lashes batting.

Stella is Greek, and the direct translation to honey mou is *my honey*, a pet name I, not so secretly, adore. Truth be told, I melt every time I hear it, and she undoubtedly uses it as a secret weapon.

"Dammit, babe. I never intended for them to see that. Not yet, anyway."

I assembled the log a long time ago. I intended only to show my girls when they were old enough to understand. I hoped I would never have to show them at all, but I needed it, nonetheless. After all, it wasn't only for them, it was documented evidence of Corina's behavior for the court.

It outlined her relentless attacks and my consistent attempts to make amends. I wanted them to see through my eyes and understand everything their mother had put us through. Her constant attempts to alienate me and use our children as a weapon shattered their vision of who their father was. She used their innocence against them.

As time went on, however, I realized it wouldn't make me any better of a father to them than Corina was a mother. She finally remarried, and things slowly leveled off. After all, a person's psyche can still be harmed as an adult, and I don't want them to hate or resent their mother. On the contrary, I don't want them to hate anyone. I want them to be happy, secure, and well-adjusted, and that's all I've ever wanted.

It takes enormous amounts of energy to hate. It drains you and emotionally tips the balance in your life, infecting you like a disease. When you succumb to it, darkness engulfs you like a cloud, and everywhere you go, your anger follows, transmitting your disease to everyone around you.

It was necessary for me to continue adding to the log because it became a form of therapy for me. I wrote detailed notes on all the printed pages about what I was feeling, the truth behind Corina's words. It became a diary of sorts, and I felt as though I were talking to my children through the pen. I never looked back through those pages, not once. I couldn't bear to relive it. It would stir up too much anger, and I knew it would open the door and invite the hatred back in.

There must have been thousands of pages in that binder. I had to buy a second one five years ago so I could keep adding to it. It must have taken Haley an enormous amount of time to get through it.

I look up, and Stella's eyes watchfully wait for me to speak.

"Well, it's done. It is what it is. I'm not going to sit here and blame you. If they didn't find it now, one of them was bound to have found it eventually. I probably should have burned it, or at least digitized it, locked with an iris scan years ago when I decided I wouldn't show them, but I always kept it as a sort of insurance policy."

"I know, love. So, what do we do now?" Stella asks.

"I don't know. I need to talk to her and hope I can right this somehow. It was late. I told her we'd talk in the morning. Somehow, I need to change this from a negative to a positive."

"Is she awake?" Stella asks.

"I don't know," I say, feeling nervous, a kaleidoscope of butterflies fluttering in my belly. "I know it's wrong, but there is still a part of me that's relieved she read it."

"I can understand that," Stella says.

"I mean, of course, I wish she hadn't, but having her know everything... well, it almost makes me feel validated as her father."

"What do you mean? You've always been a great father to those kids, and ours. You can't think that way, Dylan."

I did my best with what I was dealt. I saw them and spoke to them every chance I could. I tried to be a role model and instill values in them with the time I was allotted. I did my best to be a father, even though I couldn't see them or speak to them every day.

Haley has always wanted to be an astronaut, and I credit that to our weekend ritual of star gazing, searching for different constellations and planets on my virtual pad and trying to identify them in the night sky. We'd search and study for hours during the summer months. Her grades have always been exceptional, until this recent slip, and she has always involved herself in science clubs and even won the school science fair when she was in the 8th grade.

I sigh, releasing a gust of wind that could extinguish the Olympic torch, rest my hands on my hips and look to the ceiling for answers. "Why did you take it out of the drawer in the first place?"

I'm ashamed to think that, perhaps, she left it out on purpose. As much as I loathe Corina, Stella had to witness years of the man she loves endure her abuse. She struggled through it alongside of me, and without her support, I would have crumbled years ago. She is a strong woman, and I can't imagine anyone loving me the way she has.

My friends warned me I shouldn't jump into another relationship of this magnitude so quickly, and I knew it was sound advice, but there is something so magnificently special about Stella. I immediately felt a connection unlike any I have ever had before. She is my best friend, the partner I always wished Corina had been. Stella was the wife I had always wanted.

"I was reading it," she says.

"Why? You wanted a road map on how to destroy my life and secure yourself a place in hell right next to Corina?" I chuckle, making light of the situation. Our relationship has never been devoid of sarcasm. We thoroughly enjoy witty banter, and I knew that as harsh as it appears, it was sure to make her smile.

"No, you ass," she says, hurling her pillow at me as hard as she can.

"Which was your favorite part? When she claimed I abused her and filed a restraining order, or when she claimed I was cheating on her throughout our ten years of marriage? Oh wait, it was probably when she tried to set me up and make me look as if I was a negligent father and took me back to court for the second, oh, and third time to try and get sole custody of our children!"

"You better shut it before I punch you in your thyroid!" she says, holding her fist to my chin.

"In all seriousness, though, why?" I ask.

"I was just cleaning out the drawer, filing our taxes away, and I took it out. I opened it and just started flipping through the pages and kind of got hooked."

"Yeah, it's a real page turner. Wait until you get to the end when I burn her alive, and we're all laughing and singing around her, roasting marshmallows and singing, "Kumbaya.""

"You're an idiot! No, there were just so many memories, it took me back. Of course, they weren't good, but it brought me back to a different time. I was thinking about us. I guess that stuff triggered the good memories from that time. Then I went to the smartwall and started swiping through our old pictures, and when you got home, I ran upstairs to greet you. I totally got sidetracked and forgot all about it. I'm really sorry, honey mou. I seriously fucked up this time."

"I'd like to talk to her together. I could really use your support," I say.

"Does Annabel know?"

"I don't think so. We spent a lot of time together last night. It was nice. She didn't bring anything up, so I doubt it, and I want to keep it that way."

I hope Haley is mature enough to keep this to herself because, even at seventeen, she is too young to comprehend and objectively break down what she read. She doesn't have the experiences to understand and dissect the raw emotion from both sides. Hell, I don't know if I fully understand it all. I'd like to think I do, but I can't pretend I realize the true workings of Corina's mind and the different compartments that have distorted her reality. I'm sure that, somehow, she feels justified in her actions.

We walk down the stairs, and I breathe heavily, unequivocally anxious. I'm going to have to relive things that would be better if left buried. The more I think about it, the more stressed I become, and with each step, my anxiety builds.

I can't in good conscious justify or defend Corina's actions because, truthfully, I did little to deserve them. We didn't have a healthy relationship, but we didn't have to be enemies, either. That was her choice, and a choice that brought us to where we are today.

How do I change the way Haley feels about her mother after reading the Cunt Log when I believe her feelings are warranted? Perhaps I'll explain that her mother was hurt and people have a tendency to let their emotions get the best of them, and although I don't excuse her actions by any means, we are all human.

Hopefully, Haley will use this as a learning experience and ascertain it is important to forgive and realize that nobody is perfect, even her parents. In her youth, she idolized her mother, but perhaps now that she nears adulthood, she can accept her for her flaws.

I'll say, "Don't be like your mother, but accept she is your mother and you love her, faults and all, but strive to be better than her."

Who am I kidding, this is all so undeniably cliché. Not that it's wrong, of course, but it does sound like something you'd watch on a Lifetime afternoon special. I have to remain hopeful she will listen and be receptive, but the more I think back to the contents of that book, the more I cringe at the thought of her reading it.

Stella and I walk cautiously into the kitchen and see Annabel eating a bowl of cereal at the countertop. Our dog, Shane, sits in the seat beside her as if he were one of the kids. I swear, that dog is more human than some humans I know. When I look into his eyes, I feel he is Sigmund Freud reincarnated, analyzing my relationship with my mother. If Shane could speak, he'd undoubtedly know what to say to Haley.

"Morning, Annabel bear. Is Haley up yet?" I ask.

I bend down and kiss her on the forehead and run my hands through Shane's coat. Annabel shovels a spoonful of cocoa crisps into her mouth, stares into her bowl, and her eyes widen.

"Annabel? Did you hear me?" I ask.

With her mouth full, she says, "Dad, don't freak out."

"Where is she, Annabel?"

She slows her chewing, looks down at her cereal bowl, and *clanks* her spoon against the side.

My patience already thin, I holler, "Annabel! Where is she?"

She startles, dropping her spoon onto the floor, and Shane rushes down to lick it.

"I don't know where she is, but that idiot Jared picked her up super early this morning. I mean, like, Dad, it was still dark out and stuff."

I place my hands on the side of my head and grab two large clumps of hair and release a growl that slowly builds into a bark. I snatch my phone from the counter, take in a deep breath, and slam the phone back down.

Annabel and Stella in unison say, "What?"

Our conversation from last night comes back to me, and I recall Haley's vow to confront her mother. Would she really be so bold to do that before she gave me a chance to speak with her? Before a few months ago, I'd say no, but now, I'm not so sure. I need to call her before it's too late! My mind races, and I tremble as I look for her contact in my phone.

"Please, tell me she didn't! She wouldn't! Would she?" I vent aloud, and Stella and Annabel with a look of concern, remain silent and bite down on their lips.

I hasten down the stairs and run to my desk, yank open the top drawer, and scour it for the key to the file cabinet.

"Goddammit! Where the hell is it? Stella, where's the key?"

"What?" she yells from the top of the steps.

"The key! It's not here. I'm going to have to break it open!"

She scurries down the steps, and when she reaches the bottom, she says, "You think she would take it?"

"She told me last night she was going to confront Corina. She seemed pretty fucking determined. I told her she would only make things worse and to wait until after we could talk this morning. She said she had proof now. I didn't think she meant that literally! How could I be so careless and leave the key in my desk drawer? What was I thinking?"

Stella gnaws on her fingers and says, "Wait! I think we have the second key up in the bedroom safe." She turns and runs up the stairs.

Stella always kept anything of perceived value in that safe. She was always under the assumption our identities would be stolen, our valuables and anything dear to her could be taken in an instant. If I bought and installed a bank vault, she likely would fill it with items of discerned value. I always considered that her place to file away her crazy, but now, I wish I had kept the log locked within it. Maybe then it would still be safe and Haley's innocence along with it. How could I be so careless?

Truthfully, her obsession has saved my ass on several occasions. However, it is a false security. I bought the safe for a hundred dollars on Amazon, and I never properly secured it to the floor. Frankly, anyone could walk right out of the front door with it and crack the safe with a household drill. It was one of those projects I always intended on getting around to but never did.

She was always preparing for possible, although unlikely, tragedies. She keeps a one-month supply of bottled water and canned goods in the storage closet. She said it was just in case a bad storm hit, but I often wonder if she is secretly preparing for the possibility of a zombie apocalypse because her obsession began after we binge-watched the classic television show *The Walking Dead*. Either way, I adore her and all her eccentricities because that's what makes Stella, Stella.

Out of breath and gasping for air, she descends the stairs in a huff.

"OK, here it is!" she says.

"Dad?" Annabel yells from the top of the steps. "What's going on?"

"Nothing, Annabel. We'll be up in a few," I say.

I pluck the key from Stella's hands, take in a deep, penetrating breath, followed by a long, exaggerated exhalation, insert the key, and jiggle the lock open. I'm about to pull the drawer out when I hear, "Ugh, you again?"

A whiney voice from an old movie clip I use as a ring tone for Corina.

"Oh, you've got to be fucking kidding me!" I slam my hands onto the desk in frustration.

"What?" Stella says.

"Corina just fucking messaged me!"

"What did she say?"

"I don't know," I say and toss my phone to the side. I don't want to look at her message until I know what I'm dealing with. It feasibly could be nothing. She often messages me when I have the girls, sending random pokes. The girls are now seventeen and thirteen, but she still acts as though I'm leaving toddlers unattended. If the log safely rests in its labyrinth, it could be a mere coincidence.

I slide the drawer open, and my heart sinks into my stomach. She actually took it. I rustle through all the folders, thrash the contents in every direction, searching for a binder that is twice as thick as *Gone with the Wind*. There is no chance it's buried beneath but, regardless, I keep searching as if it will magically appear. In fact, I knew by the weight of the drawer it was gone before I even looked.

I feel betrayed. How could Haley be so incredibly insolent? Warmth begins in my gut and travels to form a pit in my throat. I concentrate on my breath and attempt to regain control of my blood pressure.

"Honey mou? My love? It's going to be alright, Love. So what? So, she took it and probably showed it to Corina." Stella chuckles. "Oh, boy. She is going to be furious."

"This is deeper than Corina. This isn't about her!"

"OK, but still, what's the worst she can do? Take you back to court? For what? Truthfully, she deserves this, anyway. I don't feel bad for her. It isn't as if you made those things up. She's been an absolute witch," Stella says.

"That's not why I'm upset. This could have a serious, lasting effect on Haley. And, what if Annabel finds out? What then? This isn't how this was supposed to go," I say.

"I get it, but I'm just saying, if she wanted to take you back to court, you have a binder of evidence to show the judge how awful she's been. Look on the bright side, you also have Haley as a witness now."

"No! I would never put Haley in that position. It's one thing to have it out with your mother, it's another thing entirely to testify against her in court! And…what if Haley gives her the binder? Then what? That's the only evidence I have!"

"OK…so, you go back through your emails and your messages and you make another one," she says softly, squeezing my shoulders to alleviate my stress.

"We're talking about twelve years of emails that may not even exist anymore, and the messaging app that we've used has shut down and been changed to a different service twice. Some of that shit is irre-fuckin-placable!" I say, slamming the desk drawer in a huff.

"OK, babe, I'm just saying, who cares how this all affects Corina?"

"Listen, I don't give a shit about Corina or how this makes her feel. I really, really don't! Of course, there is a part of me that feels justice has been served, but what I care about…all I've ever cared about, is how all of this will affect my kids, and it won't do them any good to feel like their lives have been a lie."

"Corina had this coming, and I for one, am happy Haley finally knows the truth. I hope she's miserable and filled with regret for all those years she has relentlessly attacked you, and for what?" Stella says, locking the labyrinth door.

"You know she'll retaliate. It's been her life's goal to make me miserable, and this is going to set off another storm of bullshit."

"So? Ignore her. She's pathetic! She's always been pathetic, and she will be deplorable until someone puts her out of her misery and buries her like the worm she is," Stella says. She shakes her head and smooshes her lips together as if she has a bad taste in her mouth.

I know that she's right, but it doesn't stop the anxiety from swooping in like an eagle and taking my breath away.

"Here goes nothing. Let's see what the witch has to say," I say.

I open the app and feel my heart *thump, thump, thump*.

Stella rubs my back and tries to calm me, "It's OK, love. Nothing real will come of this, you'll see. The girls will be fine."

> *From: Corina Rosario*
> *To: Dylan Grady*
> *9:22 am Sunday, March 10, 2032*
>
> *Need I remind you that, first of all, the divorce agreement states in section 10:7, paragraph 3 that neither parent should attempt to alienate the other from the children, and that we are not to discuss or show the children any of the documentation pertaining to the divorce proceeding? You are in violation of the agreement.*

"Is she serious?" Stella laughs. "Whatever, babe. That's not so bad. If she wants to waste all that money taking you back to court, let her. She's alienated you from the start! You are alienating her? Oh, that's classic!"

I can't help but laugh, and the tension eases. Stella's right, it is funny. It's the same hypocrisy I have had to deal with for the past twelve years.

Out of nowhere, and as if she heard our conversation, my phone rings. It's Corina.

"Is she serious?" I say.

"Don't answer it, babe. She has a restraining order out on you, and you're not supposed to speak to her. She could be trying to entrap you."

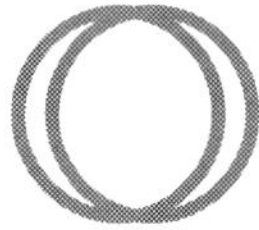

# CHAPTER 3

Corina was, in fact, rewarded a restraining order on me, but before you judge me as a monster, no, it wasn't warranted. It was merely a power play to use in our divorce. Nothing in my life has been quite as humiliating before or since. Your life is suddenly rerouted when two police officers knock on your door, awakening you from a deep sleep and instruct you to pack a bag and get out of your own home. How much of a life can one pack in five minutes?

The truth is, we had a horrible argument that night, tempers flared, and things were said and done by both of us that were regrettable. However, I am not a threat, and she was never in any danger. I'm not a violent man, and if she were to be honest, she would surely admit that.

Her plan was put into motion long before I had come home. It was an attempt for her to gain control of the house and have me physically removed from it. She had a game plan and executed every detail as if it were a jewel heist. Everything from where I would meet her down to the conversation and key words she knew would push my buttons.

You learn a lot about each other through ten years of marriage, and you certainly know what things will get the desired reaction. She knew I was never a threat to her personal safety. I loathe the animals who abuse their wives and children, tormenting the ones they are supposed to love and protect.

Corina alleged I hit her, strategically stating I punched her in the stomach, so she didn't have to provide physical proof of the abuse. When the officers arrived, I ask them, "You're telling me she can make a claim I did something without any valid proof, and you'll come and order me to leave my home?"

Their response, "Yes, sir. I'm sorry. Your wife didn't have any signs of abuse and, between you, me, and the wall here, she was in rather good spirits at the station. Not too typical of someone who had been a victim of domestic violence but, nevertheless, we are required to follow through with the claim. I suggest you get a lawyer, Mr. Grady. Your court date for the final restraining order is printed right here. We'll give you five minutes to grab some belongings. Do you have any guns or other weapons in the house, sir?"

"No, I don't. Nothing," I said. My heart sunk into my stomach, and a ball of fire replaced it in my chest.

I walked out of my house, and the officers reached out their hands and confiscated my keys. It was clear everything that was once mine was now hers. I staggered my way to my car with a small bag and a ringing in my ears. A buzz zipped through me as though my soul had been shaken, and I had trouble focusing my eyes while my limbs felt separated from my wits.

I couldn't believe that after ten years of marriage, she had succumbed to this. I saw my neighbors peeking out of their windows. I could feel them judging me as if I was the monster she painted me as in the months and years to come. She formulated a tale of abuse and adultery she leans on like a crutch, thriving off the attention and pity of others. She has always been an artist, and this was her masterpiece, her fairy tale that helps her sleep at night.

At the final restraining order hearing, she declared she was fearful of me and claimed multiple instances of abuse. She was so fearful of me. However, she was willing to drop the whole charade for more money in pendente lite support. I truly had no issue with the money, but she also demanded I agree to essentially giving her sole custody of our children, along with supervised visits. That was the moment our children became a weapon in her war. A weapon she would use often, relentlessly trying to diffuse the relationship I had with my children.

I would not sacrifice my children for any price. A father's role in his child's upbringing is important, and I wanted to have influence in their lives. I wasn't a dead-beat dad. Quite the contrary. I always paid and wanted as much time as I could get with them. I love them, and to this day, I still regret that I couldn't have played a larger role in their lives.

Corina was combative on the stand and let the water works flow like the Nile. I should have known who I was dealing with but, at the time, I was still shell-shocked and oblivious to her strategy. I knew she was nasty, but I didn't understand her true demonic potential.

She had her friends and family lie in court, testifying and bearing witness to several of her allegations to give them merit. With the help of her attorney, events were twisted and contorted to make normal arguments appear sinister.

I was a broken man. My life was being torn from me, and my future was uncertain. It had already been over two weeks since I had seen or spoken to my children, and I didn't know when, or if, I would be able to speak with them again. Two weeks to a toddler is a lifetime, and the damage had already begun to creep its way in. The visceral pain when going through a divorce is agonizing, and it shouldn't be underestimated.

Judge Cummings was a newly appointed judge, and she hadn't attained tenure yet, so she had no intentions of taking any chances. When Corina used key words in her testimony, the primary being *fear*, she sealed the deal. In these cases, the court will always rule on the side of caution. She ruled in her favor but awarded her the lowest level restraining order. I was to keep thirty feet from her at all times, and we were ordered to communicate through email, or a messaging app specifically created for divorced parents with strained relationships.

If she had dismissed the case, and I had returned to my former residence and killed or maimed Corina, it would have been a blemish on the judge's career. On the other hand, if my council truly had my best interest at heart, they would have advised me to settle and forego a trial, which would have resulted in the dismissal of the final restraining order. The disputed issues should have been tackled at the settlement table or at the final divorce hearing. After all, at that time, everything was temporary.

I came to find out I lost the case before Judge Cummings ever heard a word of testimony. The cards were stacked against me. It was all a charade, and I'm convinced my attorneys were aware of what the outcome was going to be well before they marched me into that courtroom. They only saw green. I was only the commodity who foolishly thought he was a human being. I have often speculated our attorneys were in cahoots.

In a divorce, your lawyer's assignment isn't to help you. Rather, their mission is to instigate hostility and keep you fighting. The more you hate each other, the longer your divorce and the more income they generate. Was this the beginning of their grand design for Dylan Grady's financial extermination?

This is a question I will never have an answer. However, it certainly complicated and prolonged our case, resulting in thousands of dollars in unnecessary legal fees and, all the while, awarded Corina a false power that, in the end, was destructive for everyone. The only people who benefited were the attorneys. It is an ugly profession.

Still, after all Corina has put me through, I have always dreamt we could put it all behind us and become friends. It would have benefited our children enormously. We brought out the worst in each other, and our divorce was a blessing, and I wish she could see that.

We can't go back and make different choices, so we might as well make the best of things for the sake of the children. Despite that, in the end, she was driven to punish me and determined to make herself a victim. Awarding her a restraining order only fed her demons and drove her villainess behavior to climax.

On November 7, 2025, I had filed a motion to have the restraining order removed, but I was denied by the court because she claimed to still fear me. She said my kind demeanor in my messages was for the court's eyes and that, on several occasions when picking up the children, I had made implications I was going to kill her by gesticulating my pointer finger, dragging it across my throat.

Of course, there was no truth to her allegations, but she would never voluntarily give up her superpower. She told my lawyer she worked too hard for it, just to give it up. She wore it like a badge and used it as a weapon.

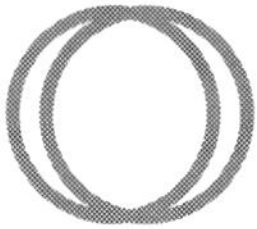

# CHAPTER 4

I sit on the floor with Jay. His three-year-old body contorts in multiple directions, gasping for breath as he squeals with delight. We're playing his favorite game, the tickle monster. He tries to run past me, but I fire my arms out and grab ahold of his waist mid-stride. I slam his little body onto the couch and tickle him until he is no longer able to breathe. When the air has been depleted and the fun breaches the cusp of obnoxious, I release him back to his feet. He runs away, only to return seconds later, screaming with enjoyment and begging for more.

Ileana still joins in from time to time, but I suspect it's only because she desires the same level of attention as Jay, and I can certainly appreciate that. She's getting older, and her interest in childish games appears to have diminished.

I've put on my best face, despite today's unpleasant events. I feel torn between worlds. My past and present have, once again, collided. Part of me feels badly for Corina, but a larger part relishes in her nightmare because, after all, what goes around comes around. Everyone told me she would eventually get what's coming to her, and maybe this is fate rearing its ugly head. I just wish I did not have to play a part in it.

"Aaaaargh," Jay hollers as he whizzes by. I reach out my left arm, and he crashes into it with extreme force.

"You can't escape the tickle monster," I say, swinging my right hand around to meet my left, securing both sides of his waist, lifting him high into the air, and spinning him like a helicopter.

Jay screams, "Put me down, Tick-le Mon-sterrr!"

"Your wish is my command," I growl in my most gruesome monster voice and slam him onto the couch.

His laugh is incredibly contagious, and when he loses control, he makes a noise similar to a hiccup. Stella and I can't refrain from belly laughing every time we hear it. Sometimes, I think I enjoy playing the tickle monster more than they do. I'm starting to feel better, but my conscious remains clouded. I need to speak to Haley to see what happened and what exactly was said but, either way, damage has been done, and there is no escaping it.

I get up and release Jay from my grip and signal for Stella to meet me in the kitchen. Annabel loved the tickle monster when she was young and happily takes over the duties when called upon, crowning herself the tickle minion. It will keep her busy while Stella and I talk. I have always adhered to my strict rule of not speaking negatively about Corina in front of any of the children.

I lean in on the counter and ask Stella quietly, "Do you think I should even bother responding to Corina?"

"Don't call her. If anything, send her a message," Stella says.

"No, I would never call her!"

"Just tell her that it's unfortunate Haley found it, and you never intended for her to see it."

I look into the living room and see they are still busy torturing Jay.

"Yeah, maybe," I say.

"If Corina intends to take you back to court again, you should at least document a response to show it wasn't intentional, 'cause you know she's implying it was."

"Yeah, I suppose You're right," I say. "I just don't want to deal with her shit today."

I pick up my phone to draft a message and see I have Facemail from Corina.

"Oh, good God," I say. "She sent me a Facemail. This should be fun!"

"Turn off hologram mode! You don't want the kids to see her face ballooned on top of the kitchen counter," she says.

I let out a resentful groan, clear my throat, and hold my phone up and prepare myself for ugliness. Corina stands by a blazing fire.

"Hi, I just wanted you to see me introducing your Cunt log, is it?" She clears her throat. "To my fireplace. It says bye-bye, asshole!"

She tosses the log into the fire, and the hungry flame devours it. She zooms in on the blaze, and I watch it burn. She flips me the bird, and the video ends abruptly.

I close my eyes and sulk after witnessing what, rather pathetically, feels like my life's work being incinerated. It amounts to a pile of ash in none other than Corina Rosario's fireplace. Hatred and resentment loom, and I try not to allow it to consume me.

"How could Haley be so shortsighted?" I say, feverishly rubbing my temples. "How could she just give it to her? I begged her to give me a chance to explain."

"Was it that bad? What did she say?" Stella asks.

"It's not what she said." I hand her the phone, "Here, watch for yourself."

Her brows lift, and her jaw drops open while she watches and listens to the devil sing. "She threw it in the fire? Oh, boy. Sorry, honey mou."

"What other method would Satan use?" I ask. "I know it's pathetic, but I feel like she just killed my dog. I worked so hard on that. It meant a lot to me, and I know it's ridiculous, but I felt like it validated all she put me through."

Stella puts her arms around my neck, "I know, honey mou. I'm so sorry."

"It was my only proof of the shit that has gone on all these years, and now look at it…a pile of fucken ashes."

My mind is saturated, on the verge of venting all of my emotions onto Stella like a Hurricane when, suddenly, the front door squeaks open and the smart alarm scan announces, "Visitor approved. Welcome home, Haley." My eyes spring open, I skirt around the island and see Haley standing in the foyer, clutching her bag to her chest. She stares back at me with a crooked smile. Relief and anger tussle within, uncertain whether to scold her or embrace in a warm hug.

"Haley, do you have any idea what you've done?" I say.

She looks at me conflicted, as divided on how to approach me as I am with her. The last thing I want is for her to feel as though she's unwelcomed at whichever home she arrives. I decide it is wise to shelve my anger for now. I pull her in and wrap my arms tightly around her.

"I love you, Haley, but why in the hell wouldn't you give me a chance to talk to you before you go and do a thing like that?"

"Dad, I'm sorry, but… I'm not sorry. I just had to," she says, lowering her head and staring at her foot that nervously taps the floor.

"Do you realize the spot you've put me in? This is surely going to set off another shit storm with your mom."

Annabel appears behind me, seemingly out of thin air, "What did she do?"

"Nothing, Annabel. Honey, please, this is between Daddy and Haley. Please, baby, go in the other room and watch Jay," I say.

"No, Dad. I'm not a baby anymore. I heard you say something about what Haley did is going to get Mom angry. What did she do?" Annabel demanded, eyes firm and unwavering.

Another conundrum presents itself, one that has repercussions, regardless of the path I choose. I promised my children long ago I would never lie to them and now I curse myself for not controlling my outburst until we were in private. I also vowed that no matter how poorly Corina spoke about me, I would not add to their mind fuck by speaking poorly of her in their presence.

My house would be a safe haven. A place where they could openly love both Mommy and Daddy and without fear or guilt. Do I tell her the truth and deal with that profound mess, or do I utter my first lie? The answer is an obvious one, but a white lie is a lie nonetheless, and I suspect Annabel will find out sooner than later and when she does, I don't want her to question her father's integrity. Perhaps I can tell her without divulging any details.

"Annabel, honey. Haley found a book of mine. Kind of like a diary I've kept since your mom and I separated. It upset her, that's all. Now, please go back in with Jay love, OK?"

"Well, can I see it?" Annabel asks.

"No, Annabel, please go," I say, pointing my finger towards the living room. "You're too young to understand and, frankly, so is Haley. It doesn't matter, anyway. It's been destroyed so—"

"Destroyed? Oh, you mean this?" Haley whips the log out of her bag and shakes it in the air as if she were a cheerleader with a pompom. I stare in disbelief, utterly confused. I imagine I look like a puppy with my head tilt on its side.

"What, you thought I'd actually be dumb enough to give her the only copy? As if! I made a copy…two actually. One for Mom and one for me," Haley says with a wink.

"Oh, you did, did you?" I say, standing tall, crossing my arms in front of my chest.

Why would she tell me that she made an extra copy? She must know I would, in no way, be agreeable to her keeping one. I'm relieved to see that the Cunt Log lives on. However, it concerns me that Haley is so hell bent on destroying her mother.

"Wait, if you have the original, how did Mom know the title? It was only on the front of the binder. That binder," I say, pointing at the one clutched to her chest.

With a wicked smirk, she says, "It was catchy, I had Staples add a title page when they made the copies. Actually, it was Jared's idea. You know, Dad, you'd really like him. He hates Mom, too," she says with a wink.

"Why would you hate Mom?" Annabel insists.

"OK, OK, OK! Haley, that's enough! No one hates Mom. Haley's just confused because of some things she read." My tone deepens. "Things she wasn't meant to read in the first place."

"As if I wouldn't read it?"

"OK, Haley, let's go for a ride."

Stella rests her arm around Annabel. "Come on, sweetie. Maybe your dad can pick us up some lunch while he's gone?"

"Sure," I say softly.

"Pizza!" Ileana yells from down the hall.

“Pizza again?” I say.

Ileana could never get enough pizza. It’s all she ever wants to eat. Thankfully, Stella and I are on the same page with their feeding ritual. They eat what we eat or they don’t eat at all. A few missed meals are all it takes to show them that their food strikes just end in hunger. We tame the beast and order takeout on the weekends, to give us a break and to give Ileana her fair share of pizza nights.

“OK, OK, pizza it is. I’ll pick up the usual from Dante’s?”

“OK, honey mou,” Stella says. She leans in and whispers into my ear, “Don’t be too hard on her, she’s going through something.”

Haley’s world has been shaken. She’s confused, hurt and stumbling down a dangerous path. She needs to understand that life isn’t always easy and each relationship between a man and a woman is unique. Sometimes, people just don’t complement each other, and when things implode, the way a person reacts isn’t always rational. Lord knows Corina isn’t rationale.

Haley has never had her heart broken, and her inexperience demonstrates she lacks the necessary means to pass judgment. A broken heart, especially when you feel as though you’ve been maltreated by someone you’ve given a large portion of your life to, isn’t easily mended, and it can poison your spirit if you let it. When you go through a divorce, animosity has a tendency to take over. You fight in court because your angry, hurt and, of course, greed tends to rear its ugly face.

The thing is, Corina was horrible, and I can’t make excuses for her. I’ll try for the sake of my children because it wouldn’t be fair for them to live with a vex resulting from our shortcomings as husband and wife. The least we could do is attempt to be good co-parents and not entangle them in our feuds.

“Come on, Haley, let’s go for a ride. Stella, could you take this and put it somewhere safe? Somewhere where no one can ever find it again.”

I hand her the log and grab my keys.

“Hell, maybe we should burn it after all!” Stella says as Haley and I walk into the garage.

We pull out of the driveway, and Haley gazes out of the passenger window and off into the distance. I can see the conflict in her eyes, reflecting off the window. I drive in silence for the next ten minutes to allow her to decompress.

"Dad?"

"Yes, sweetie?"

"I thought you wanted to talk?"

One of us had to break the silence eventually, but I was sure it would be me. I have been running through different scenarios and ways to say what I want to but, unfortunately, they are all intertwining in my mind.

"OK, first tell me how it went with your mother?"

"Exactly how you would expect it to go," she says sharply and with a hint condescension, though her voice broke, signaling she is resisting the urge to cry.

I make a right onto Maritime Avenue and continue to drive aimlessly. The traffic signals roll out the red carpet and seem to turn green for us as we approach them.

"Listen, divorce is a…"

"Dad, spare me the divorce is a difficult and complicated animal that comes with years of conflict talk. We've had it before," she says, rolling her eyes and returning her gaze out the window.

"Haley, I just want you to understand that when people get married, they do so because they love each other so much that they can't imagine living their life without the other person. Your mother and I got married young, probably too young and as we got older, we grew apart. You don't intend for it to happen but—"

"Blah, blah, blah, blah, blah," she interrupts.

"Haley, cut the crap and listen to me, please! When I'm finished, you can vent all you want, and I will just listen to everything you have to say," I say.

"Fine!"

I pause to regain my train of thought and remind myself that she is, as Stella put it, going through something.

"Look, love can be fantastic, but when it falls apart, it can also really suck. People get hurt in relationships, and a broken heart is nothing to laugh at. It truly can be a physical and emotionally painful thing. I hope you never have to go through it but truthfully, it's pretty unavoidable. It's an unfortunate part of life, but you know what's worse?"

"What, Dad?"

"What's worse is when people can't let go of their anger. Your mother is angry at me, for whatever reason, and she hasn't been able to move on from that. I don't know why. We haven't actually physically spoken since the divorce, but it's clear from what you can see in the log, she feels justified. I don't know if she resents my happiness or if she really thinks I was unfaithful. Either way, she thinks she has reason to hate me. I'm not condoning her behavior. In fact, I think it's truly disgusting, but if you hear only one thing from my rant, hear this..." I pause to see if she will interject. "You and Annabel are wonderful girls and both your mother and I love you very much. We are also human, and even though we're adults, adults make mistakes. It's OK to make mistakes as long as you learn from them. People are constantly growing, changing, and learning, no matter how old they are. If you stop learning, you're dead. You should always aim to be the best version of yourself that you can be because you are the only person you will have to answer to one day."

"OK, sure, Dad," she says with a snort.

"I know that sounds cliché, but it's true. You'll have to look yourself in the mirror one day, and you don't want to have any regrets. As much as you might hate your mother right now, she's your mom, and you will regret throwing that relationship away because of our mistakes. Learn from them, understand them as best you can, and aim to be better. Better than her and better than me. Be yourself and learn to forgive."

"Do you forgive Mom?" Haley asks.

I have to pause before I answer because, truthfully, no, I don't.

"No...I don't," I say.

"See?" she says as if she has outwitted me.

"No, what I see is that you weren't listening. Be better than me, and be better than your mother. I don't forgive Mom, but I've let go of my animosity. I've come to understand that your mother has reasons for feeling the way she does. They may be misguided, but they're her reasons. I don't understand what drives her hatred and, frankly, at this point, I don't care. All I want, and all I've ever wanted, is for you and your sister to not be harmed by our mistakes. I want you both to be happy and secure and understand that, although you may have gotten caught in the crossfire of our divorce, it isn't your burden to carry, it's ours!"

"That's a bunch of bullshit, Dad! Are you done?"

"Go ahead, Haley, give it to me."

"Mom lied to us our whole lives about everything. Do you know how hard it was to be five years old and have your mother telling you that Daddy hit Mommy and that he is a bad man? Then drop us off to you for your weekend? For what? So she can punish you? Do you realize what kind of a mind fuck that is?"

"I do," I say calmly.

"I was afraid to stay with you on your weekends."

"I know, I remember."

"She painted this picture of you I never really fully let go of. I have always loved you, but… I've always felt guilty about it. I thought you were a bad person, and I could only trust Mom. She said you were abusive, a liar, a cheater, and she said you didn't want to be with us because you didn't have the patience for children!" Her voice cracks, and tears gush.

It's hard to finally let these emotions out. She has kept them bottled up for so many years, especially when she feels like everything she had known and trusted was a lie or, at the very least, an extreme exaggeration. She can finally see her mother for who she is: weak, selfish, and ruthless. She knows she was used as a weapon as often as she was treated as her daughter.

"I understand, sweetie, I really do. I just don't—"

"I hate her, Dad! She has totally fucked up my head. Ahhhh," she groans. "I'm so confused!"

Several minutes of silence pass, and with each moment, my heart breaks, watching her cry into her sleeve. I feel responsible and not at all, all the same. I can't come up with anything to say to console her.

"I love you, Haley."

Her tears reduce to sniffles. I can only imagine how frustrated she must be.

"I understand, baby. I do, but she is your mother, and she can't be replaced. I also know that you love her, and I don't want to see this destroy your spirit. I can't sit here and tell you that the things that your saying don't burn in my gut. It brings me back to when you were so young and all of the challenges I had to overcome with you. The senseless crying when I picked you up, and the things you would say to me that broke my heart. I understood you were just repeating phrases you heard from Mom, but they still hurt like hell. What she did was horrible, but I want you to understand her intent was to hurt me, not you. Yes, it's true she used you girls against me, but her ignorance blinded her from seeing she was hurting you in the process. She let her anger control her, it poisoned her soul."

"She has no soul, Dad!"

"Haley, you need to process this, and in time, I think you will have a different perspective," I say.

"Yeah, when?"

"It may take years Haley, but I think when you're older and you've had more life experiences under your belt, you may look at this whole thing differently."

We drive the rest of the way to Dante's in silence. Haley's eyes are glued to her phone. Her fingers slam the keyboard, moving at lightning speed, messaging who I presume to be Jared. I can only imagine what she is saying.

If I could only read them, perhaps then I would know exactly what she is thinking. Her reality has been altered, her mind restructured, and it will take time for her to make sense of it all, and she will have to do so on her own terms. I'm just hopeful she will grow from this and not regress.

"Dad?"

"Yes, sweetie?"

Can Jared pick me up at Dante's? Please, Dad, I just need someone to talk to."

"Haley, talk to me. You know, you may not believe it now but, one day, you'll see I am truly your best friend. You can talk to me about anything. I'm actually a pretty good listener."

"I know, Dad. I love you, but I need to get away for a bit. I feel like someone died, and the more I look at you, the more I think about it. Please, Dad?"

"OK, but you're supposed to go home to Mom's tonight. You're still a kid, and you need to go home," I say.

"I'm not a kid," she cuts back.

"I'll rephrase. You're under eighteen, so you're not legally an adult, and if you think I'd let you stay out all night with Jared, you've officially lost your mind."

"Can I stay at your house for a while?"

"My house? My house is your house but, somehow, I don't think your mother will approve. She would likely call the police and tell them I kidnapped you."

Haley snickers and looks out the window again. "Yeah, you're probably right, but I really can't talk to her."

"I'll tell you what, text her and ask if you can stay with me for a few days and tell her to message me if she is agreeable to it," I say. "OK?"

"She'll never go for it," Haley says defeated.

"Probably not, but you won't know unless you try. If you ever feel unsafe in any way, you come to me immediately. I know John has a bit of a temper."

John Rosario, Corina's husband, is a short-tempered little bulldog with an inflated perception of himself.

I pull into a spot at Dante's and see Jared's classic 2006 Subaru Impreza is already in the parking lot. It's unmistakable. You don't see many of those around anymore. A few years ago, they mandated all cars must be converted to full electric. It was a real blow to the oil industry, and it nearly crippled the economy, but they were left with little choice after global warming could not be contested any longer.

Wars were being fought over it and countries like China and India were forced to reduce industrial pollution, while the United States, among others, were mandated to limit beef and dairy consumption and find a way to limit environmental waste. Data was finally made public that cattle methane was a major contributor, along with non-recyclable, non-biodegradable materials like plastic bags were banned. The Earth would no longer take a back seat to capitalism, and I, for one, couldn't agree more. The Earth should always come first.

Jared is a product of a silver spoon play acting a role of a hoodlum. His parents paid an obscene amount of money to have his Impreza converted over to an electric motor to meet environmental regulations. He had it painted the most hideous yellow color and outfitted with matching yellow and black rims. It looks like an immaculate pile of bee shit. I really don't know what Haley sees in this kid.

I see a scrawny little runt with reddish brown hair, riddled with acne scattered about his forehead. He leans against the side of his car, smoking a cigarette. He thinks he is the James Dean of the new age. He has a beard that he has no business growing, filled with patches and a shine to it, which gives the appearance that he doesn't practice good hygiene.

Haley on the other hand, has beautifully flawless skin, high cheekbones and gorgeously thick, flowing brown hair. She could be a model, if that were her desire.

"Haley, I really don't care for this kid. You can do far better!" I insist.

"You don't know him, Dad. He's really great."

"He smokes cigarettes and marijuana from the looks of it. He hasn't been very respectful when I've spoken to him. I really don't think he's the catch you think he is."

"He doesn't smoke marijuana, but so what if he did, it's legal," she says.

"Maybe so, but not for a seventeen-year-old, and I don't like the idea of you hanging around someone who's drinking and smoking weed, especially when you're getting into his car."

"Relax, Dad. Jared doesn't do that stuff, and besides, he wouldn't drive if he were drunk or high."

"Be careful, please. Be smart! I raised you to be smart. Don't get in the car with anyone who has been doing anything. It isn't cool to be dead," I say.

"Yes, Dad," she says, rolling her eyes. "I have to go. He's waiting for me. Bye, Dad."

She gets out of the car and slams the door.

I lower the window and yell loud enough for both of them to hear me, "Call or text me later and let me know where you will be staying tonight, with me or your mom. And text your mom, Haley. I don't want a visit from the police tonight because you never went home! If I do, it will be the last time you spend time with Jared!"

She turns and waves me off and runs into Jared's arms.

"Go home, Haley! Tonight!"

I remember what it was like to be young and in love, but it makes me sick to think she's already seventeen and what she might be doing with this boy. She's obviously taken by him, but I just have to have faith in her and pray she isn't sexually active. The thought of it runs through my head and makes my stomach turn.

*

Dante's is the only real pizzeria left in this part of New Jersey. The millennials have transformed the pizza restaurant industry into trendy internet cafes, serving brick oven, single serve pies, smothered with ingredients like figs, quinoa, and kale, along with overpriced lattes and imitation Italian espresso.

"Hey, Tony, pick up for Grady," I say.

"Sure thing. Give me a few minutes, pal. It'll be out in just a sec."

I walk over to the refrigerator and grab two liters of soda for the kids. Out of the corner of my eye, I see a couple in the back of the restaurant cuddled in a booth. The man's face is buried in the woman's neck, and they clearly aren't hiding their affection for one another. When the man lifts his head, I immediately recognize him. John Rosario; Corina's husband, and the women is clearly not Corina.

"Oh, just perfect," I mutter under my breath.

They sit way too close to be casual friends, and I've never fed pizza or suctioned my lips to a casual friend's neck before.

"OK, Dylan, all set," Tony shouts from behind the counter.

I politely nod to Tony and shift my gaze back to where John is seated. Our eyes lock, and his demeanor becomes uneasy. A preverbal "oh shit" expression manifests upon his face, and he noticeably fidgets in his seat. He leans over and whispers something into his companion's ear, and the woman awkwardly forces her eyes up to look at me. I meet her guilt-ridden face with a half-cocked smile, and she abruptly scoots out of the booth and scurries into the ladies' room. John confidently stands up and puffs his chest, adjusts his already too snug jeans around his waist, and with a cocky swagger, makes his way over to me.

"Hey, Dylan, what's up?"

"John," I acknowledge him, but I don't offer my hand.

I've met John on a number of occasions over the years. Most of them were at my parenting time exchanges when picking up the girls curbside at their mother's home. I've always found him to be brash and never particularly kind. However, I imagine from the stories Corina has concocted over the years, he doesn't think much of me, either. He is passive aggressive and attempts to assert his dominance, like a dog marking his territory.

On one occasion, after I finished situating the girls in the car, he reached out and offered me his hand. I obliged, although, when our hands met, he firmed his grip, squeezing my hand as tightly as he could and says, "Now, be a good boy this weekend, you hear?"

I chuckled, instantly becoming flush. It ignited the beast within me, and I wanted to pounce on him. My adrenaline would have allowed me to rip metal like paper, but I reminded myself his plan was to provoke me. They would love nothing more than for me to give them a reason to involve the police. To add another scene to the drama they have scripted.

John clears his throat. "Just having lunch with an old college buddy. What brings you down this way?" He offers me his hand, but I continue to stare blankly at him and reject his phony gentlemanly offer.

"Just pizza, John. Looks like you two are quite the, uh, old acquaintances," I say with a wink.

"Oh, Dylan boy, don't be getting any stupid ideas. I'm not someone you want to fuck with in your, uh...position."

"Are you threatening me, Johnny...boy?" I take a step closer, closing the gap between us.

"Guys, guys, guys, please? Not in the store. Let's keep things cool. *Capisce*?" Tony says, reaching for the house phone. He jiggles it in the air, insinuating he will call the police if he has to.

"No worries, Tony, I'm leaving. Here, scan an extra twenty, buy the happy couple a round of drinks on me," I say smugly, opening my eye and leaning into the iris pay scanner. I smile at him as I back out of the door, holding my pies.

The door swings closed behind me, and John reaches his hand out to catch it and yells, "By the way, I love your logbook. Great read!"

"Alrighty, John, learn anything?" I holler back as I continue to walk to my car, but I refuse to turn around and engage him any longer.

I start the car and set my music to my most serene playlist. I titled it "Because it's Beautiful" because I filled it with gorgeous, calming music like Sigur Ros, new age classical, and Joselyn Stars. John stands in the center of my rearview mirror, holding his phone to his ear, staring me down as I back out of the parking space. What a pathetic little man. I zoom past him, and he steps into the street with his arms spread, slamming his fist to his chest, challenging me like a gorilla.

With my foot on the pedal and the window open, I wave to him, fluttering my fingers. "Bye-bye, sweetie!"

Good for Corina. Her second husband seems to be everything she painted me to be. Karma is certainly an ugly bitch, isn't she? I turn down Jarvis Lane, and I can't help but salivate over the pizzas' intoxicating aroma, and I fight every urge to take a slice. It's been a long day, and Dante's is a great way to cap it off. I'm looking forward to cuddling up with Stella and the kids on the couch, renting a movie, and indulging in a little heaven.

I close my eyes, sink into the heated seat, and let autopilot take over when a flash of blue and red light up the sky all around me. I look to my rear and see two police cars, sirens blaring, accelerating up behind me, and I pull to the shoulder, slow down to allow them to pass. Someone is about to have a rough night, I think.

At the rate they're traveling, someone is either in grave danger or in a heap of trouble. I decelerate but note their speed also decreases rapidly, and they appear to be veering behind me on the shoulder. Confusion and mild trepidation infuse when the *whoop-whoop* of the sirens sound, signaling for me to pull over.

I search my memory, but I can't think of anything I did that would warrant a traffic stop. However, it isn't uncommon for suburban police officers to treat minor traffic infringements as though a felony had been committed. The crime rate is low, their pay is high, and many love utilizing the power they have been bestowed.

The officer gets out of his car and unlocks the holster of his firearm, rests his hand on the pistol grip, and cautiously makes his way to my driver's side window. I proceed to lower my window but am startled to hear a knock at the passenger door. I didn't realize there were officers approaching my car on both sides. Darkness crept in early today, and the squad lights blind me as they reflect off my rearview mirror, so I reach my hand up to avert it.

"Sir! Both hands on the wheel! Where I can see them!" he yells, and both officers simultaneously draw their firearms.

I raise my hands, but then feverishly slam them down on top of the steering wheel, eager to comply.

"Sorry, the lights were blinding, I just wanted to—"

"Driver's license and registration, sir," the officer at my window says, growling, gritting his teeth together.

I upload my license to the cars I-shield, and he shines the flashlight down, studies it for a moment, and then nods to the other officer.

"Mr. Grady, please step out of the car sir," he commands.

"I'm sorry, but can you tell me what I've done, Officer? Why do I need to—"

"Sir! Get out of the vehicle now!" the second officer barks and sticks his gun through my passenger window.

The first officer attempts to open my driver's side door, but my doors remain locked, and the handle releases with an anticlimactic *thud*. I better comply.

"Can I move to unlock the doors, Officers?" I ask. My voice shakes, and my hands tremble.

The officer nods, takes a step backward, and maintains his gun pointed at me. I unlock the doors, and he immediately swings it open. My nerves have taken control and when I attempt to step out, I am abruptly halted by my seatbelt, which remains engaged.

I move to unbuckle it, and the officer scolds, "Slowly, Mr. Grady!"

His gun and flashlight follow my hands, and I cautiously reach to my side to unclip the seatbelt using only my right hand and maintaining my left on the wheel. These officers appear to be jumpy, and I want to demonstrate my submission. I slowly step out and glimpse the second officer scurrying around to the front of my car. The first officer grabs me violently, twists my wrist, spins me around, and slams me with great force onto the hood.

Furious, I belt out, "Is this really necessary? What's this all about?"

I've just entered my neighborhood, and I'm being slammed up against my car and frisked by the police as if I were a hardened criminal. In a quiet neighborhood such as this, excitement is sparse, and this is quite a spectacle.

"When was the last time you saw your ex-wife, Corina Rosario, Mr. Grady?" the second officer interrogates.

"Uh, like twelve years ago!" I answer truthfully and let out a sardonic laugh.

He snickers. "Oh? So, you didn't just have a run-in with her at Dante's Pizzeria? Sure smells like pizza in your car. O'Sullivan, you hungry?"

Suddenly, it rains down on me like a monsoon. John. That motherfucker! He called the police and alleged I violated the order of protection.

"No, I saw her husband, John. Corina wasn't there!" I insisted.

The first officer pulls back on my wrists until I squirm.

"OK, well, we can talk about it down at the station. Do I have to cuff you or are you going to come—"

"Cuff 'im," the second officer interjects. "I don't like his tone."

I glare up at the officer and catch a glimpse of his badge: Joseph Rosario. Rosario? Could he be related to John? I study his face and note he has the same crooked Italian nose and olive complexion. Clearly a resemblance, although this man is much larger. His back, like John's, is a bit kyphotic, pushing his shoulders forward and giving him a slight hunchback. The resemblance is striking, and I have little doubt about their relation.

"My car. What am I going to do about my car?"

"We'll call a tow," says the first officer.

"I live a block and half from here, can I just have my—"

"Tow!" Officer Rosario snaps.

Officer O'Sullivan looks hesitantly at Officer Rosario and says, "Joe, maybe we could just call his..."

"Tow, O'Sullivan, goddammit!" He glares at his partner, warning him not to challenge his authority.

The heat builds in my chest, and the veins pulsate in my temples. My hands clench into fists, and my blood pressure blasts off. I need to calm myself as best as I can because the worst thing for me to do right now is lose my temper or be combative.

The injustices I have experienced have brought me to a boiling point, and it amazes me I haven't snapped yet. It's been one thing after another for the past twelve years, and I think back to all of the abuse that I've suffered at Corina's hands. I've powered through all of it, but this is fucking humiliating. It brings me back to that ugly day when I was served the temporary order of protection and escorted out of my house by two officers. At least those officers were somewhat sympathetic, but Joseph Rosario has already convicted and sentenced me for a crime I haven't committed.

"Am I under arrest officer?" I ask.

Officer Rosario hisses and reads me my rights while O'Sullivan secures the cuffs behind my back. He stands me up, grabbing the back of my shirt, and yanks me upright.

"Let's make sure those cuffs are secure. This one appears dangerous. After all, he likes to beat up women," Rosario ridicules with a half-cocked smile.

He squeezes both cuffs and tightens them so hard I feel them cutting into my wrists, and I wince in pain but remain silent.

"Alright, alright. Enough, Cap, let's get him into the station," Officer O'Sullivan says.

O'Sullivan guides me to the back seat of his squad car. "Sorry, bud. I guess Captain Rosario don't fancy you much. OK, in you go, watch your head."

Captain? Oh, dear God! This pompous ass is the man in charge? The utter doom of my situation settles in, and without options, I accept my path. As we pull away, I glance down my street and can see my house lights on. I think about how Stella must be starting to wonder where I am and if I'm alright. Everything happened so fast I wasn't able to grab my phone, although I doubt they would have let me take it with me, anyway.

My mind races through multiple scenarios, and I imagine Stella calling me, over and over, only to be greeted by my voicemail again and again. As the night pushes on, her worry will shift to panic. I should be allowed to call them when we get to the station. I think about Ileana, Jay, and Annabel. They will surely be worried also. It has always been difficult for Stella to keep her emotions in. She needs to release them. We are very similar that way.

"Can I call my girlfriend when we get to the station to let her know that I'm alright?" I ask.

Captain Rosario turns around and looks me in the eye with a villainous gaze. "Girlfriend, eh? No, you can't call your girlfriend. Maybe if she were your wife it would be different, but no girlfriends!"

My voice deepens, but I try and control my tone. "Listen, we've been together for twelve years. She is my wife, just not legally. We have two children together, and they're going to be worried sick."

"Buddy, all we do is legal. What about *no* don't you understand? You think I give a shit about your girlfriend or your two bastards?"

A pain strikes my chest, and like a furnace, I incinerate Rosario, limb by limb in my mind's eye. How dare he call my children bastards. I'm left with little doubt that Captain Joseph Rosario is Corina's brother in-law. His resemblance to John is uncanny, and he clearly has every intention of playing a key role in Corina's theatre. To make matters worse, he really has the power to fuck me. Corina would have never played this hand when I was still paying her alimony. After all, I was her meal ticket. If I were to get locked up and lose my job, her payday would be lost along with it.

"Aren't I entitled to a phone call?"

"You'll get your phone call when I say you get your call, *capisce*?"

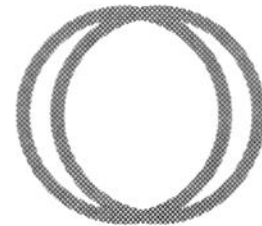

# CHAPTER 5

Have you ever tried walking while your hands are cuffed behind your back? Let me tell you, it is no easy task. My equilibrium is thrown off and walking straight is no longer mundane. I find myself attempting to focus my eyes on a fixed point to maintain balance, and I realize that the only thing that will break my fall is my face. Of course, it doesn't help that Captain Rosario is shoving me every which way, using the back of my shirt as if he were a ventriloquist and I was his puppet.

He shoves me into a small square room that resembles one of those interrogation rooms you see in movies from the 1980s. It has a small, square metallic table bolted to the floor, three chairs, and what I presume to be a two-way mirror. The lights are incredibly bright. One beams like a spotlight on my chair, hot and blinding, and another is shone at the mirror. He shoves me in, and I stumble to the ground and with a wicked smile he orders me to remain seated.

They leave me in solitary, cuffed and bruised for what feels like an eternity. Waiting and worrying in utter silence, in a room filled with nothing but my pain and anxiety.

Several hours later, the door swings open, and Officer O'Sullivan comes in and removes the cuffs, looking over his shoulder to make sure no one sees him.

"I'm sorry, he shouldn't have left you cuffed like this," he says.

I glance up at him and nod and gawk down at my raw, lacerated wrists in gross disbelief, and I try, but I can't flex or extend them without significant discomfort. I work them in circles to loosen them without any relief. This is certainly police brutality, but I know better than to make a commotion. At least officer Darby O'Sullivan appears to be a good apple among a rotten harvest.

I think about Stella and the kids, and I know they are undoubtedly panicked by now. I imagine Stella must be losing her mind. It really infuriates me they won't allow me to call them. I estimate I left the house a little over three hours ago, and I imagine she has called me multiple times and is more horrified every time she gets my voicemail.

Suddenly, I hear muffled voices. Several officers, including Captain Rosario congregate by the door, and I watch them with a sardonic grin as they strategize behind the small square window. Their nods and shakes are enough to tell me they are plotting my interrogation.

Captain Rosario opens the door and takes a step towards me when I hear a familiar female voice down the hall. He stops in his tracks and circles back, slamming the metal framed door shut behind him. It's Corina, that bitch! I'd recognize that entitled voice anywhere! She is much shorter than Rosario, and I can only see the top of her head, but the unmistakable wicked librarian bun adds confirmation to my suspicion.

Moments later, the door swings open with a *squeak*, and this time, Rosario enters looking down into a folder. He licks his fingers and flips through them one by one as he strolls slowly to his chair.

"Mr. Grady," he says, slamming the file onto the table, "you left quite a shiner on your ex-wife. Let me ask you, how does that make you feel? Like a big, powerful man? I mean, after all, you outweigh her by what, two to one?"

I look up at him, cocking my head to the side. Corina has a black eye? Would she really go this far to put me in jail? Does he sincerely believe I assaulted her or is he, the dear brother in-law, in on their scheme?

"Shiner?" I ask with my mouth hung open in disbelief.

"Yeah, numbskull, from where you put your fist into her eye," he says, pausing between each syllable. He leans back into his chair, crosses his arms in front of his chest, and winks at me, grinning ear to ear.

“Bullshit! I told you, I haven’t been within fifty feet of Corina since the day we separated!”

“Uh huh,” he mutters and proceeds to narrate his story. “You see her at Dante’s picking up some pies. You two get into it about some logbook you wrote. Ring any bells?”

“The logbook? No.”

“She tells you she torched it. You exchange words, and when she follows you out to your car, likely provoking you, I’ll give you that much. Then *boom!* You spin around and sock her! Got her good, too!”

“Are you kidding me?” No! Like I told you before, Corina was not there! I saw her husband John and—”

Rosario cuts me off and reaches into his folder and flings three pictures, one after another, onto the table. “OK, Dylan, you can tell it to the judge. The evidence is clear cut.”

I stare at the photos on the table, spread out like a crime scene, showcasing Corina’s battered eye from three different angles.

I place my hands down on the table and lean into him. “I didn’t hit anyone!” I yell.

“OK, sure,” he says. “We also have a credible witness.”

“Who?” I ask.

“Her husband, John Rosario,” he says.

“That’s your credible witness? Oh, give me a break!” I shout.

“I’ve known John, uh, quite a while, I’ve never known him to be a liar. And I certainly have no—

I disrupt him mid-sentence. “Hey, you’re Joe Rosario? John Rosario? You two look like you could be twins, any chance you’re related?”

“Johnny is my little brother, but that has nothing to—”

“Isn’t that a bit of a conflict of interest?” I say.

“Conflict of interest?” he hisses.

“Yeah, I’d say you’re biased, to say the least. I mean, shit, you already have your mind made up, and you haven't even begun to investigate!"

I see the anger cultivating in his eyes. His brow arches, and his fists clench, and I can see the folder wrinkle within his grip.

"This is some pretty damning evidence, wouldn't you say?" he says, jabbing his pointer finger repeatedly onto the photo of Corina's battered eye.

"You haven't even asked me my version! You just keep repeating their nonsense!"

I'm what you would call hangry at this point. I haven't eaten in about twenty-four hours. I'm irritable, and I've had enough of this bullshit!

"Did you review the CCTV at Dante's? Did you speak to Tony? I mean, Jesus, he witnessed the whole damn thing! You have nothing! You'd see that I'm innocent if you just did a little bit of police work!"

Rosario laughs at my insult and, smugly, he says, "OK, so let's hear your version, sport."

"Hear this," I say. "I want my lawyer." I raise my battered wrists into his view.

"Lawyer, Dylie?" he asks, releasing a wicked laugh.

"I'll say one more thing before I stop talking altogether."

He sits back into his chair and returns his arms crossed in front of his chest. "Yeah, Grady, what's dat?"

"Hey, Corina! Yup, I know your there! Your husband is cheating on you with some redhead. That's who he was with at Dante's, and I'm willing to bet that John's the one who gave you the shiner! Eh?"

"OK, tough guy, let's show you to your accommodations," he growls and pops out of his chair, knocking it backwards onto the ground.

"I want my phone call!" I demand.

"Sure, you said you wanted to call your lawyer, isn't that right, sport?"

*

I awaken in the precinct's holding cell at 6:48 in the morning. The giant clock on the wall, adjacent from my cell has kept me awake all night with its inordinately loud *tick, tick, ticking.*

"Mr. Grady, your lawyer is here!" the officer yells from down the hall, and he escorts Susan Duncan in.

She stops in front of my cell, tilts her head, and thins her lips sympathetically. "Dylan, I'm so sorry you're still dealing with her in this capacity. Hell, your case was one of my first when I was shadowing Jerry at the beginning of my practice, and you're still being tormented by her? What has it been, eleven years?"

"Twelve," I say. "It is what it is, but thank you for your, um, condolences."

"It's good to see you. You look good. Well…all things considered."

"Thanks. The bars are slimming," I say. "I also haven't eaten in about thirty-six hours, so, I may be able to slide through them by this afternoon."

Her mouth drops open. "They didn't give you any food?"

"Or water! I'm dying of thirst here," I say, followed by a dry swallow.

"Well, we're going to get you out of here soon. Let me see if I can get you some water."

Susan walks down the corridor and speaks with the officer on guard duty. I can't hear what they are saying, but I can tell she is giving him an earful. The officer glances up, and then down at his feet, nods his head as a boy who had just been scolded by his mother would. She spins around and confidently walks back down the hall, shaking her head in disgust. She approaches my cell, silent and confident, opens her briefcase, and pulls out some documents. She flips through them, scanning them one by one, glances up at me between pages.

"They're bringing water now," she says. "So, let's get to it. They claim that you hit your ex-wife outside of Dante's pizzeria."

"Susan, she wasn't even there," I appeal.

I proceed to tell her everything that happened yesterday evening, and she listens in disbelief. I told her about Haley finding the Cunt Log, though she didn't find the name quite as amusing as Haley did. How I ran into John with his mistress and being pulled over by Rosario and detailed the treatment I received from him. I also unloaded my suspicions of collusion and unfolded the drama that Captain Joseph Rosario is John Rosario's older brother, and that Corina was not only at the station, but I suspect she was watching and listening to them interrogate me.

"It's all a scheme to destroy me! Susan, I don't give a shit about Corina! She has put me through so much shit over the years, you think I'd hit her now?

They locked me up and didn't even allow me to call my..." I gasp. "Stella! She must be worried sick! Please, Susan, can I use your phone to call her?"

"They should've let you call her last night. You're legally entitled to it. Listen, I shouldn't be passing you a cell phone in here, but I'll call her and let her know what happened, OK? You just relax and let me handle this. If what you're telling me is true, and I'm sure it is, you have nothing to worry about. We'll speak with Tony at Dante's, get the CCTV footage proving your innocence, and we'll see about getting you out of here by early this afternoon at the latest. OK?"

"OK," I say, feeling a little relieved.

"Here, write Stella's number down, and I'll go and call her immediately," she says, passing me a pen and one of her business cards to write on.

I write her number down as clearly as possible, but the pen argues with my trembling hands. My nerves, along with my blood pressure, have been put to the test, but if I haven't had a stroke yet, then I'm evaluating myself to be as healthy as a cow during lent. I pass her back the contraband and instantly feel a release. At least I know Stella and the kids will get word that I'm alright.

"OK, I'll see about getting you some food. Anything else I can do for you?" she asks.

"No, Susan, thank you. Susan? Please call Stella. Let her know that I'm alright?"

"As soon as I'm out that door, hang tight."

She walks down the long, concrete corridor, leaving a trail of confidence and overpowering perfume behind.

I sit and replay everything that has transpired over and over in my head, and I can't help but feel numb. How could anyone sink this low, even Corina? I knew she would retaliate after reading the log, but I didn't imagine, in my wildest dreams, I would be sitting in a holding cell, awaiting judgment for another one of her heinous schemes.

My spine cracks, and it feels as though it has separated from my body. The muscles hang like dead weight, pulling on my facet joints until the connective tissue holds on by a thread. The cell's bed is, what amounts to, a steel bench with a couch pillow and a thin, dirt-laden blanket. I decide to do some yoga stretches on the concrete floor to loosen up and overhear the guards making jokes at my expense as I enter into my downward dog. I don't care. I must alleviate this nagging pain.

A guard approaches my cell and slides a tray through the feeder. A crusty stale bagel, a cold cup of coffee, and a half-eaten container of yogurt sits on top of a faded blue plastic tray.

"Here you go, twinkle toes. Hope you're enjoying your stay at our fine establishment. We accept tips."

I wanted to give him a tip alright. How about innocent until proven guilty? You shouldn't judge anyone until you have all the facts and have heard both sides of the story. How about doing some investigating before locking me in a cage? I overcome my urge to react and understand it would be a pointless argument and would certainly do more harm than good. I keep my lips sealed and graciously accept my scraps.

I guzzle the coffee and devour the stale, crusty bagel, however, it's been so long since I've eaten anything that I begin to feel nauseous, as though my body were rejecting it. My shoveling reduces to nibbling and my gulps to sips. I don't touch the potentially tainted yogurt, and when finished, I sit anxiously and await word from my lawyer.

In a world where we are always an iris scan away from entertainment, you rely on these things to keep your mind occupied. It's sad actually. Everything these days is robotic. I recall when I was a child, sitting for hours in my room with no television, robots, smart phones, tablets, or video games; they simply didn't exist. I had a few toys and would play for hours, using nothing but my imagination. I'd pretend that my bed was a mountain and that the radiator were a fortress.

Life, as I remember it, was much simpler then. Kids don't even know how to use their imaginations anymore. There is too much access to entertainment, and every toy does something, leaving little to the mind's eye. The world is filled with miniature computer engineers and computing code is taught more than spoken languages. After all, people communicate far more with devices than their tongues these days.

Annabel and Haley often sit at the kitchen table messaging each other instead of engaging in conversation. At first, I thought they just wanted to talk about me or Stella but after poking and prodding them, they showed me it was just mindless banter, sending each other holographic memes and interesting facts.

I sit and stare at the empty concrete wall, and I can't help but feel sorry for myself. I need to trust that Susan will work diligently to get me out of here, and I need to have faith she was able to reach Stella, and she and the children know now I'm alright.

"Mr. Grady," I hear his voice and my stomach turns, "how'd ya sleep?" Captain Rosario says.

Startled, I fling my head up to meet his arrogant smile. I didn't hear him coming over my self-pity.

"Jumpy today, I see," he says.

"Yeah, I guess that's what injustice does to you," I mutter.

"Uh huh," he says. "So, Mr. Grady, please…accept my apology. It turns out your story checks out after all. Must have been someone else that gave ol' Corina the eyeshadow. Just a case of mistaken identity, I guess." He shrugs his shoulders, trying to resist the urge to smile, but his cheekbones involuntarily flex.

"Really? Mistaken identity, huh?" Doing my best to resist the urge to lash out at him.

"Yup! Appears to be," he says, liberating a chuckle.

"I hardly find this funny, Captain. Isn't it a crime to lie to the police and frame—"

"Mr. Grady, I'm not hearing, 'Thank you, Captain, I'm just so happy this has been all cleared up, I'll be on my way now.' It would be best that you drop it and move on. You see, sometimes people see what they want to, rather than what actually is, so just let it go."

I can't hold back any longer. "So, then it has nothing to do with you protecting your brother and sister in-law after committing a crime? And what about police harassment? Let's talk about that!" I lift my bruised wrists to his eye level so he can get a good look.

Officer Rosario looks down and takes a deep breath, glances back up at me with a grimace, and says, "Well, I still think you did it. My brother ain't no liar. You see, we just can't prove it. It's her word against yours, but the CCTV and Tony seem to corroborate your story, so I have no choice but to let you go, but let's just say, I'm not convinced."

"Yup, got it." I snicker. "Un-fucken-believable!"

Rosario takes a challenging step towards me, puffs his chest, and places his hand on his baton as I move to take my first step out of the cell.

"Watch it, Grady," he tells me.

The adrenaline pumps so hard in my veins that I feel as though they may burst. However, there are some battles you just don't have a choice but to concede. No matter how right I am or how much of a jack ass he is, this would only end disastrously for me. I have to keep my cool. I need to get out of here and live free to fight another day.

With all the will I can muster, I say, "Thank you, Captain, for all of your hospitality. May I please go home now?"

"Better," he says, stepping aside and allowing me to pass. I reach the door at the end of the hallway, and as my hand reaches for the knob, Rosario shouts, "I'd offer you a lift, but I think a walk may do you some good. After all, you had a big breakfast! Walk it off, sport!" He laughs, and his laughter echoes through the small precinct cell block. What a couple of assholes. Joseph and John Rosario are two peas in a pod.

There is nothing quite as disheartening as a police officer who abuses the power he is bestowed. It's no wonder why so many Americans look at the police as their enemy, often deemed guilty because of the color of their skin or perceived socioeconomic status. Police are there to preserve the peace, enforce the law, and reduce fear. What does it say about the local police when they instill fear in the innocent? I am guilty because they say I am, even though the evidence contradicts their charge.

The air hits my face as I walk out of the precinct, and I marvel at how good it feels to be free. I can't imagine what it must feel like after being incarcerated for a lengthy period of time.

A droplet of water explodes on the top of my head. It's raining, and I don't have an umbrella or a coat, and my phone remains locked inside of my car, wherever that might be. I won't waste my breath asking to use the station phone, and it would be senseless to look for a payphone as those have been obsolete for a long time now.

I begin the long, cold, wet, three-mile trek home, and it feels good to stretch my legs, but I must admit that I'm anxious to get home to Stella and the kids. The rain picks up and, in an instant, I find I am soaked, so I pick up the pace. I always walk as if everything I do is emergent, anyway. It's an unfortunate byproduct of being from the New York metropolitan area.

I find myself rushing through everything in order to have a little more time to relax at the end of the day but if I really think about it, I have a difficult time winding down, and perhaps it takes me longer to wind down than time I had presumed to have saved.

I turn down my block, shivering, soaking wet, when a siren blares behind me, startling me. I spin around, maintaining my hands in my pockets only to see Captain Rosario wave as he zooms past, adding insult to injury. I concede to it all and allow the rain to cleanse me, washing away the fury. I'm just happy to be steps away from my home, from my family, the people who truly bring me happiness.

I stumble up the steps, approach the door, and raise my finger to the bell when, out of nowhere, the door swings open, and Stella stands in the doorway. Her mouth hangs open, and she stares in disbelief for a moment at my dripping silhouette but, within seconds, she slams her body into mine, embracing me with the warmest hug I have ever received, and I instantly feel the relief melt off her.

"Oh, honey mou. Are you OK? What the hell happened? I was so… Thank God you're home!"

She frantically kisses my cheeks, neck, and chest, and then she rests her head on my soaked shirt that is stuck to my body like latex.

I step into the doorway and am greeted by the smart homes alarm system, "Welcome home, Mr. Grady."

I sigh and caress Stella's face. "Let me put on some dry clothes, and I'll tell you all about it," I say. "Where are the kids?"

"It's Monday, honey mou. They're in school."

"Right," I say, shaking my head. "Where did you tell them I was?"

Stella glances up at me, pulls me in close again, and cries uncontrollably.

"I was so worried! There was no way for me to hide it!"

"Shhhh, shhhh, shhhh. I know. It's OK."

I kiss her and rest my chin upon her head and bask in her love.

"Dylan, they could see it. They knew something was wrong when you never came home, and I couldn't…I just couldn't."

"It's OK, my love. Where's Annabel? How did she get to?"

"Well, no one called, and I didn't know what to do, so she stayed here, and I took her to school this morning. I called every hospital, and the police, and no one knew anything. I was freaking out. I didn't sleep a wink, and I don't think the kids did, either. I had no choice, I had to tell them! I didn't know where you were! I couldn't lie, I just couldn't pull it off."

"You called the Weston Police?"

"Yeah, like a dozen times," she says. "And Scotchfield, Franklin, you name it!"

It's clear now they intentionally kept my location from Stella. I have to think that breaks some kind of law. Surely, they aren't above the law? They can abuse me all they want, but what animal would make innocents suffer? Stella and the children didn't deserve to be terrorized, and by none other than the local police. There is nothing worse than the unknown and the mental torture your racing mind can inflict.

"They didn't even let me call you. I was so worried about you guys!" I say, pulling her in tighter.

Tears run down my cheeks like a winding river, moistening every crevice, and before I know it, I am crying like an overtired toddle. We embrace in the doorway, sobbing in each other's arms for what feels like an eternity. When we finally manage to pull away, I see the clouds part, the rain stops suddenly and the sun peeks through the clouds, beaming through the doorway. It's moments like this that force me to reconsider the possibility that God exists and that, perhaps, he is sending me a message.

"I'm drained," I say.

"Me too. I need a glass of wine." She sniffs and tries to stop gasping for air. "And a cigarette."

We both quit smoking years ago but often have a pack lying around for moments of extreme stress; moments precisely like this.

I change my clothes and open a bottle of wine, and Stella grabs the pack of cigarettes out of the safe, securely locked away from the children. I pour two tall glasses, and we head out onto the deck with our wine and cigarettes. We drink and smoke, and I tell her all about what happened, and she listens, her jaw dropping open as her cigarette burns down to the butt.

"Oh, my God. Where's your car?" she asks.

"They had it towed. I don't know where, either. We passed a Franco's tow truck when they were bringing me in. Perhaps I'll start there. Maybe they have it."

"They didn't tell you where?"

"Nope, and I was so eager to get out of there, I forgot to ask. Likely wouldn't tell me, anyway."

"Can't blame you," she says.

We sit in silence and savor the solace.

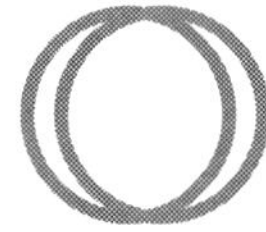

# CHAPTER 6

"Hi, I'm Dylan Grady. I'm here for my car."

"License and plate number," the man behind the desk says without taking his eyes away from his Holographix game.

I take my license out and lay it on the table. "Plate number is YZB49R," I say.

"Give me a sec," he says but frantically continues his hand gestures, swiping and swatting his Holographix projected from his phone.

Ever since they released the technology, addiction has reached a new high. A three-dimensional holographic video game that is completely interactive through voice and hand gesture control. I must admit it blows the Xbox and PlayStation from my youth out of the water. It's amazing how realistic it is, and I can't help myself from getting sucked into it for a moment.

People can play games, access personal trainers, and even pornographic material that gives the semblance that everything has been transported, happening in real time in your living room or wherever you are for that matter.

Most people can contain themselves until they get home. However, you do see people swatting and yelling in the trains, walking down the street or, in this case, at work, getting paid to play.

"You know you can pause that thing," I say.

"Shhh, shh, shh." He waves me off.

"Holographix pause!" His game ceases mid-swipe. I have taken enough abuse for today, and I'll be damned if I'm going to sit here and take anymore.

"Yooooo! What the fuck, ole man? That was the final boss, and I was in da zone!"

I look him in the eyes, mine with fire ablaze. "I've had a really long day, and I'm done waiting for you to acknowledge me. Now, my car...please," I growl.

He sighs and says, "License plate?"

"YZB49R."

"$684.74," he says.

"Dollars? Six hundred and eighty-four dollars? That's ludicrous!" I lean over the counter to get a look at his screen.

"And seventy-four cents, please. We take cash or credit, no iris pay.

"For one night? Seems a little egregious," I say.

"Two days. The car got here at 6:45 yesterday evening," he says.

"It's 6:47, that's only twenty-four hours."

"Any time past twenty-four hours and you pay an additional day," he says casually.

"I've been standing here for five minutes while you played your damn game!"

He looks up at me and folds his arms, rests them on his giant beer belly, leans back into his chair, and stares back at me blankly.

It's not about the money, it's the principle of it all. When my father passed away, he left some investments to my mother, and she lived off their dividends until she passed last year, and when she passed, my sister Cheryl and I inherited a good sum of money. Dad had great intuition, but he had no idea what he had invested in would blow up to be the monsters they are today.

It was just a few small companies named Google and Amazon. He didn't invest much, but he got in early, and they have continued to dominate the world. Google, Amazon, and Facebook continued to expand their business models and service everything from consumerism, home security, the food industry, and now, even healthcare. Amazon eventually put healthcare giants like Cardinal and 3M out of business.

Once the United States finally converted to a universal healthcare system, Amazon unanimously won the government bid because they were able to provide healthcare products at a fraction of the cost. At first, companies like Cardinal and 3M were forced to use Amazon as a middleman, but Amazon drove their prices down to such depths they discontinue products or use cheaper, lower quality materials.

Eventually, Amazon strategically produced their own versions of products as competitive patents expired and put them out of business altogether. Even Walmart, the once retail giant, has filed for bankruptcy because they weren't able to compete with Amazon's same day delivery to your door business model. Everything has become based on consumer convenience to the point that storefronts have largely become extinct. Some grocery stores remain. However, Amazon and Google both sit at the top of the leader board in that industry with their self-checkout stores.

Thankfully, I had inherited my small fortune, long after my divorce and didn't have to worry about Corina trying to stake her claim in it.

"You're a crook, you know that, right?" I say, slamming my American Express card down onto the counter so hard his Holographix shimmers.

"No Amex," he says.

"Here." I hand him my Visa, scoop up the American Express, and place it neatly into my wallet.

"Oh, fancy pants, huh?" he says, studying the bill. "You drive one of those new Porsche, self-driving cars, huh?"

"Yep."

"Well," he snarls, "then you can afford it, pal."

I look up and give him the most hateful look I can muster. I loathe lazy degenerates like this.

"It's around back, Daddy Warbucks," he says, tossing my key fob into the air.

I pull out of the parking lot and am so exhausted I set the car to auto-drive, sit back, and watch the streetlamps whip by through the translucent roof. I feel myself beginning to doze off, so I shake my head and position my seat upright. A few more blocks, and I take the wheel and turn off the auto-drive feature, fearful I may fall asleep if I'm not active.

Even though cars have auto-drive features, it's still a violation to sleep behind the wheel. You're supposed to be alert in the event you need to take control of the wheel. Oddly, you're allowed to use the feature to escort you home if you're under the influence, but you're not allowed to sleep if you're too tired to drive.

"Porsche, disengage auto-drive."

"Auto-drive will be disengaged in five seconds," the onboard computer responds.

I grab the wheel, turn up the volume, and feel the car move through the turns with ease.

*Whoop-whoop* blare the sirens behind me, and as if thrown into a bout of déjà vu, red and blue lights fill the sky. I pull over, and the officer shines his spotlight into my rear window but, this time, I avert the mirror to deflect the light from blinding me before they approach. I sit with my hands on the wheel in the ten and two o'clock position and await my fate. My heart pounds, I feel flush, and I notice I'm beginning to perspire.

Within what feels like seconds, the officer knocks on my driver's side window. I look up and immediately recognize Captain Rosario glaring down at me with a contemptuous smile. Did I really expect it to be anyone else? I lower the window, a man on his final thread, but a man who learned from his experience the day before.

"Officer?" I condescendingly greet Captain Rosario.

"Captain, Grady. It's Captain Rosario," he says, lowering his voice. "Mind rolling down your other window there for Officer O'Sullivan?"

I lower my passenger window. "Mind telling me why you've stopped me, Captain?"

"Enjoying your evening, Mr. Grady?"

"Yes, Captain, it's been lovely, thank you!" I say enthusiastically, and my smile widens from ear to ear. "Now, whatever have I done to warrant such prestigious company this fine evening?"

Captain Rosario chews his gum and glares at me for what feels like an eternity, and I refuse to look away or release my exuberant smile. I intend to show him that he hasn't broken me. "Speeding, Grady. Where are you headed in such a hurry?" he asks.

"My good sir, I wasn't going more than twenty-seven mph," I say.

"That's correct, Mr. Grady but you see, the speed limit is twenty-five. Put up your license and registration," he clears his throat, "good sir," and taps on the windshield with his scanner.

"Why certainly, Captain. Here you are."

I upload my documents to the cars I-shield, and he scans them, never removing his grimacing eyes from me. I am thoroughly enjoying the dialogue. Kill them with kindness, Stella always says. I'm not sure if this is exactly what she meant, but I think it's open to interpretation.

Captain Rosario and Officer O'Sullivan walk back to their vehicle, presumably to fill out an e-ticket for a bullshit violation. Whoever heard of getting pulled over for driving a measly two miles per hour over the speed limit?

About ten minutes later, they return, and a summons instantly appears on my I-shield. "Mr. Grady, it appears to us that you may be under the influence. Have you been drinking or using anything you'd like to make us aware of?"

"Oh, no, no, no! Hugs not drugs! You see, Captain, I'm just high on life. I'm so blessed and incredibly grateful to be here with you and the good Officer O'Sullivan today. Oh! And I've seen you've uploaded an e-ticket, allowing me to contribute monetarily to this fine town? Fannnntastic!"

"Mr. Grady, then I'm sure you wouldn't object to an on-site toxicology test?" he asks.

"An on-site drug test?" I ask, baring my teeth. "Well, I've read those are vastly unreliable. Perhaps you should ask my lawyer for permission and explain what cause you have?" I say.

"Your lawyer? No, I don't think we'll be calling your lawyer," he says with a chuckle.

"Oh, you don't have to, Captain. You see, when you pulled me over, I called her and asked her to listen in. Susan?" I look up, stare into his eyes with 'check mate asshole' plastered all over my face.

"Hi, Captain, this is Susan Dunleavy. As my client appropriately asked, what cause do you have for an on-site toxicology test? I didn't hear anything that would warrant it."

Captain Rosario turns red instantly, and his expression turns to rage while all forty-three muscles in his face seemingly flex at once.

He flings the ticket into my lap. "Enjoy your evening, sir," he says, gritting his teeth and makes his way back to the squad car.

"Thank you, Susan. Sorry to bother you, but who knows what they had planned for me tonight," I say.

"It's no bother. You did the right thing," she says. "Clearly, they have it out for you. Do you want me to stay on the line until you get home, or do you think you'll be OK?"

"I think I'll be alright. I'm going to turn on auto-drive. I'll call you if I need you again. Please, keep your phone close."

"OK. Hope things get better for you and, remember, record everything," she says.

"Thanks, I will. Good night, Susan."

For the remainder of the drive, I cautiously peer through my rearview mirror and down side streets, expecting Rosario to pop out at any moment. I should get used to it because I certainly don't expect him to give up. He is intent on locking me up, and I know he will do whatever it takes to do so.

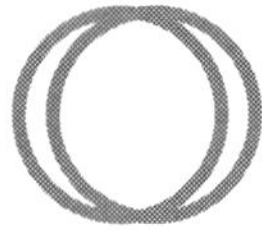

# CHAPTER 7

Stella and I sit on the porch and wait for the pizza to arrive. I ordered it as a peace offering. A make up for the one that never arrived on Sunday night. Perhaps if I had ordered delivery, then that nightmare would have never taken place.

I find myself studying Ileana and Jay as they run and play in the park across the street. It seems like it was just yesterday I was changing their diapers. Now, I count my gray hairs as Ileana is about to enter a new school and Jay learns a new word seemingly every day.

Stella, the new age hippie she is, demanded that we use washable diapers to save the Earth. What a royal pain in the ass those were! Laundry was literally done daily. Save the Earth but waste valuable water in the process, seemed like an oxymoron to me. However, when Jay was finally potty trained, I missed the soothing sound of the laundry machine running outside of my bedroom door while I fell asleep. I eventually supplanted it with a fan, but it isn't the same.

I sit quietly in awe, having trouble conceptualizing how fast they've grown. Ileana's voice, though still childlike, has matured. Her beautiful dirty blonde hair has grown just past her shoulders, and she has developed thick, naturally flowing curls. Her feet appear too large for her growing body, and her legs seem to be lengthening by the day. She has a very chiseled jawline for a girl with dimples. I can see them indented under her high cheekbones, perched upon her porcelain skin from all the way across the street. When she smiles, the Earth smiles with her, infectious and innocent.

Jay's shaggy reddish-brown hair, and the freckles under his eyes remind me of my father, a Grady family trait. I, too, had them as a child, but they've seemed to vanish over the years. I miss my dad, and I deeply wish he could have met my children. They are all beautiful and unique. He would have had a ball watching and playing with them. He always said that he wanted to have a girl, and we have three of them for him to fawn over.

His death really rattled me, and my sister Cheryl, too. He had returned from a trip overseas and had become violently ill. His visits to the toilet became longer and more frequent as the supposed bacteria spread throughout his system. He sought doctor's advice and was prescribed numerous antibiotics, though none provided any resolve.

As his body melted, fat and muscle dissolved, and he was unable to hold down a sustainable diet. Cheryl and I had begged and pleaded with him to go to the hospital but, in those days, America had a commercial healthcare system, unlike the government regulated system we have in place today.

His insurance lapsed, and insurance plans were outrageously expensive when purchased outside of a group. Hospital bills could leave you bankrupt and send your life into financial spiral. While his investments were sound, they were young, with little growth, and he didn't have the foresight to see they would develop into the riches they have become today.

Arguments ensued week over week until he finally caved and went to the hospital. He was there for three days. Tests were run and treatment was administered. He appeared to be improving, so his doctors sent him home to recover, and thinking that this was all behind us, Cheryl and I visited less frequently, reverting back to phone call check-ins. Unbeknownst to us, his condition only improved for a few days, likely due to the intravenous fluids and steroids he received in the hospital.

He quietly continued to fail and seemingly accepted the fate he had chosen. Meanwhile, he would tell us that he was improving and getting stronger every day. He was doing exercises to slowly rebuild the muscle he had lost, was keeping food down, and bathroom visits were normalizing. All had appeared to be progressing, and we laid our fears to rest. However, a random visit would prove to be one of the worst days of my life. A life fuck that would knock the wind clear out of me.

On that day, time stopped, and a numbness crept in and at times, I wonder if it had ever left. The vision of his shallow breath, my final, 'I love you Dad,' and my attempts to bring him back to life while his vitality petered away replays in my mind's eye like a skipping record. I can still hear my mother cheering him on, hoping he can hear her plea to fight his way back to us, "Come on, Joseph!"

A piece of my soul was taken that day, and my life had been altered. When I look back on it, perhaps I never really absorbed the appropriate message. We get so lost in life, so tied to the things we have and the things we want, that we lose sight of what is truly important. We think everything that happens every day is so crucial, but the truth is, most of it isn't important at all.

You should save your stress for the things that truly matter. The things you truly give a fuck about, not whether you have to work late tonight or if someone hurt your feelings. Live every day as if it's your last because, you never know, it just might be. I stress too much about the mundane. It's difficult to keep this ideology in the forefront of your mind, especially when life beats you down again and again. I have to work on that.

The year following Dad's passing, I had a recurring dream that seemed to follow me like his ghost. Cheryl and I are hauling his coffin through a forest. It's dark, filled with dense, suffocating fog, and Dad pleaded with us to get him to where he needed to be. I could see him and speak with him, but I was also aware his body was in the coffin we carried like two pallbearers on a mission in the underworld. The weight of it was punishing, and we struggled with every ounce of strength not to let him down.

"Don't drop me!" he would command.

Up and down tiny hills and in and out of marsh-like puddles. I call them puddles because they were small in diameter, however, many were deep enough to cover our heads, and we struggled to hold our heads above the water. Our arms stretched overhead, bearing the weight of what was once our father, and I could hear Cheryl's cries, feel her pain and anguish as if it were my own.

Eventually, I understood it was necessary for me to rise above. I needed to bear the weight of my father on my shoulders. I need to power on, put my back into it, and take the load to relieve her of the crushing weight. I must carry on as my father would, step into his shoes and lead.

I don't recall if we ever reached our destination, but perhaps that was the destination. Maybe he wanted me to know he needed me to step up and be the patriarch in his absence. I don't know if I have lived up to his expectation, but the dream faded, and it never returned. As eerie as it was, I miss that dream because I felt connected to him when I awoke.

I think that when our loved ones pass on, they visit us in our dreams. I haven't had a dream with him for quite some time now, and I feel like I've lost him. Is he disappointed in what Dylan Grady has become? I may not have the wisdom to recognize some of the mistakes I've made but, conceivably, he's just resting and finally at peace.

"What are you thinking about love?" Stella asks.

"Oh, nothing," I say.

"Doesn't look like nothing. Everything alright?"

"Yeah. I was just thinking about how Jay looks a lot like my dad. He has the same freckles under his eyes, hair, and even his ears remind me of him. It's like he has been reincarnated."

"Yeah, he does look a lot like him, but then again, so do you," she says. "I wish I could have met him."

I reach over and grab her hand. "He would have adored you," I say. "I can't place Ileana, though. I see a lot of you, but I don't see me at all."

"Oh, I do," she says. "She certainly has your laugh and sense of humor."

"Yeah, but that's stuff she picked up from me. I'm talking about the way she looks, family traits, stuff like that. I just don't see it."

Stella rolls her eyes and looks to her glass of Chianti.

"Relax babe, it's just an observation. It's not like I don't love her to death. Look, neither Haley nor Annabel look a lot like me, either. Maybe girls typically look more like their moms and boys their dads? I don't know. Who cares, really?"

"Perhaps," she says. "Hey, have you been paying attention to that Alter-life thing?"

"A bit. I never thought we'd see the day they can actually transport people into an alternate reality."

"Reality? How real could it be? It's like you'd be living in a computer game. That's crazy!" she says in a huff.

"How do you know we aren't living in a computer simulation right now?" I challenge her. "Who knows, the world as we know it could just be one big computer simulation."

Stella glares at me, takes a sip of her wine, and says, "We're not."

"How do you know? We could all be living in a simulated world, like the old *Sims* games. A character in someone else's creation, playing games within a game."

"This sounds vaguely familiar to the time when you tried to convince me it's totally conceivable that we all see colors differently," she says with a sneer.

"Well, why not? How do you know that when I see blue, it isn't what red is to you? How do we know that we see the same thing? We're taught that the car over there is blue, an apple is red, and a lemon is yellow, but how do we know our mind processes the colors exactly the same way?"

"That's stupid! You're stupid!" She laughs. "But I love you."

I smile at her. "Stupid? Or brilliant?"

Our laughter continues. We *clink* glasses and sit in silence, gazing into the sun as it sets over the hills, beyond the park. The world is so beautiful, so why does it have to be so damn complicated?

"But, seriously, could you ever really consider Alter-life?" she asks.

"Me? No, but I guess I could understand why someone would want to."

"Really? How so?" she asks.

"Suppose I take the kids to their swimming lessons. A normal day. But on the way home, we get sideswiped by a drunk driver. Dead…all of us. Everything you know and love is gone. The pain is overwhelming, and you—"

"Stop!" she says, hitting my arm. "I don't even want to think about that! Now spit!"

"Spit?" Stella's superstitions have a tendency to overwhelm her. Perhaps it's a Greek thing? If you say something, it will come true if you don't spit to cleanse your mouth of your filthy words. I spit to appease her, "But think about it," I say. "Would living in an alternate reality where that horrific, life-altering event never happened, and you never even knew it happened, be appealing? You could live out your days happy as a pig in shit ignorance with everyone by your side."

"Mmmaybe," she says, tapping her index finger to her lip.

"I don't know why people are protesting. Why do they give a shit if someone wants a chance at being happy again? What's so wrong with that? Who cares if it's in a simulated world? Sometimes, I think people just need something to bitch about," I say.

"Well, what about the people you're leaving behind? You're lying in a room, strapped to a bed with tubes keeping your body alive and living the, quote-unquote, life of your dreams, but what happens to the people you've left behind? You just leave everything and say fuck it? fuck them?"

"I guess if they were that miserable, barring an undiagnosed mental illness, then those people probably contributed to their misery," I say with a wink.

"And how would they know if their clients don't have a mental illness, like severe manic depression or something? They'd be miserable anywhere."

"I read that they do a DNA test and rule all that stuff out on the spot. If they do suffer from a mental illness, they need spousal consent if you're married and a written order from a psychiatrist. They can change things about you in the alternate reality. If you suffer from depression here, they can rid you of it there."

"Jeez, honey mou. You've really researched this, huh? Something you want to tell me?" she asks leaning back into her chair with a half-cocked smile.

I laugh. "Shut up, babe! It's just interesting, that's all."

A car pulls into the driveway, and a lanky, shaggy-haired teenage boy climbs out of the driver's seat, pizza in hand with Stella's Caesar salad in a bag looped around his wrist. I grab the pizza, and he scans my iris for payment.

"Add ten for yourself," I say.

I remember when tipping two or three dollars was sufficient, but inflation has soared over the years. Iris pay was created by Jetcoin, and it's a way to auto pay using a cryptocurrency. Jetcoin has developed scanners to scan your iris' and provide them to establishments that sign up for their payment service. Consumers download an app, scan their iris, and convert dollars to Jetcoin.

It has largely contributed to the decline in the value of the dollar because it is used globally and has created a unique, world-shared currency. In a world where the consumer market is vastly online, it is a perfect and secure way to pay worldwide. There has even been recent discussion to make Jetcoin the global reserve currency, which has led to major economic problems within the United States and a rapid decline in the value of the dollar.

You can even opt to get paid directly in Jetcoin and bypass the dollar completely. After the second bank bailout of 2023, it is arguably more secure than keeping your money in a bank. It's sad but inevitable. Come to think of it, I don't know anyone who uses standard currency anymore.

"Ileana! Jay! Dinner!" Stella shouts, making her way across our quiet neighborhood street. The kids shoot down the slide, entangled together like a train, and I can hear Ileana celebrate her infamously favorite pizza night. As I set the table, I see Dante's logo imprinted on the pizza box and am immediately flooded with emotion. I sigh deeply and involuntarily play back flashes of the events that had taken place there and after.

I wonder how Haley is managing at home with her Mom and John. I presume they've spun their web of lies and told them I hit their mother. I don't think Haley will buy into it, but what about Annabel? Could this ruin our relationship? How would I handle that?

I suppose if Corina's willing to stoop that low, then I'll have to take the gloves off and fight. I couldn't possibly allow Annabel to believe I actually hit her mother, and I'd have no choice but to tell her everything. I may have to show her the log after all. I'm willing to sacrifice a portion of my children's affection for their sanity, but I'm not willing to lose their love and trust entirely over another devious lie.

We sit down for dinner, and Ileana is at full attention, like a member of the royal guard. Stella unleashes the magnificent beauty and aromatherapy of a Dante's pepperoni pizza, and it tames Ileana's inner beast. As the box opens, she springs from her chair and slings her hand forward to grab a slice.

Stella swats at her hand and says, "Down, girl! I'll get you one. Plain or pepperoni?"

"Peeeepperrooooooniii!" Ileana belts out like an opera singer on opening night.

"How about you, sweetie?" she asks Jay.

"Cheese, please!" he says enthusiastically through his teeth with an exuberant smile.

We all dig into our pizza as if it were the first meal after a long fast, and I can already foresee a food coma in our futures.

"Honey mou," Stella says with a full mouth, "do you think you could take Ileana to her school testing tomorrow?"

"Testing?" I ask.

"Yeah, remember? She needs to get updates on her shots, and they do full blood work and a DNA scan," she says.

"DNA scan? What, if she's not of the highest genetic code or susceptible to a disease, they won't let her in? What the hell do they need that for?" I ask.

"Dylan, we talked about this! It's for placement. They check her health, too, but that's more for us. They look at her DNA and base a course curriculum on her natural genetic strengths."

"You're kidding me?" I say.

"Nope. Look, we decided since we can afford it, the kids should go to the best schools, right?"

"Well, yes, but..."

"Well, Barron Academy has proven to be the best, and their DNA-based curriculum is largely responsible," Stella contests.

"OK, OK, OK, love, but just promise me that we won't push them onto a path that makes them miserable. Regardless of her strengths, I still want her to be happy. Even though she may be good at math, that doesn't mean she would be happy being a mathematician."

"Listen, all the best colleges are only accepting kids who meet their major's DNA profiles these days, anyway. She'll just be ahead of the curve. Anyway, there is more to math than just being a mathematician. She could be a teacher, accountant, or an engineer to name a few."

"True," I concede.

Ileana interjects with a strained look on her face, "But I don't think I'm good at math!"

"Oh, no, baby. Daddy and I are just using that as an example," Stella says.

"But I don't think I'm good at anything…well, except playing," Ileana says glumly.

"Oh, my baby girl, you're great at lots of things and, typically, you don't know what they are until you're older. You have to give them time to develop, but you'll find things you love, and you'll work on them," I say.

Ileana drops her pizza onto her plate, and with a puzzled look, she says, "But how will I know to work on them if I don't even know what they are?"

"It will come naturally, don't worry. You'll love doing it, so it won't feel like work. You'll do it because you enjoy it," Stella says.

"OK…I guess," Ileana says, deep in thought. "But what if I fail the DNA test?"

"Oh, sweetheart, you can't fail it," I console. "It isn't that type of a test. It looks at what you're made of, and they put your results into a computer and, somehow, but don't ask me how, they are able to see what you're likely to excel at. Don't worry, lucky for you, I'm not one of those maniac father's who'll ever make you be something you don't want to be. In the end, Mom and I just want both of you to be healthy and happy. You only have one life to live, so you might as well be happy."

"Well, sort of," Stella retorts.

"Sort of what?" I ask.

"Alter-life," Stella jokes.

"Oh!" I chuckle, "Yeah, I guess...kind of one life."

"What's Alter-life?" Ileana asks.

"Just something in the news. It's nothing to concern you," Stella says.

Suddenly, my phone rings and just in time to avert another series of sticky questions. If a DNA test is going to send her into a tizzy, I'd hate to take a stab at Alter-life. I'm still unsure if I understand it, and I'd rather not try to explain it to an eleven-year-old.

"Who's that?" Stella asks.

"I don't know. I don't recognize the number."

I would often send the call to my voicemail, but something inside of me commands me to answer it.

"Hello?"

"Mr. Grady?"

"Speaking."

"Mr. Grady, this is Officer Darby O'Sullivan. Listen—"

"You've got to be kidding me, Officer! This is harassment—"

"Mr. Grady," he cuts me off, "this is serious!"

A chill runs down my spine. It stiffens, and I wait anxiously for him to go on.

"Your daughter," he sighs, "Annabel."

*Gush*. My adrenaline releases like a tsunami, and my eyes spring open, and my heart pounds in my chest.

"She's had an accident. She's at St. Peter's Hospital," he says.

"What kind of accident?" I say panicked and pop out of my chair. "Is she OK?"

He pauses for a moment, and it feels like an eternity in Hell.

"Officer! Dammit, is she OK?" I say.

"What? Dylan, is who OK?" Stella asks frantic.

I raise my hand, signaling for her to wait, but she continues to talk, though her voice muffles inaudibly in the background.

My mind spirals down a black hole, and I feel as though I may pass out when, suddenly, his voice echoes within the tunnel bouncing me back to the chaos, “I don’t know, Grady, but I think you should get down here, now.”

“What?” I say.

“I said I think you should get to St. Peter’s as soon as possible,” he says.

I hang up the phone, race to the closet, and throw on my shoes and a coat. I grab my keys and head for the door in a huff.

“Dylan! Wait! What happened? Where are you going?”

Suddenly aware my family is staring at me as worried as I am, I say, “Oh, I don’t know. Annabel, it’s Annabel! She’s been in some sort of accident. She’s in the hospital!”

My words are choppy, and I hear myself skip over syllables. It may all be palaver.

“Is she OK?” Stella asks.

“What?”

Stella grabs my shoulders and looks at me dead in the eyes.

“Is Annabel alright?”

“What? I-I don’t know!”

“We’re coming with you!” Stella says.

“No, stay here with the kids…please?”

“No, you’re in no shape to be driving!” Stella insists.

“I’ll use auto-drive. I-I-I have to go!” I rush into the garage and yell, “Porsche, start!” As the garage door opens, I yell, “Go to St. Peter’s Hospital, Montclair, New Jersey. Engage auto-drive!”

My mind is racing, and my hands shake uncontrollably, and I’m gnawing on my lip like a rabid dog. I want to take over the wheel and speed as fast as the car will allow, but I concede I am in no condition to drive.

O’Sullivan didn’t give me any real information on Annabel’s condition. Naturally, the worst is cycling through my mind at an inhuman rate. Perhaps it’s a defense mechanism, but I convince myself this could all be another elaborate setup. A plan concocted by Captain Rosario and Corina to entrap me into a plot where I would violate the restraining order. That, sadly, is my best-case scenario. I would happily spend an eternity in jail in return for her safety.

As the car approaches the hospital, I take over the wheel. “Auto-drive disengage." I pull up to the valet and jump out and abandon it with the car still running. I zip past the parking attendant and into the hospital to the visitor information desk.

I am greeted by an older, stout woman, built like a fullback with brightly artificial golden-colored hair.

"Annabel Grady!" I blurt out, out of breath and it sounded more like, 'AnnaFul Gaydy.' I take a deep penetrating breath and try again, "I'm here for Annabel Grady, G-R-A-D-Y."

"Are you an immediate family member?"

"Yes, father," I say.

"Identification please," she says flat, staring through me with disinterested eyes.

I fumble through my wallet and hand her my driver's license. She takes my identification and glances down at my trembling hands, snaps my picture, and prints out a visitor's ID Badge.

"OK, sir, she's in the ICU. You need to go down—"

"ICU?" I interrupt her.

"Yes, go down the—"

"Like, intensive care?" I say in disbelief.

"Yes, sir. Go down the hall, past the bathrooms, take the first set of elevators on your right to the fifth floor. Make a right outside of the elevators and check in at the nurses' station. They will direct you from there. She's in room 551. Next in line, please."

"OK," I utter and step to the side.

I am caught in a nightmare. Is this real? Annabel is in the ICU? I walk down the hall and enter a door to a world of the unknown. The one I have always feared could show its face and alter my life forever. A mysterious door, locked, but one day would open, letting all my demons in.

I repeat the room number out loud so I don't forget it but also as an exercise to expel my nervous energy, "551, 551, 551, 551, 551, 551, 551, 551..."

I approach the nurses' station, heart pounding in my chest, and the tone of the life support monitors harmonize from room to room, humming a song that no mother or father should ever have to hear. I feel the drum of my pulse beating along in my ears, and the room spins.

"Breathe, Dylan, breathe," I say out loud.

Across from the nurses' station, I see a sign that reads room number 551 hanging above the door. That number will forever be written in my memory and might as well be 666.

I draw another deep breath as I enter the room, and I see Annabel hooked up to all sorts of tubes, wires, and machines. She is intubated, a large bandage wraps her head, and another on her arm with pins poking out of it. This isn't a trap, this is my worst nightmare. My eyes water, and my heart sinks into my stomach.

I scan the room and see Corina sitting in the dark, huddled in the corner, scowling at me with tear-welled eyes. I can't determine whether her expression is sinister or broken, but I don't rightfully care. In this moment, we are two parents filled with angst for one another but connected by tragedy. Our immense love for our children binds us, and whether she wants me here or not, I will remain.

"What…happened?" My voice cracks, and the tears persist past the barrier of my soul. The first words I have spoken to Corina since the day we had separated. The day she had me removed from my home and claimed it as her dominion. It was the first act of her play, and the first day of her passion story but, for me, it was the first day of my new life. When I look back and reflect, it was the best damn day of my life because it took all that pain to release me of her toxicity.

After a long pause, she speaks, "Haley…she was pulling out of the driveway… she didn't see that Annabel…she backed into her. She fell back and hit her head hard. Really hard!" She buries her head into her hands and howls and, for a moment, I almost feel as though she were human.

"What did the doctors say? How bad is it? Will she be alright?" I ask.

She sits silent, sniffling back her tears, and stares at Annabel. I give her a few moments to regain her composure, and I, too, take time to be silent and numb.

I hear the squeaking wheels of a hospital bed being rolled down the hall and it breaks me from my trance, "Corina? Please, what did the doctor say?" But again, I am met with silence and pursed lips.

"Corina!" I raise my voice frustrated, "Where is her doctor?" She stands from her chair and strolls over to the window, turns her back to me, and stares out into the dark night.

I gawk at her in disbelief. How could she be so cold?

"Corina, please? Tell me something!" I shout.

I glance over at Annabel, lifeless and undeserving, and close my eyes to dam the tears. A single tear breaks free, glides down my cheek and falls, cutting through the air like a missile and glistening in the dim light. It explodes onto the black and white checkered tile floor.

Sucking back my tears, I walk out of the room, down the hall to the nurses' station.

"Excuse me, I'm Dylan Grady, Annabel Grady's father. Can I speak with her doctor?"

"Dr. Lin is rounding on his patients at the moment. Let me see if he's been to your room yet. Just give me a minute. I have to page the resident."

I wait at the desk, fidgeting until the nurse returns moments later and says, "Mr. Grady, Dr. Lin hasn't been to your daughters' room yet. He should be there shortly. Please, be patient."

"Yes, OK…thank you. Uh, is there anything you can tell me about her condition?" I say.

"I'm sorry, sir. You should really speak with Dr. Lin."

"OK," I say.

When I return to Annabel's room, Corina is still staring out of the window. Same old Corina. Too wrapped up in her own emotions to consider anyone else's. In situations like these, nothing is worse than the unknown.

I walk over to Annabel and kiss her bandaged forehead and caress her cheek with the backside of my hand.

"Annabel, baby? It's Dad, love. Come back to us, sweetheart."

I look over and see Corina watching me, and her expression has softened.

"Corina, please, what did they say? Will she recover?"

She exhales loudly and replies coldly, "Ask the doctor."

Even in tragedy, she can't resist an opportunity to be wicked.

"Don't you ever get tired of this bullshit? I mean, shit, wouldn't life be easier, for everyone if we were civil? Instead, you continue to manufacture ways to punish me?"

I stop myself from going on a rant, and for the next hour, we sit in silence on opposing sides of the room, two separate dimensions bound by the same misery.

"Hello. Mr. Grady, I presume?" I pop out of my chair and see a man I surmise to be Dr. Lin standing in the doorway. He wears a white lab coat and holds a clipboard in his hand, accompanied by two young gentleman I assume to be his residents.

"Dr. Lin?"

"Yes. I'm sorry to have kept you waiting. Has your wife filled you in on your daughter's condition? Are there any questions?"

"Ex-wife, and no, nothing." I glance over at Corina and catch her rolling her eyes.

"OK...well, let's start from the beginning then. Annabel suffered a traumatic brain injury from when her head hit the pavement. Sometimes, when you hit your head hard enough, the brain crashes back and forth inside the skull, causing swelling and bleeding. It can swell and push against the skull, which can be life threatening. I had to perform a craniotomy to relieve the pressure."

"Craniotomy?"

"I removed a piece of her skull, Mr. Grady. It was necessary, in order to decompress her brain and allow it to heal."

"So, she'll be OK?" I ask.

"Listen, Annabel presented with some very serious injuries. She's on a ventilator and a feeding tube and, at this time, we are unsure if she is able to breathe on her own. I'm sorry, Mr. Grady, but if Annabel wakes up—"

"If?"

"Yes, Mr. Grady, if she wakes up, there is a high likelihood she will have permanent injury. It's likely she'll never regain full neuro-cognitive function and remain in a vegetative state."

"Oh, my God!" I become lightheaded and fall back into the chair.

"She's also incurred a nasty fracture and an orthopedic surgeon, Sebastian Cordiale, put an external fixator on her arm while she was still under anesthesia. I can't speak to her arm, you'll have to speak with him, but I believe they expect her arm to fully recover. I'm sorry, folks, I know how very difficult this is. I wish I had better news for you."

"How long will she be hooked up to those machines?" I ask.

"Well, you folks will have to discuss end of life plans. I'll be honest, Mr. Grady, it doesn't look good. Although, we have seen cases where these patients make partial recoveries, it is rather unlikely. Her head took a devastating blow. I'm so very sorry.".

I try to voice the words, 'Thank you, Doctor,' but I'm paralyzed. I can't speak, I can't move, I can't do anything but stare at the cracked tiles on the floor. *My baby, my Annabel Bear. how can life go on without you in it?*

"Well, folks, I'm going to get her nurse to change her bandages and clean her up, but I have to move on to my next patient. Any other questions you have for me right now?" He pauses for a moment, but I imagine he realizes I am muted by the trauma. It occurs to me that perhaps Corina didn't relay anything to me because she physically couldn't. It's conceivable that she, too, has been muted by the trauma. Vocalizing it is unimaginable because, perhaps then, it would make this nightmare a reality.

My anger dissipates, and I appreciate that Corina and I are both living the same tragic nightmare. Our anger with each other is pointless and petty. We have a much larger problem than each other, and for the first time in twelve years, I feel as though I understand her behavior. If I make peace with the things that have vexed me, they will no longer control me.

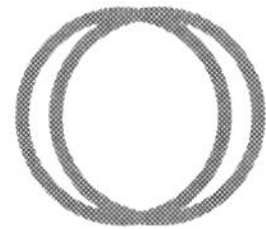

# CHAPTER 8

It's been two long days, camped out in room 551, catatonically staring into the abysmal. The *beep-beep-beep* of the machines is entrancing, and the nurse visits to refresh the intravenous fluids and empty the catheter have been the only thing breaking me from a state of permanent hypnosis.

Corina often comes and goes without saying a word. We sit on opposing sides of the room in awkward, miserable silence, and I imagine that she, like me, is continually punishing herself with memories of our beautiful girl. I shuffle images of my Annabel bear through my head like an old slide show and each memory is more painful than the last.

As a baby, she would grab a hold my index finger whenever I held her and fall asleep in my arms, never easing her grip. Corina absolutely hated it! She always resented the love our children had for me, and even in marriage, she competed with me for their love. She would love nothing more than for their love to be transformed into hatred. There is nothing worse than feeling like your spouse is consistently rooting for you to fail. It's no wonder Corina tried to alienate me from my children after the divorce. She alienated me from them in marriage.

Three-year-old Annabel would always run up to me, hug my leg, and say, "I love my daddy!" Oh, how I adored those moments. Other times, she would randomly grab my hand, kiss it, and when I held her, she would caress my face and look into my eyes with adoration. She played my heart like a violin. A composer of my love, so genuine and pure.

The love you have for your children is the truest form that exists. It is unconditional. I place their lives ahead of my own, and there isn't anything I wouldn't do to trade places with her. Haley, Annabel, Ileana, Jay, and Stella, they are my happiness, and without them, I am nothing more than a worm in a hole.

I pray Annabel isn't in pain. I pray her mind is at peace. I can't bear the thought of her cognizant and fearful, frozen in darkness, awake but unable to move. *I beg you, God, please let her dream of unicorns and rainbows, in a world filled with love and happiness. Let her be the princess she has always wished she could be. We love her so deeply, and although I can't imagine a world without her, please accept her into your world and lead her to happiness.*

This is the first resemblance of a prayer I have uttered in years, and perhaps my first acknowledgment of God, though, I admit, it is manifested out of my desperation, and I doubt He will listen to an agnostic. Tragedy can make even the most unlikely people suddenly religious, and I suppose I am guilty of this. *Please, God, show me your mercy.*

I find myself begging for forgiveness but also challenging him to prove his existence. "Demonstrate your worthiness of my worship!" I command.

If He could grant me this one miracle, I would surely be a believer. Devout, serving him in any way He commands.

My mind continues to wrestle with itself. Corina enters the room and blows past me in a huff, stops dead in her tracks, and lets out a long, painful groan. "Can't I just have some peace with my daughter? Don't you ever go home?"

It takes a moment for her remark to register. I glance up at her from the green chair that has become an extension of my body, and although I feel a momentary escalation of anger, I have no energy to fight. I'm so tired of being at odds with her.

"OK," I say calmly. "I'll go get some food and come back later. Have you spoken to Haley?" She refuses to meet my gaze or utter a single word. She releases a long sigh and looks up to the ceiling, and the irritation radiates off her like steam.

I don't want to sit here in awkward silence as she glares at me from across the room, anyway. We have become strangers. I don't know this person, and regardless of how much she thinks she knows about me, I have changed enormously since our separation. When I'm around her, however, I think and feel like my former self. I don't like that person.

I gather my things and place them in my bag, walk over to Annabel, and kiss her on the forehead.

"How about you go home, and I'll message you when I'm going to leave, and when you want to come back, you can check in with me? I'll let you know if you can return!"

"Corina, you can't keep me away from my children, and you can't dictate when I can come and go! How about you message me, and I'll let you know when I leave and when I'm coming back?" My breath accelerates, and my nostrils flare.

Her eyes intensify, and I can see the fire blazing and the raw, sweltering anger morph her face into the angry little troll I remember. The evil witch who could terrify children in fairy tales and foster sleepless nights. I will no longer allow her to control me or to dictate when I can see my children, just as she has done for all of their lives, hiding behind a divorce agreement that has awarded her a false sense of empowerment.

"None of this would have happened if it weren't for you! This is on you, Dylan! You and your stupid log! If you hadn't made that stupid thing, then none of this would have ever happened!"

She points to Annabel and holds her arm out, marching over to her bedside. "Look, Dylan! Look! Look what you did to our little girl!"

My blood pressure surges, the veins in my neck and temples pulse, and I stare with bloodcurdling hatred as the devil sings and dances her song of denial. I can't summon a word. I just stare at her in disbelief.

"Nothing? You have nothing to say for yourself? You horrible, maniacal asshole!" she hollers.

Corina is a disease, a chronic illness that has plagued me for as long as I can remember. She hides and lives dormant within. A parasite that resurfaces time and again, nibbling at my soul and feeding off my pain. The love I have for my children makes me vulnerable, allowing her to multiply, infecting my body and possessing my soul.

I can't hold it in any longer, "Goddammit, Corina! Why?"

"Why what?" she asks. Her head whips around, face scrunches and her forehead sculpts a perfect V.

"Why must you always be such a horrible bitch? What have I really done? What did I do to deserve these years of torture?"

"What have you done?" she says, leaning back and placing her hand over her heart.

"Yes, what? Please, tell me! What in the fuck did I do to deserve all this… shit?"

She scowls and scoffs. "Oh, that's fresh! Well, for starters…you're alive!"

"Before we got a divorce, we hadn't gotten along for years. We had nothing in common, and any hint of romanticism vanished shortly after we were married! What is it? Why couldn't we have just gotten along? If for nothing else, the sake of the children?" I say and realize suddenly I am shouting and uncontrollably spitting as I scream. The years of meaningless abuse has resurfaced and is exploding in me like a fireworks display. "Is it because you thought I cheated on you with Stella? News flash, I never cheated on you!"

"Oh, yes you did!" she shouts back.

"No! No, I didn't! Besides, even if I had, you cheated on me for years with Tom in your office! Years! And I had proof! I had witnesses, copies of messages and old phone records, and if our divorce had made it to trial, it would have all come out, and you would have looked like a goddamned fool!"

"Bullshit! Then why didn't you?"

"Because I just wanted to move on! Don't you see that not everything is worth a fight? I came to terms with the fact we weren't meant to be, and in the best interest of everyone, I settled! I settled hoping we could move on in peace and our children could be less scathed."

"Just remember you are the one who left! You filed for divorce!" she says as if that meant anything at all.

"You didn't give me a choice! You set me up! You called the fucken cops on me! You had me tossed out of my house and filed a restraining order! But here's the kicker, ladies and gentlemen, if I paid you more money and agreed to see our children less, you would have dropped the restraining order altogether? Are you kidding me? Come on, Corina, you know I would have never hurt you. You planned the destruction of our marriage, and then you spent the last however many years trying to destroy me! For what? What did it get you? I'll tell you what it got you. It got you one daughter who hates and resents you, and another in the goddamned hospital with tubes stuck down her throat! Congratulations!" I clap obnoxiously loud, spinning in circles, effectively cheering myself on. This is who she brings out in me, who I become. We make each other worse people.

Nurse Elsa walks into the room, and like boxers at the end of a round, we both walk to our corners, falling silent.

"Sorry, folks, I'll just be a moment. Don't want our little princess here to get any bed sores."

Pacing back and forth, running my fingers through my hair, I walk over to the window, gaze out over the awful view of the hospital mechanicals and air ducts. I suppose it's more important for patients who are alert and recovering to have the more pleasant views the hospital has to offer, but this is rather depressing.

Nurse Elsa finishes her work in awkward silence, and I cool down and return to Bruce Banner. I realize how unimportant and petty this all is. There's no point in arguing about it now. It won't change anything. It seems clear to me that we are merely venting our frustrations and releasing our raw emotions on each other, just like we did throughout the final years of our marriage. We never learned to separate our anger and support one another. I never felt appreciated, simply a workhorse, paycheck, provider, and an entertainer.

I'm sure she has her story to tell, and I suppose she would say I wasn't the best husband to her, either, but I tried my best. It's hard to look inward, to truly be critical of one's self. Our conscious justifies and rationalizes our behavior, and we always find a way to excuse the things we do. After all, we're both human, and we grew apart. There was a critical piece in our relationship that was broken, and it was simply irreparable. Divorce was a prerequisite to happiness; happiness 102, and it was an inevitable tragedy.

"OK folks, all set," she says, scurrying towards the door. Before she exits, she stops suddenly and turns to face us. "Listen, folks, I know it's none of my business, but positivity seems to really help patients here. I don't know if they're listening, but I think they absorb the chi, if you know what I mean. The ones who do best are usually the ones surrounded by positivity and love. Whatever's going on between the two of you isn't as important as your daughter. I'm sorry if I'm out of line."

We both nod in acknowledgement. She nods back and exits the room with her head down. I return to my chair, and we sit at opposing corners in silence. My elbows perch on my knees, hands clenched in fists under my chin, and I watch Corina swipe left and right on her phone.

Nurse Elsa can't be more than twenty-five years old, but she just schooled us on life. It's terrifying to think that, although slim, we may be hurting Annabel's chances of recovery. Can she hear us? Can she feel us? Has our resentment and anger for each other been impeding any chance of recovery? How could we be so selfish? How could we have been so selfish all these years? Is there something I could have done to repair our broken relationship? Something I could have said to make things more amicable? Perhaps all of these years, Corina has felt as wronged by me as I have by her.

It's too late, isn't it? Our stubbornness has made us arch enemies. Once lovers, linked in matrimony, reverted into lifelong adversaries, and what has it accomplished? Only misery, anger, and resentment for everyone; our parents, friends, new spouses, but most of all, the onus was laid upon our children. We should have been better. We should have been stronger and less selfish. Divorce was in the cards, but how we handled the divorce and how it affected our children was a choice, and we failed. If we made different choices, none of this would have ever happened. Our children would be happier, better adjusted and, likely, not in the ICU.

In a moment of compassion and regret, I reach out. "Look, Corina, I'm sorry if I hurt you. I'm sorry if you feel I wronged you in some way. I can't go back and change it. It's been so long I don't even remember how we ended up here, but I always hoped we could move past all the ugliness and be friends."

"Ha!" she says.

"OK, maybe friends is pushing it, but civil at the very least. Speak from time to time and raise our children together, without all this animosity. Most of all, I'm sorry for not apologizing to you earlier. I know I wasn't the perfect husband, but you know I'm a good man. I hope you can find it in your heart one day to forgive me, and we can finally be at peace."

She sits in silence, but I see her face soften. Her lips, once hard and pursed, have eased. She glances up at me, then quickly back down at her phone, and the lines on her forehead release their grip. Perhaps I finally got through to her.

"OK, I'll leave you. Please, let me know when you leave so I can come back," I say.

"No, it's fine…you can stay but just…for Christ's sake, please stop talking," she says, followed by a giggle. A hint of humor, and for the first time in twelve years, I think I may have finally reached her on some level.

"Fair enough," I say. "Do you know where Haley is? I need to speak with her."

Corina looks down at her hands and mumbles softly, "I spoke with Maddy's Mom. She has been there, mostly."

We sit in silence for a while, but I still feel miserable and mournful looking over at my Annabel, but a weight has been lifted. A weight I have been hauling around for the past twelve years, and I've come to realize it doesn't matter who I feel is right or wrong or how much I feel victimized. What matters is stopping the venomous cycle that has been tormenting everyone's lives. I don't know if it has made a difference or if it meant anything to Corina, but it meant something to me, and I meant what I said. Hate controls you, it gnaws and eventually consumes you, and everyone around you falls victim to it.

*

I walk out of the hospital and feel the cool air touch my face for the first time in two days. The crisp air is refreshing, but nothing would be better than a long shower to rinse the depression off me, but first, I must find Haley. I can imagine how she must be struggling with guilt. I need to hold her, coddle her like I did when she was a child, and tell her everything will be alright.

I pick up my car at the valet and head over to Maddy's house. I catch a glimpse of myself in the rearview mirror. *Who are you?* I look like a homeless person. My hair disheveled, unshaven, and my mouth reeks of two-day-old morning breath. As the car cruises on autopilot, I pass my hand through my hair and wipe the crust from the corner of my eyes.

I take the water bottle that was left on the passenger seat, cup my hand, and splash it over my face, but I am unable to rinse the broken from my soul. I try to hold back tears but it's useless. My face scrunches, my brow indents, and the river flows once again, but as quickly as it began, I dam the tears and wipe my face dry. However short the episode may have been, my eyes are bloodshot. My light-colored eyes are offset with jagged red lines covering the whites and add to my zombie-like appearance.

I pull up to Maddy's house. A cute colonial with a perfect lawn, perfect, neatly trimmed hedges, and an arched door that makes the house somehow look as if it were smiling. I walk the golden brick walkway, paved for the perfect family, and when I reach the door, it swings open before I can raise my hand to knock.

"Hi, Mrs., uh… I'm sorry, Maddy's mom?" I say becoming flush. I can't recall Maddy's last name for the life of me. In fact, I'm not sure if I ever knew it. I have met Maddy on many occasions, but Corina has done her best to poison my reputation with all the girl's classmate's parents for so many years, and it became so awkward that I made little attempt to involve myself with them socially.

"Yes?" she says and tilts her head to the side studying me.

"I'm sorry to bother you, I'm Haley's father, Dylan Grady," I reach out my hand and she immediately grabs it and slings her free arm around me.

"Come in, come in! Poor thing. I'm Grace McFadden. I'm so sorry to hear about what's happened."

"Thank you. That's OK, really. Is Haley here?" I say.

I imagine I look like a lost puppy.

She looks down to her hands that interlock in front of her abdomen. "No. Poor little Haley. We love her so much. Think of her as one of our own. She and our little Maddy have been the best of friends since they were in elementary school."

"Yes, I know. Maddy is a wonderful girl. Are they here?"

"No… I mean, she is staying here, but they went out. A boy by the name of Jared picked them up in some godawful yellow vehicle. Didn't say where they were going. I'm so sorry. Would you like to come in for a drink and wait?"

"No, thank you. Here is my number." I tap my phone twice on the side of her door and sync my contact with her smart home. "Please, if she comes here before I find her, please call me. It's extremely important I speak with her."

"Of course," she says. Her cheekbones rise into a crooked smile, and her brow sulks, meeting in between her eyes.

I return to my car and think about all the places she could be. She could be at Jared's house, but I don't even know where Jared lives. I could drive by Chippy's Deli where a lot of her school friends seem to congregate. If she isn't there, perhaps she is in the woods behind the high school doing God knows what? I remember Annabel telling me once that Haley goes there a lot to be alone and think.

I pull up to Chippy's Deli, but even though there are a handful of kids congregating in the front, Haley and Maddy are not among them. I drive through town and scour the streets, but other than a few kids dribbling a basketball, the streets are bare.

I pull into the high school parking lot, swing around back, park by the baseball diamond and look out past the field to the line of trees that act as a barrier to the school grounds. I scan down the line and spot a small opening to the far-right corner of the field, where there appears to be a hole in the chain link fence. Someone appears to have clipped the links and spread it apart.

That must be it. I walk across the field and crawl under the opening in the fence. My shirt gets caught on one of the rusty links, tears a gaping hole and takes a chunk of my skin along with it.

"Shit," I say, reaching my hand to my back and feeling a stream of blood touch my fingers.

I stand up and feel the cool breeze run up my shirt and it adds to my misery, sending a chill running up my spine. Suddenly, I smell a scent I am not familiar with. It smells of chemicals, almost like Vicks VapoRub burning in the air. My nasal passages clear in an instant. I have a bad feeling about this.

I continue down the beaten path, and the smell becomes even more potent. I do my best to avoid the sticks and leaves that are scattered about because I don't want whoever is here to be warned of my presence. When I was a teenager, I used to meet my friends in the woods. We would each bring a joint, a bowl, even a bong, each packed with a different strain and smoke. If I heard someone coming, the first thing I'd do is hide and, at times, take off running as if my life depended on it.

I come upon a fallen tree, slowly climb over it, and hear voices off to my right. I creep slowly in between the trees, careful as to where to place my feet until I see three silhouettes huddled in a circle, passing a bowl among them, but I still can't see their faces. The smell that I smelled upon entering the path is surely whatever it is they are smoking, and it is something unfamiliar from my experimental youth.

There has been a new drug all over the news called Rooster. It is a designer drug developed by some graduate students at Arizona State University. They were attempting to develop a new antipsychotic. One intended to treat people suffering from bipolar disorder and extreme depression. The drug was successful. However, people became dependent on it because it depleted them of all their serotonin, making them even more depressed when taken off it, resulting in elevated suicide rates when doses were missed. It also has a psychedelic effect when smoked through a vaporizer, and people become so euphoric they have a greater chance of an overdose.

"Cock-a-doooo-dle-doooooo!" the boy squawks with his hands cupped to his mouth like a megaphone.

"Shut the fuck up, Jared!" Maddy says, slapping him on the shoulder.

"Maddy, stop being such a herbivore. Join Hales and expand your consciousness. Here, take a hit," Jared says.

Hailey sways back and forth and leans her weight against a tree. My heart breaks.

"Oh, no, Haley," I whisper to myself.

Haley reaches for the bowl, puts it to her lips, and spins in a wobbly circle, puffing it incessantly. Smoke billows out of her mouth like a chimney, and she barrels over and coughs.

I storm out of the brush with my arms flexed, fists tightly clenched, and yell, "Haley!"

I sounded angrier than I intended, and the growl of my voice startles them.

Haley stumbles, throws her head back, and falls clumsily to the floor.

"Oh, shit!" Jared says and lets out an obnoxiously coy giggle.

"Oh, shit, is right, Jared," I say. "You'll be lucky if I don't kick the living shit out of you before I leave here.

"Wha—" he says with an obnoxious high-pitched squealing laugh. He throws his hands up in the air in surrender. "It was Haley's idea!"

"No, it wasn't," Maddy interjects and pushes Jared with both hands in his chest.

Haley hops to her feet and dusts the debris off her pants with her hands. "What are you doing here, Dad?"

"I've been looking all over for you! Haley, we need to talk about what happened."

"No, we don't! I fucken killed her, Dad. What else do you want me to say?"

I look at Haley and reach out for her, but she smacks my hand away.

"What is this shit, anyway?" I snatch the bowl out of her hand and sniff the stream of smoke, my head revolts, and my eyes release back into my head.

"Just a little weed, Mr. Grady. Relax, dude," Jared says.

My eyes widen, and the vein begins to twitch in my neck. "Don't tell me to fucking relax…dude! In fact, if you know what's good for you, you won't breathe another fucking word! Got it?" I sniff it again. "This isn't fucken weed.

Is this Rooster?"

Maddy looks down to the ground, and Jared tries to prevent a smile from curling up on his stupid, pompous, pimple-ridden face.

"Haley? If shit wasn't bad enough, this is what you choose to do?"

"Who cares, Dad? Life is over, anyway. What the fuck is the difference?" she says, wiping tears from her eyes. "Does anything really matter anymore? I killed her, Dad! The only person I could ever truly trust! The only person who absolutely loved me unconditionally and I-I, me, Haley. I fucken killed her! I did that!"

"What happened?" I ask, kneeling beside her.

"She, she… Mom happened!"

She begins to unfold the story in broken, sniffling words, and I sit and listen, piecing together what I can. "Mom. John. He, she…" She coughs, chokes and spits mucus off to her side.

"It's OK, baby. What is it?"

"They said you hit her! Dante's. Bullshit! 'Cause I was there," she says, pointing to herself. "You dropped me off, and we saw the whole thing," she whines, pointing to Jared, and then herself. "Mom wasn't even there! I told her I knew it was all a lie. I told her I was leaving to go live with you. Bella must've heard, Dad!" She throws her hands up to cover her face and smears dirt across her cheeks as she moves to clear the tears. "Aaaarggg. Oh, God!" she wails.

"Haley, come here, my love," I beg, holding my arms out and plead for her to enter my embrace.

"I didn't know she was out there! She must've gone out the back. I hit her so hard! Sounded like a fucking bowling ball hitting the pavement!" She screeches, screaming so loudly the birds in the trees take flight.

"Oh, no, no, no!" I cover my ears. I can't listen to another word. "Haley, it was an accident. A horrible accident," I say. My eyes well up. I reach for her, but again, she swats my hands away, drops to the ground, and curls into a ball.

Maddy runs over to her and throws her arms around her and looks up to me. "Mr. Grady, I'm so sorry for all of this. I didn't smoke anything…promise. I'll watch her. She just needs some time. I'll make sure she gets home and gets to bed. She'll come around, but I don't think now is a good time."

I put my head down, and I feel my heart sink into my chest. The emptiness I felt since the moment I was given Annabel's grave prognosis suddenly becomes even more hollow, but as hollow as I feel, I can't imagine what Haley must be going through.

"OK. Haley, baby? My love? Please, come home and stay with me and Stella. We love you. You always have a home with us."

"What's there to love? How could you ever forgive me? I killed your little Annabel bear." She cries into Maddy's sleeve.

I nod to Maddy. "Take care of her."

I swallow the massive pit lodged in my gullet and begin what feels like the longest walk I have ever taken back to my car.

*

I pull into the driveway, greeted by Stella on the porch, drinking a glass of wine and smoking one of our reserve cigarettes.

"Hi, honey mou. Any news?" Stella says, unintentionally exhaling a cloud of smoke into my face.

"No, same," I say, wafting away the smoke.

"Nothing? Nothing happened today?"

"No."

"Really?" she asks as if I were keeping something from her.

I'm becoming irritated, and I feel myself getting ready to snap and unload all of my raw emotion. I just can't bring myself to talk about it right now. I realize it isn't Stella I'm angry with, I'm just overwhelmed, frustrated, and angry with the world. I want to climb a mountain and yell to the heavens as loud as I can, hoping that, above all the lemmings, God will hear me.

I can't let the toxicity of my current situation poison the people around me. I love them, and they are suffering with me. They suffer because of their love for Annabel, and also because of their love for me.

"No, love, I'm sorry. Nothing has changed. I'm just drained of emotion, and I don't really want to talk about it. I promise I'll tell you if anything changes, OK?" I open my arms, inviting her in for a hug, and we embrace each other in silence.

"I rescheduled Ileana's genetic test for tomorrow. I know you wanted to be there. If you aren't up for it, I can take her," she says.

"No, I'll go. I need to keep busy. It won't do me any good to sit around the house and sulk all day. What time?"

"I made it for eleven, but I think we can change it to later if you want. She seemed pretty open," she says.

"No, eleven is fine. I'll do that, and then I'll stop by and see Annabel again. I want to speak with her doctor and see what his plan is. I haven't seen or heard anything from him since the first day. It's as if the nurse is her doctor now. Plan? What plan?"

"Well, it's like you always say. This universal healthcare system has destroyed medicine. Less doctors, less surgery, more drugs," Stella says.

It's true. Universal healthcare has severely limited the number of healthcare providers and reduced the incentives for doctors to treat their patients. Demand for care is limited to supply, and people have to wait to receive care. Annabel had emergency surgery but is now viewed as stable, and they will get to her when they get to her. She is no longer a priority, simply a number at the end of a long line.

I also fear they may remove her from life support prematurely, simply because she has reached the maximum dollar the government is willing to spend on her. Her life is worth all I have, and I want to make it clear I will pay, and continue to pay, until I feel it is appropriate to let her go.

I can't stop thinking that if healthcare remained private, then there would have been a lot more research conducted on her condition and health care focused companies would have spent more money on research and development to find answers. Innovation stops when there is no money to be made.

The United States' decision to socialize healthcare effected healthcare throughout the entire world. Like a domino effect, the research and development in the healthcare industry across the world came to a screeching halt. Companies foreign and domestic, focused their attention on making products cheaper and streamlining current technology rather than investing in the next generation cure. New technology ceased because even foreign companies relied on the sales in the United States in order to supplement the prices they received in their own counties with socialized medicine already in place.

The number of multinational companies soared, and most healthcare products were produced overseas in China and India. The quality of these products had tremendously been reduced, and there are more reported failures on fewer surgeries than ever before.

Nothing is better under government control because, let's be honest, the United States government does not have the best interest of its people in mind. Follow the money and you'll find the problem. A recent study has shown that over forty thousand Americans have died unnecessarily due to the long waiting list for necessary procedures like coronary bypass.

Many people assumed that socialized medicine meant that they were going to receive free healthcare but when their taxes spiked so egregiously and continued to spike, year over year, the once middle class was succumbed to poverty levels thus, increasing the need for more social programs, resulting in bigger government. They said it would balance over time, however, it has only worsened and created an economic crisis, essentially eliminating the middle class altogether.

America is no longer the country it once was. A country created and prospered on the idea of freedom and capitalism is in turmoil.

"Love, you know I may need to use our money to keep Annabel..."

"Of course, love, I know. I wouldn't have it any other way. Whatever you have to do. I love her, too, honey, you know that," she says. Her face immediately distorts, and she cries.

"I know," I say and, in that moment, I have a complete and total meltdown. The rush of emotion passes through me like a ghost. I'm possessed with utter sorrow; tears gush and soak every crevice of my face. The numbness retreats, the grief sets in, and I feel like I could cry for days.

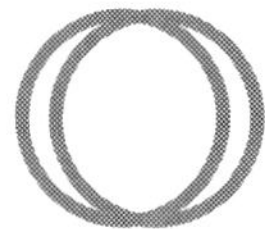

# CHAPTER 9

I tossed and turned all night. It was the first night I have spent at home since Annabel has been in the hospital, and I feel overwhelming guilt for not being there with her, but I have a responsibility here, too. Ileana, Jay, and Stella need me also, but I'm haunted by the *what ifs*. What if she were to wake up and I'm not there? What if she were to...? No, I have to remain positive.

I fall in and out of prayer, to a God who doesn't owe me a thing, and worse things have happened to better people than me, but Annabel? Annabel is one of the best people I know, and not just because she is my daughter. She truly is good.

I recall when she was around six years old, we would go to the playground, and she would always seek out the younger children who were fearful or shy. She would help them, hold their hands, and guide them through the jungle gym. She has always had a nurturing, calming presence. I have always admired her empathy, confidence, and ability to push past her insecurities and do what she feels is right. To take her away from this world would be the biggest sin of all. Even at thirteen, she has a profound effect on people. She has profoundly affected *me*.

As night shifts to dawn, I toss and turn until the sheets beneath me have more ripples than the sea. It is pointless to continue to try and sleep, so I open the news app to distract myself from my self-destructive thoughts. Nearly every other article is an opinion piece written about Alter-life. It has become the most controversial topic in the media, and they have latched onto it. Many deem it to be sacrilegious and spew their hatred for founder Donald Morgan all over the page.

Am I alone in thinking this could help people that are suffering, tormented and alone in a world that has turned its back on them? What about those burdened with severe depression or who are mentally disabled? They can lead a happy, *normal* existence in Alter-life because they will be the norm. People who are terminally ill could live without pain, suffering, or memory. They could live out their days, half their age, and in ignorant bliss, and when they pass, they will do so without pain, fear, or regret.

People are so quick to judge others for the choices they make. However, everyone is faced with different circumstances and paths can be veered by the things we are forced to endure. I believe we are all products of our unique experience. The world molds us. Born in innocence with a unique personality, though our path shapes which direction our energy flows, and perhaps some people truly don't have a reason to smile. It's easy to say it's a state of mind, but until you've had your entire world collapse, you wouldn't understand.

In this particular article, the media depicts Alter-life as a product of the devil. They make outlandish comparisons to late term abortion. "Alter-life aborts mothers and fathers out of this world, taking them away from the children who need them." They claim that Alter-life creator, Donald Morgan, is playing God. A world within a world, he is the, "Alpha and the Omega, the first and the last, the beginning and the end," quoting Revelation 22:13.

Of course, ole Donny boy asked for it. He probably should have had the foresight to see that putting the Alpha and Omega symbols at the beginning and the end of the Alter-life logo was bound to stir up some controversy. The implication and reference to a biblical passage was inevitably going to ruffle some feathers.

The media has irresponsibly rallied the far-right wing Evangelicals, and they are picketing in the streets in front of the Alter-life facility. People in hordes gather in one of the biggest religious demonstrations recorded in the last fifty years. God's advocates spitting on future Alter-life clients, dousing them with holy water, loaded into semi-automatic water guns.

Protestors shout, "One world, one God!" Others raise picket signs picturing Donald Morgan's face inside of a pentagram.

It all seems rather extreme to me and not very, well, Christian. The hypocrisy is blinding, but I guess if you feel that you are doing God's work, then perhaps you feel justified. I have a theory that some people believe their church attendance washes away their sins, and if you sin in the name of God, somehow it isn't a sin at all.

"What the hell is with that look on your face?" Stella asks, startling me out of my deep thought, and I nearly roll off the bed.

"Oh, my God! You scared the shit out of me!" I say, holding my hand up to my chest, feeling my heart pound within.

She laughs from her belly, so hard that mucus inflates like a balloon at the tip of her left nostril. She sniffs it back in and chokes as it collides with the back of her throat.

"Do you need me to put Depends on the shopping list? You look like you might have shit your pants!" she manages to say, still gasping for air.

"No, you asshole. I was just deep in thought and trying to be quiet. Couple that with a major life crisis and a nervous breakdown and, well, that's what you get!"

Even in the face of tragedy, we still manage to make each other laugh. One of the reasons we have always gotten along so well, our sense of humor is intertwined. We truly are as close to soul mates as two people could possibly be.

"Don't forget, today is Ileana's big day," she says.

"Big day?"

"Yeah, her DNA placement test."

"That's her big day?" I ask.

"Well, yeah, it could map out the rest of her life! This could be the day she discovers what she loves to do. What she's going to do for the rest of her life!"

Stella says practically jumping out of her shoes.

"OK, OK, but listen. Like I've said before, I'm not going to force her onto a path she doesn't want to take because of what some stupid test says she would be good at." I say. "I understand that they may go hand in hand, but I just want her to be happy and follow a path that is going to make her happy, not one just because she may be good at it."

"If she's good at it, she will like it," Stella says, matching my irritableness.

"Not true," I contest.

"How so?"

"How so? OK, I'm good at grammar. I have always excelled at it, but I'd be miserable as a writer or a teacher. It isn't what would make me happy. If I took this test when I was her age, my parents and teachers may have pushed me into a career that, yes, I probably would excel at, but in the end, I'd be miserable," I say.

We stare at each other for a few moments in silence. She often does this when she knows I've made a valid point, but she will never concede.

"That's asinine," she says.

"OK."

"OK? OK?" she says, partially joking and hits me with her pillow.

"Alright, Stella my love, we'll force Ileana to do whatever the test says, OK? I mean fuck her happiness. In the end, it isn't as important as our own, right?"

"You're an asshole, you know that?"

"Yup!"

*

"Ileana Grady?" a voice calls out from an empty doorway.

We stand in sync, and my knees let out a loud *crack*. We have been sitting in this perfectly square room for what feels like eons, with only ancient e-magazines and an eerily quirky receptionist to keep our minds occupied. There are signs posted throughout the school that read: No Electronic Devices.

I assumed they were intended for the students, but I was scolded shortly after we sat down by the quirky woman behind the desk who couldn't stop fidgeting in her chair, picking her nose and eating it.

We cautiously walk towards the door, unsure if we should enter. I glance over at the receptionist for direction, though she remains fixated on her computer, with her finger up her nose. We peek our heads through the door and are greeted by an attractive woman with red hair, fair skin, and green eyes.

"Hi, Ileana?"

"Yes," Ileana replies, glancing up with timid eyes.

"I'm Ms. Patrice. I'm going to be your talent guide here at the school."

"Talent guide?" I ask.

"Oh, yes. Mr. Grady, I presume?" she asks, offering me her hand. "A talent guide is an advisor here at Barron Academy. Essentially, it's what a guidance counselor was when you went to school. However, we offer more of, well… customized guidance. Follow me, please."

We follow Ms. Patrice down a long corridor, filled with classrooms that resemble college auditoriums with less seating. Most of the rooms are decked out with high tech equipment from wall to wall, with seats spread about. It isn't your stereotypical classroom layout. The Astrophysicists/Astronomy studies lab is an actual planetarium, equipped with a giant telescope that extends down the center of the room.

Haley would have loved that at Ileana's age, and I wish, at the time, I could have afforded to send her to a place like this. Perhaps her love for astronomy would have excelled her in a direction that would have filled her life with meaning and focus and kept her away from the likes of Jared.

As we near the end of the hallway, we are led into a room with a sign on the door that reads: Testing Laboratory. It's a small room, resembling a doctor's exam room with a large wooden desk in the center, bolted to the floor. There is one chair for the examiner and two chairs on the opposite side for the student and parent.

"Take a seat, please," Ms. Patrice says. "So, today is your big day! Are you excited?"

"Um, yes, I guess," Ileana says.

"Can I ask a question?" I intervene.

"Sure, of course," Ms. Patrice says.

"What if the test comes back and says Ileana's path should be something that, well…something she doesn't want to do? Something that won't make her happy."

"I see we have a skeptic." She chuckles.

I can't help but feel as though her response, though plastered with a smile from ear to ear, is loaded with condescension.

"Listen, I just don't want to force her onto a path that doesn't make her happy. Success may be important, but happiness is more important," I say.

"Well, Mr. Grady, it is our belief here at Barron Academy that a career in what you've been biologically gifted will make you happy. Isn't that why you applied Ileana to our institution?"

Institution? I've always hated that term. When I hear institution, I immediately think of a building with few windows and its inhabitants in straitjackets.

"I understand the philosophy but, to be honest, it's more Ileana's mother that is sold on the curriculum," I say.

Ileana hits my leg and shoots me a look of distress.

"I see. Well, Ileana, do you want to attend Barron Academy?" Ms. Patrice asks softly.

"Yes! Yes, very much!" Ileana says, placing her hands together in prayer.

"OK! Well, that's great because that's…" she raises her finger and points to a sign that reads: Happiness is Success, "the most important thing. Students who don't want to participate in the program often don't excel," she says, glancing down at the chart in front of her. "Give me a sec, I'll be right back," she says, still smiling like a robot. I presume she has been trained to do so but, strangely, it makes me feel dirty inside.

She exits the room, and as soon as the door *chirps* closed, Ileana smacks me in the chest. "Dad! What are you doing? What if they kick me out? Or…or give my spot to someone else?"

I look to her adoringly, "OK, sweetie, I'll stop. But I just want you to be happy. Your happiness means everything to me."

"I know, Dad, but just stop…please?"

Ms. Patrice enters the room with a testing kit in hand, identical to the one on her desk, marked Ileana Grady. She sits down, folds her arms on her desk, and clears her throat, "Mr. Grady," she says nearly singing, "I've obtained permission from Principal Meisner himself to offer you a free DNA scan! We can run it simultaneously with Ileana's."

"No, no that's alright. You don't have to do—"

"It may put your mind at ease when you see the types of data we receive and how we would use that data towards a curriculum at the institution."

"Please, Daddy? Do it with me?" Ileana pleads.

I look at her and am met with enormous puppy dog eyes. I know she's nervous but, truthfully, I don't like the idea of anyone having my DNA. Who knows what they could do with it.

"No, baby, this is for you and—"

"Pleeeease?" Ileana begs again.

I'm a sucker, and I may be too empathetic to effectively parent. I'm always considering others feeling before my own.

"Well...alright, what the hell? Let's do it, but Ms. Patrice, promise me this is confidential and none of the information is shared with anyone or any groups outside of this school."

"Yes, Mr. Grady, I promise. You must sign this form for both of you that explains our privacy policy, and no, we can't share any of this information unless you release it. You are just authorizing us to view and use the information solely for Barron Academies academic purposes. We won't clone you, LOL."

I cringe. I loathe when people talk in text shorthand, especially shorthand that dates them. LOL? LOL hasn't been used in nearly a decade. It's one thing to write it to demonstrate emotion but another to say it out loud in a conversation. I suddenly realize I'm smiling at her awkwardly, so I laugh and say, "Of course not! Who'd want to clone me, anyway? LOL!"

Did I really just do that? Did I just use LOL in a sentence? Ms. Patrice nervously clears her throat again and says, "Well, OK then, it's settled. Any more questions before we get started?"

"How long before we get the results? Do we have to come back to review them or do you call us?"

"Oh, no, it takes about fifteen minutes for us to chart the DNA and then the computer spits back a thorough analysis of your strengths and weaknesses," she says.

"Today? You get them back in fifteen minutes?" I ask, eyes wide.

"Yeah, it's amazing what these new super computers can do. Would you like to have us map out which DNA markers you share? In other words, we can, with pretty close accuracy, see which traits Ileana received from you, and the remainder is safe to assume is from her mother. Oh, and Mother Nature herself."

"OK sure, that could be fun," I say.

"Alrighty then, let's get started!" She opens the kits and, to my surprise, I see they only consist of two sterile packed cotton swabs, a plastic test tube filled with solution, sterile gloves, and a disposable sterile razor blade.

"Now, I need each of you to swab the inside of your cheek for approximately thirty seconds. Make sure not to contaminate the swab by putting it down. I will take the swabs, cut off the cotton, and insert it into these tubes."

She hands us the swabs. We stare at each other and make funny faces with our eyes as we vigorously swab our cheeks for the next thirty seconds.

"Remember, keep turning the swab. Try and get it fully saturated," she says.

When the timer sounds, Ms. Patrice carefully takes our swabs, cuts off the cotton with the razor blade, inserts them into the test tube with the solution, and carefully places them into a unit under the computer terminal.

"Alright, we have fifteen minutes or so. I'll be back! Can I get either of you anything? Coffee, tea, water?"

"No, thank you," we say in unison.

For the next fifteen minutes, I have no choice but to submit to a barrage of questions about Annabel. I don't want to talk about it. However, she has a right to know. She is her sister after all. I fight back tears, and my lip quivers, wrestling through my emotions, and tell her as much as I can manage, although some of her questions I just simply don't have answers to.

I'm ashamed with myself. I have been so selfish!

"I'm sorry I haven't come to you to talk to you and Jay about all this. I know it must be hard for you being left in the dark. I remember hating that as a kid," I say.

"Hating what?"

"When I was your age, and Grandma or Grandpa would keep things from me. I always knew what was going on, but I needed clarity, and no one would give it to me, so, I'm sorry, I really am."

"It's OK, Daddy," Ileana says, moisture clouding her eyes.

"I think it's because we think we're protecting you, but if I really think about it, I think it just confuses you. It's a little selfish on our part, your mother and I."

Moments later, the door squeaks open, and I stiffen in my chair. For some nonsensical reason, I'm nervous. I feel like I'm back in school and a figure of authority just entered the room, test scores in hand that weigh heavily on my future.

Ms. Patrice scoops the back of her red and white skirt, flattens it to the back of her legs, and takes her seat. "Alright! I love this part, it's so exciting! Your life could literally change in the next few minutes!"

I feel my heart beat harder. The release of adrenaline cools my chest with a gush and sends me fidgeting in my chair again. I pray to myself the results excite her. Something that invigorates and motivates her through her life. I don't want her to be a prisoner to her DNA.

"OK, let's see here, Ileana. Now, keep in mind, I am not a geneticist. I just read the computer analysis of your DNA. There's a lot that goes into getting these results, though I'm told they are done with 99.8% accuracy. There have only been two cases we know of where a child has successfully deviated from the course curriculum the computer has mapped out."

I can't help but think that it's because most people who attend this school are sold on the technology so, naturally, they don't believe they would be good at anything other than what the computer has told them. Without confidence, you'll fail more than you succeed.

"Oooh, Ileana. It says here that your ideal profession would be in healthcare.

Perhaps a nurse or even a doctor is in your future? How do you like that, Dad?" Ms. Patrice says with a wink.

"As long it's something that would make her happy. I don't care if she is a garbage man, so long as she wakes up smiling every day." I look over at Ileana, and she seems to be pleased. Her smile is loud and proud. She hasn't said a word but looks like she is on cloud nine.

"She has a high level of empathy and a desire to care for people. She also has excellent fine motor skills and analytical thinking. It states her ideal career would be a surgeon."

This isn't a surprise. These traits run deep on my side of the family. Who knows, if DNA scans were available when I was Ileana's age, perhaps I would have become a surgeon. Maybe it would have put me on the correct path and eliminated the doubt and insecurities that can play a part in holding one back. I didn't think I was smart enough to become a surgeon, but if someone told me it was my destiny? Hell, I think I would have had the confidence to rise to the challenge.

"As for you, Mr. Grady..." She picks up the paper. "Hmmm, I uh...um... well...so, it says," she clears her throat again, looking perplexed at the results, and her eyes spring wide.

"Is there something wrong, Ms. Patrice?" I say.

She looks up with a giant smile, but anxiety attacks her eyes like a violent storm.

"Ileana, would you mind stepping out of the room for just a moment?" Ms. Patrice says.

"Really, whatever it says is OK. If it says I'm an imbecile, so be it," I say.

"No, actually it says your ideal career would have been an investigator or a detective," she says quick and flat. Clearly, there is something else.

"Really?" I ask, intrigued.

"Yes," Ms. Patrice says and places the results down, looking at me apprehensively. "I really need to speak with you in private, Mr. Grady. Ileana, would you please go sit in Mr. Meisner's office at the end of the hall? It's the last door on the left. We will come get you in just a few minutes. Uh, when I'm done with your father."

"Uh, OK, sure." Ileana locks eyes with me and lifts her eyebrows as if to say, 'This is strange.'

I smile and nod at her. "All good, baby doll. See you in a few."

We sit in silence until Ileana is out of harm's way. The uneasiness is clear on my face. I feel flush, extremely confused, and nervous, and I perspire. What could it possibly be? Why would she ask Ileana to leave? Were they able to see a genetic disease? Am I dying? I'm dying! If it isn't a disease, the suspense will surely kill me.

Just as I'm about to say something to break the silence, Ms. Patrice says, "I'm sorry, Mr. Grady but…I'm not sure if you knew but…"

"What? Know what?" I snap back, unable to contain myself any longer.

"Ileana is not your biological child," she spits the words out so quickly as if they were burning a hole in her soul.

"No…no, no…you must be mistaken!"

"I'm afraid not." Her voice cracks.

I see only red.

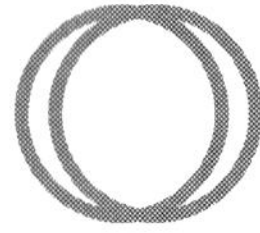

# CHAPTER 10

"Daddy, what's wrong? What was that all about?" Ileana asks.

"Ileana, put on your seatbelt, I'm not going to ask you again!" I snap.

Silence consumes us, but the noise is louder than ever in my head, and I feel like I am losing my mind. First Annabel, and now this? I'm cursed. The news that Ileana is not my biological daughter is devastating. How could this be? Has Stella known all along?

I grit my teeth, clenching my jaw so tight that it aches, and I see my bloodshot eyes staring back at me through the rearview mirror. My shoulders feel as though the weight of the world is resting upon them.

We sit at the traffic light, and with every second that passes, I grow more agitated. A car pulls alongside of us on the shoulder, blaring mariachi music intrusively loud. So loud my seat vibrates violently and tickles the cilia within my ears, causing me to shake. Another car pulls behind me and stops short, almost rear-ending me.

*Breathe! Take a breath,* I tell myself.

The light changes from red to green and, like a bullet, I fire the gas pedal to the floor when, unexpectedly, a man walks out in front of my car. I slam on the brakes, bringing us to a screeching halt, and the man scowls at us as he strolls past my car out of turn. The heat that was already at a dangerous simmer, rapidly boiling in my chest.

My eyes widen, teeth grind together and in an instant, I change from Bruce Banner into the Incredible Hulk. When the man is barely past my car, I slam onto the gas, exceeding the speed limit in an instant. I am no longer in control. My emotions have taken over and are at the wheel. I should engage auto-drive, but you can't reason with the Hulk.

"Daddy, what's wrong? Please, slow down," Ileana screams, holding on for dear life.

I realize I'm frightening her, and I soften and decelerate, but it's too late. I slam my hands onto the wheel. "Great, just great!" I scream.

Ileana shudders in her seat. "What?"

"It's the police, I'm getting pulled over."

"Oh," she says quietly staring into her lap.

I veer the car to the side of the road and slow onto the shoulder. My left eye twitches and extends rapidly to my temple. My blood pressure skyrockets, and I can't seem to swallow it down. I continue to take deep breath after deep breath, and in my state of madness, I meet Ileana's eyes, and she looks at me, terrified and confused. The color leaves my face, and my vision blurs.

I hear a faint knock at the window and another and another, but I'm frozen. The baton strikes my window a fourth time, and this time, it echoes inside my head like a tuning fork, but I am unable to release my grip from the wheel, unable to regain control of my body.

I tilt my head towards Ileana. She is speaking to me, although her voice is muffled, and I can't make out what she's saying.

"What?" my voice echoes and, suddenly, I feel nauseous.

I look up and see Captain Rosario whacking my window with his baton. He seethes and spits, shouting profanely and, in that moment, I regain enough lucidity to open the window. The window opens, and Captain Rosario's baton cracks the side of my head. *Pop!*

*

I wake to sirens wailing in my ear, enveloping me in a cocoon of pandemonium and rattling my pounding head. Overwhelmed by nausea when the vehicle turns abruptly, I feel something warm run down my cheek, but when I move to inspect it, I'm unable to. My wrists and ankles are bound with restraints. My left eye is swollen shut, and my head pulsates. I struggle to focus my good eye on the blurry blob to my left, but when it finally comes into focus, I see Captain Rosario and an EMT sitting beside me. Rosario towers over me, smirking sinisterly.

"Well, good morning, sunshine," Rosario says.

I stare at him long, hard, killing him with my mind, but it's useless. His cocky grin not only remains, it has grown wider. He believes he has won, and perhaps he has. I return my one-eyed gaze to the roof, close it, and return my focus to my breathing.

"If you're going to take me to the hospital, can you at least put me in the room with my Annabel?" I say.

My eye continues to swell, and I feel it branching out until it consumes the left side of my face, and with every moment that passes, it inflates.

"Not likely, pal. You're not in ICU shape…yet," he says with a wink.

"Then finish me off, would ya?"

"It was an accident, you know," Rosario says, lowering his voice, almost apologetic.

"What was?"

"You opened your window right as I was swinging ole Mickey! It really was like, well, like God just willed it to happen. I ain't never seen timing like that. Those new cars open their windows so damn quick, and because they're shatterproof, I was just wailing on it, and *bam!* Got you good, too."

"God isn't on my side, that's for damn sure," I say.

"Why didn't you just open your damn window, Grady?"

I choose not to answer, and then suddenly my memory is jarred. My eye springs open, and I try to break free of my restraints, "Where's Ileana? My daughter, where is she?"

"Hey, hey, hey, relax! Don't worry, she's fine. My officer is taking her home.

I told 'em to radio me when he gets there. I'll have him explain to your ole lady what happened and where they can find you, OK, sport?"

My head slams back down onto the gurney, and I remember Ms. Patrice's words, and I suspect those words will haunt me for the remainder of my days.

"Are these restraints really necessary?" I ask.

"Well, Grady, your behavior was a bit irrational. You refused to open your window and, shit, you looked like you were possessed or something! I didn't know what to expect when you woke up, you know, with your history of violence and all."

I relinquish a long, defeated sigh and settle into my prison.

Captain Rosario clears his throat and says, "I'll tell you what. If you can promise me and George here you'll behave yourself, and I won't have to have George stick you with that there tranquilizer, I'll take 'em off. But hey, one wrong move and George here is going to put you down, *Capisce*?"

I concede and mumble, "*Capisce*," under my breath.

He removes the restraints, and my wrists still feel as though they are bound. I suppose that it is a reminder I am a prisoner to this life. A life that less than a week ago was pretty damn great, but now, the dogs have been released, and they gnaw at my soul.

I rummage through my mind and try to find a happy place, but I feel sorry for myself, and my self-pity is punishing, reverting back and forth from Annabel to Ileana. I've been through some pretty rough patches before but nothing like this, one life-changing event after another. A sleeping beauty and a paternal revelation have swept away my will.

Perhaps this is how you become the grumpy old man who lives in the dark, scary house on the corner of Grove Street. The unkept one with the sign, that once happily read *The Grady's* now squeaks when it swings by a single nail, just as the man within dangles by a single thread. Stripped of all life's pleasures, left bitter, angry, and broken.

I just want to go home and hide, make a tent with the blankets in my bedroom, just as I did when I was a child, but I can't face her. I can't even look at Stella. She disgusts me. She allowed me to raise Ileana and led me to believe she was mine all these years. I am convinced she knew! Trapped me into a life, into another family where, again, I am left bound and betrayed. I am everyone's prisoner, and the weight of all their worlds is suspended on my shoulders. They're sore, and I can't bear it anymore. I'm going to collapse.

Stella and I dated casually throughout the first year of our relationship. I knew she had dated other men, but I didn't know she had been sleeping with them. She told me I was the only one. She lied. The relationship began with a fable, and my life amounts to a tale of betrayal and regret.

The ambulance comes to a stop and breaks me from my self-pity. I hear the driver's door open and slam shut. The rear doors swing ajar, and a rush of light punches me in my good eye, blinding me. Rosario grabs my arm and leads me out of the ambulance.

"So, what happens now, Captain?" I say.

"What do you mean?"

"Am I under arrest for something, or are you just escorting me to the hospital because you have a crush on me?"

"You wish, Grady. You may be my bitch but don't make me put you to work on your knees," he says, jabbing me in the ribs with his elbow. "No, not under arrest…yet."

The automatic door opens, and he guides me into the emergency department, unexpectedly yanks me to the side, allowing EMT's to wheel a critical patient past. A medic is mounted, working tirelessly performing chest compressions. Curious as a rubbernecker, I peer down as the gurney passes and see the victim is a young girl, seventeen or eighteen perhaps. An oxygen mask covers her mouth, mucus and vomit run down her chin and are painted all over her torn open shirt, and I think she looks a hell of a lot like my… No, it couldn't be…is it?

"Haley!" I shout, lunging toward the gurney. "Haley!" My voice cracks, and my throat burns from the ferocity of my scream.

Without a second to spare, I feel the arms of several men grab me, pulling and pushing, trying to wrestle me to the floor, but my adrenaline pumps, and I am a force, determined and fearless. Any worry of consequence has been long abandoned, and I'll fight whoever dare put themselves between me and my Haley.

I swing, twist and turn, punching my way loose, and pop up and sprint like a rabid dog towards the horde of EMTs rushing my daughter past the waiting room, scurry down a dimly lit hallway, and into a small room with a curtain closure. I am swiftly met by Captain Rosario and three security officers grabbing hold of anything they can grip on my body. My blood-stained shirt rips as Rosario wrestles me to the floor and binds my hands behind my back.

"Grady, stop! Stop fighting! Goddammit, Grady, listen to me! Whatever it is, clearly, they need to focus on your daughter! You aren't going to help by hovering on top of them!" he says, gasping for air.

I'm panting, the adrenaline surges, and I'm unable to stop fighting to free my hands.

"I know how this must be for you, but you need to let them work. You can't be in the way! Let them try to save her," he says.

Let them try to save her? The first intelligent thing Rosario has ever said. Perhaps there is a human being buried within that carcass after all. He's right, they need to work, and I would just be a hinderance. I stop fighting but am unable to stop convulsing on the floor.

"What happened to her?" I cry out. My voice is hoarse, and my throat burns.

My lip quivers, and crippling, paralyzing fear seizes control of me. Unfathomably beaten in a world I no longer recognize. I whine uncontrollably like that of a hyena's cry, growing louder and louder.

I hear a man's voice above me say, "I'm sorry, sir. We've done everything we can for her. We've lost her." I sink into the floor, melting, deeper and deeper into the perpetual darkness.

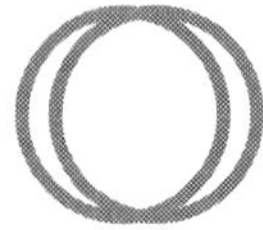

# CHAPTER 11

When tragedy strikes, friends convey their sorrow, apologetically wear their best sad face, prepare food or send flowers, but moments later, it's all forgotten. They go about their day, understandably so, although the anguish and misery torment the lives of those who are directly affected. Every hour is a battle, a war of emotions, attempting to cope with loss or the potential for it and hanging onto hope proves to be most difficult of all.

Everyone reassures you, "Everything will be alright, Dylan."

"No, Karen! Everything will not be alright. It's far from fucking alright!"

My fortress of solitude, I remain concealed under the blankets I have erected into a teepee. It was our game. The one I dragged with me from my youth, and the one that both Haley and Annabel adored when they were younger. I sit, illuminating my face with the torch from my phone and imagine they are here with me, princesses in our castle.

I keep trying to pluck myself out of this nightmare, even for just a moment. A three-headed monster. Three nightmares collide, and each as devastating as the last. My heart is broken, it hurts to breathe, and I am so alone, so…helpless.

I came home this morning while Stella was tucked away in the laundry room. I heard her operating the mechanicals, and the light was on, so I immediately crept up the stairs and locked myself in our bedroom. When she realized I was home, she banged on the door continuously for about twenty minutes. The beat echoes, *knock, knock, knock...knock, knock, knock* like a silhouette of drums pounding on my temples. I don't believe she is aware I know about Ileana, and my stomach can't handle that dialogue with her right now. I just lost my daughter; both of them. I can't speak.

The trust has been steamrolled out of our relationship, our foundation is in shambles, and I feel emotionless when I think of her. I have blocked her calls. Yes, I realize that it is childish, but I can't bear to look at her, and I don't have the energy to argue. It won't change anything. I am entombed in numbness.

"Please, Stella, just leave me alone!" I beg her.

"Why won't you open the door?"

Haley has overdosed on Rooster, and I presume it was given to her by that dipshit Jared, and when I find that son of a bitch, I will kill him. She has passed onto what, I pray, is a better place. The Grady sisters now live and love in a world of my creation: solitary.

*Haley, please guide your sister to the other side. I would rather Annabel be with you than imprisoned in a lifeless body.* I pray there isn't suffering, and they watch over each other until it is my time to join them. The thought of them in pain is too agonizing to endure. It tortures me every minute of the day.

*Knock, knock, knock*, the drum beats on. "Dylan! Honey mou! Please, open the door. I'm sorry this is happening, and I know you're in a bad place right now, but this isn't easy on any of us. We are all hurting! Come out and talk to me!" She pauses, and I hear her breath through the crack of the door. I think she may finally give up, but then, like a bullet, she fires, "Don't be so damn self-centered!"

Like a locomotive, the coals have been put to the fire. Adrenaline surges through my veins, and my heart pounds in my chest, relinquishing the beast. My emotions are volatile, and like a werewolf, aware of the full moon, I chain myself in my chamber.

I force myself to evacuate my fortress, hop off the bed, and head to the bathroom that adjoins the master bedroom. I splash cold water over my face and stare into the mirror, glare at the reflection as the water drips from my nose. A tired, old, shattered monstrosity grimaces back at me, and I think, *What have you become?* There is something in those eyes, something I haven't seen in a long time. Something frightening and transfiguring. A switch has been flipped, and it may not be possible to reset it.

"Well, at least I know you're alive! You know, you can be awfully selfish sometimes!" she says.

Selfish? Me? The fire burns like a furnace, and I tremble. I close my eyes and try to shake it off but it's too late, the embers are spreading, spreading, spreading…I combust. How could she possibly call me selfish? She has allowed me to believe I am Ileana's father all these years. She commits the ultimate act of selfishness and has the audacity to call me selfish? Me?

I slam both of my fists down onto the counter and vociferate, "Selfish? I'm selfish?"

I stomp over to the door, no longer able to chain the beast and swing it open, but when our eyes lock, I am met with overwhelming, conflicting emotion. The finality slices me again like a fresh wound. I have loved this woman so much and for so long. Was it all a lie? Haven't I given her everything? Even that which I hold most dear to me, my trust.

"Oh, my God! Honey mou, your face? What did they do to you?"

My eyes burn, and I feel my face distort, my lip quiver. I try to regain a hold of my emotions, but I can't resist the violent attack of affection and pain, inosculating branches that blur the lines of my reality. Tears fall like cannonballs, but I don't know why I'm crying. Is it anger, regret, pain, loss, or is it something else entirely? I am losing myself in a tangled web of emotional distress.

"Honey mou, calm down. Everything is going to be alright."

I penetrate her with a cold stare long enough to see her soul shiver.

"No, Stella, everything is not going to be alright!" I shout, spraying tears that have puddled within my philtrum onto her face.

"Well, not if you think that way it won't. You have to be more positive," she says.

The ferocity is evident on my face, and the pungent stench of fear engulfs us like a cloud. She fears me in my present state of madness, and I…I fear for the rest of my life. Most everything I know and love has been taken from me in a matter of days.

"I know you know," I say, snarling, trying to control the supercharged rage that runs through my veins like rocket fuel.

"Know what? What do I know? Dylan, you're scaring me!" she says. Her eyes dart back and forth, studying me, and her confusion overlaps fear.

"You've always known, and for that…for that…we can no longer be *we*," I say.

Her jaw drops open. "What in the hell are you even talking about? You're talking like a crazy person! What have I always known?" she demands, and her voice modulates from confusion to anger.

"Ileana isn't mine, Stella!"

"What? What are you talking about?" she says as though she was appalled. However, I see it in her eyes. She knows the secret she has held close to her chest has finally been unleashed. At the very least, I'm certain she has always surmised it was possible, but she would prefer to entangle herself in lies than admit to something so heinous.

"You're really going to play this game? Goddammit, Stella, I'm not Ileana's father!"

Her mouth hangs open, her neck retracts, and her left eye twitches as it often does when she has been backed into a corner in an argument.

"And what about Jay?"

"What about him?" she asks, tears welling up in her eyes.

"Is he mine, Stella?"

She places her hand over her mouth and stares at me, unresponsive.

I allow her a moment to respond, but when she doesn't, I rush past her, scurry down the stairs, loop around the banister, and march to the kitchen and swipe up my keys.

"Where are you going?" She yells from the top of the stairs.

Blubbering, I say, "Oh, and in case you're interested, Haley overdosed!"

I open the door to the garage and hear Stella race down the stairs. "What? Dylan! Wait! Dylan! Oh, my God!" she screams. "What are you talking about?"

I slam the door, hasten to my car, and zip into reverse. I see Stella running down the driveway, flailing her arms and pleading for me to stop, but I punch the car into drive and peel away, leaving another life in my rearview mirror. At the end of the block, I engage auto-drive because driving with one eye is remarkably strenuous.

I need to relax, to think, but most of all, I need to be alone. I've been here before, and I don't think I can do it again. Stella and I never married, but she was my life partner, my best friend, my everything, and my trust and faith in women, in humanity, has been obliterated.

I order the car to take me on a scenic route. It rolls me into town, like a baby in a stroller, and I whine, tucked away in my swaddle. The children's screams as they chase each other in the schoolyard bounce off the cabin and deflect off my skull. I cover my hands over my ears and curl into a ball. My second life, my chance for a do-over has pulled away from me as quickly as the car pulled away from Stella. We always promised each other we would never lie. However bad things appeared to be, as long as we were honest, we would find a way to work through it. That was our mission, and that alone is what kept us going strong all these years. It is the backbone of any relationship, but it was our oxygen, and without it, we simply cannot survive.

I pass Beso, the restaurant where Stella and I had our first date and where we shared our first kiss. I escorted her slowly back to the car, allowing me time to work up the courage. It was a magical night, and I immediately knew I was going to love this woman. Some say, "She had me at hello," though Stella had me when we passed a diner, and she threw her arms around my neck and said, "Take me. I love the smell of bacon!" I was hooked from that moment, and I never foresaw an end.

I pass Grant Park, where we took our pregnancy photos with both Ileana and Jay, and they are still on display, scattered on walls and end tables throughout the house. I remember how happy I was to become a father again. I didn't have any doubts that Stella would be an excellent mother and an excellent partner. If she had only told me about Ileana then, perhaps we could have moved past it. I will always be her father, but things will never be the same. I will always know and forever have a broken heart.

I feel as though the automobile has linked up and accessed my memories because the scenic route compels me to confront my past and, at every corner, there is a different keepsake. Block after block, more devastation and heartache settle in, and it nestles itself into the corner of my soul, tugging and pulling at my heartstrings. Escorted through the looping back roads, the car swerves and hugs the road like a glove, taking turns more precisely than any human navigator ever could, and with every bend, I whirl in and out, revolving through cycles of depression, anger, and regret.

I think about all that goes into a separation and remember the utter devastation. The destruction of our union, but also to the bond I had with my children, implodes into millions of pieces. I'll spend the next ten years trying to piece it back together to resemble something remotely close to what I once had. I don't think Stella has it in her to be so ruthless, but then again, I didn't think Corina did, either. I don't care about the money, I really don't, but I can't go through the gut-wrenching torture of alienation again. I can't…I just can't go through it again!

My breathing becomes rapid, my throat constricts, and I feel as though I am sucking through a straw. I can't breathe! I gasp for air and, suddenly, a pain strikes inside of my chest. Am I having a heart attack? I grab my throat, undo the top button of my shirt, but nothing brings any relief.

I reach out, press the park button on the display, roll down the window, and am blasted with cool air. The car pulls over and slows to a stop, and I relax my head on the window, trying to regulate my breathing and clear my mind, taking deep breath after deep breath, wheezing and forcing oxygen into my lungs.

A few minutes later, I can breathe freely again, and my hammering heart rate settles. My ears pop, and I'm flabbergasted to hear loud chanting and yelling. I open my eyes to crowds of people enveloping my car in a bubble. Protesters march up and down the sidewalk, holding picket signs, reciting chants, and seething. They crowd the street like self-righteous cockroaches.

"What the hell is this?" I mutter to myself.

I scan the scene, and when I look up, my eyes lock onto the massive Alter-life sign lit in large red letters on top of the building.

Life is a set of choices and mine…mine have led me here, to this moment… to this car, to this picket line…to Alter-life. Am I to believe this is really a coincidence? I don't believe in coincidences. No, this is fate. My chance to live in ignorant bliss, to save everyone from more senseless pain. I have nothing left. They have all been taken from me. The pain is crippling. Make it stop!

Though they may not be of my loins, I refuse to have Ileana and Jay grow up with the same baggage that led to the fate of Annabel and Haley. Make me forget. I need to forget! I'll be young again. I'll be *me* again. Surely, they will be better off if they think I'm dead, and I will make one final choice to free us all. To break the cycle that has created all this misery. Surely, my *death* would be smoother than the drama that comes with breaking up a family. I've been through it before, and I won't do it again. All the he-said she-said drivel that fucks up your kids and steals their youth. I can't. I won't.

"Thank you for calling the attorney office of Bill Wither's, this is Bill."

"Bill, it's Dylan Grady. Listen carefully, and please, do exactly as I tell you."

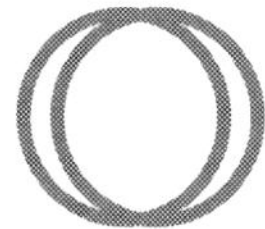

# CHAPTER 12

I am greeted by an attractive, young brunette. Her hair is wound up in a beehive, and she wears a blue swing dress, common in 1950s America. I look around the office and notice that everyone is dressed in a theme for a different time period. I see a seventies rocker, classic eighties Madonna, even a cowboy equipped with a lasso and spurs. She offers me an island cocktail, one of the ones with an umbrella that reeks of coconut.

I lounge back into a leather recliner and watch the immersive walls as they sell me on the Alter-life experience. Three-dimensional smart walls, revolving through clips of happy, beautiful people, celebrating their perfect lives together in exotic places. I feel like I just arrived at a Sandals Resort in the Caribbean and, at any moment, a busboy is going to tap me on the shoulder and lead me to my room.

"Mr. Grady?" I hear a voice behind me.

"Yes?"

"Welcome to Alter-life, where your life is our dream. I am your guide to your new life, Johan Samuels."

He offers me his hand, and when I shake his limp appendage, I can't help but notice that it's oddly smooth and delicate, like that of a woman.

"Please, follow me and join me in my office. Come, discuss the life you have always wanted but can now be your reality."

I follow Mr. Samuels to his office, and even at a modest five feet, ten inches, I tower over him. What he lacks in stature, however, he makes up for with his good looks. He reminds me of a young Brad Pitt, down to the haircut, but his demeanor is a bit less attractive, reminding me of a used car salesman, and I can't help but think that his real name is likely Jonathan.

"So, Mr. Grady, tell me what brings you to Alter-life?"

"I want to live the dream, Johan. I want to forget everything. I want to forget everybody, be twenty-eight again, happy as a pig in shit! Can you do that for me?" I ask unwavering, staring directly into his eyes.

"Well, alrighty, that's easy! We can certainly do that for you. Is there a specific reason why you've picked twenty-eight?"

"Yes, that was the year I married my ex-wife, and I want to, well, I'd like to not do that, Johan. I want to live my life without her ever getting a hold of my balls and squeezing the life from them. I want to eliminate the toxic cycle that marrying her set into motion."

"OK." He chuckles. "What made you feel that way?" He crosses his hands in his lap and leans back into his chair, obnoxiously tapping his pen to his lips.

"What made me feel that way?" I ask, raising an eyebrow.

"Yes, what did she do that made you feel that your relationship set your life onto this, uh…toxic cycle?"

"What is this, a therapy session? Listen, I want to un-fuck myself. I want to be who I was before all this shit happened in my life," I say.

Johan pauses and writes something in his chart, nervously tugs at the small tuft of hair below his lip, and says, "Dylan… Can I call you Dylan?"

"Sure."

"Dylan, we have to understand your motives for entering Alter-life so we can recreate your new life and eliminate, uhh, your balls getting squeezed." He laughs. "Your words, of course. Secondly, we need to make sure you are in the right frame of mind to enter Alter-life."

"Frame of mind?"

"Yes, you see, Alter-life is largely created by you. Your mind, memories, and your mental state largely dictate the world that will surround you," he says.

"OK, OK, OK. First things first, Johan. Please, explain to me how you recreate my life in your machine?"

"Well, the PR685 develops your world, using your own memories. Of course, because our minds tend to distort and create predispositions, delusions, and biases nestled in our versions of our memories, things won't be exactly how they would be in the world we sit in today, but don't worry, to you, it will all seem completely normal because, of course, well, you won't have any memory of this world. You'll have no cognitive understanding the world you live in is virtual."

"I see. So, how would I know not to marry my ex-wife or to make better choices?"

"We can't make you make better choices, but we can target specific people or interests and give you a nudge, per se. We can trigger your emotions related to specific things. In other words, we can make it so that when you see or think about your ex-wife, you feel extreme nausea, distaste, or even hatred. Hopefully, you won't marry someone you're predisposed to hate." He laughs like a hyena, and I cringe when the pitch is rejected by my eardrums.

He clears his throat. "We can also place you in your dream career or hell, make you a billionaire with endless funds with no career at all! Sit on a beach somewhere in the lap of luxury?" he says with a wink.

"Promise me, Johan. I need your guarantee I won't have any memory of this world…or the people in it. I need to absolve myself of everything to enjoy anything else," I say.

"Dylan, you have my guarantee. It will be as if this world never existed, and the world of Alter-life will be as real as apple pie. None of our participants have awakened with any understanding their world was a simulation."

"Wake? I thought this was permanent," I say.

"Well, yes, sort of. If you die in Alter-life, you are resurrected in this world. Of course, there is a chance you won't make it back. Your vitals are monitored closely by our team of physicians and nurses around the clock, but when you die in Alter-life, well, let's put it this way…your mind and body are intrinsically connected. If your brain thinks you have gone into cardiac arrest, your body often responds. If your vitals decline, our team will work tirelessly to resuscitate you."

"And then what? That's it, I just go back to my life here?" I say.

Johan chuckles. "That's the beauty of it. You can do whatever you want! You can remain here, or we can put you back in and you can do it again! Well, so long as you're healthy enough to pass the reentry physical, of course."

"So, suppose I live thirty years in Alter-life and die. I wake up here, eighty plus years old, confused and alone. I have nothing left, elderly, broke, and alone. What then, Johan? What if I can't afford to go back in?"

"Oh, no, no, no! First, let me assure you that our fee is for lifetime access. As long as your body is healthy enough to re-enter Alter-life, we will put you back in. Secondly, time in Alter-life doesn't operate on the same scale as it does here, uh, in this reality. One month in Alter-life is equivalent to approximately one day here. In other words, thirty years spent in Alter-life only equates to approximately one year in this reality. You'll wake up relatively unchanged!" he says.

"I see."

"A little muscle atrophy, of course, but we provide you with plenty of intravenous sustenance, amino acids, and Aqua-tens to keep your muscles active. A few short weeks of physical therapy and you'll be as good as new."

"Aqua-tens?"

"Yes, it's similar to an old TENS unit, transcutaneous electrical nerve stimulation. We send electrical stimulation to your muscles so they periodically contract," he says.

"So, conceptually, I could live multiple lifetimes within Alter-life? You could extend my life hundreds of years?"

"Sort of, yes. Well, at least it will feel that way. If your body can withstand thirty more years here on Earth then, theoretically, it will translate to roughly nine hundred years in Alter-life! You could live your life nine or even ten times over, and each time we can improve upon your last. Tweak this, tweak that, and voilà! Fresh start after fresh start! Now, what the hell could be better than that?"

"If I survive my death that is?" I say.

"Correct! There are no guarantees in that regard. We don't know how your mind and body will handle death in Alter-life. Although, with that said, we have a gentleman who has died three times already, and he's still ticking."

"Three times? I thought this technology was only open to the public a few weeks ago?" I say.

"Yup!" He laughs again with such a high pitch I can't help but shiver. "He always dreamed of being an outlaw in the Wild West, but each time we send him in, he dies…and more gruesomely than the last, I might add. But as crazy would have it, every time we revive him, he insists on going back in the same way. We've equipped him with better skills and, I mean, shit, he's almost superhuman at this point, but nothing works. Each time he dies a brutal death. If you ask me, he isn't a great outlaw, but who am I to judge? He's happy! I guess he feels as though it's worth the risk, or maybe he just likes to die. Who knows?" He shrugs.

"So, I can go back and live in different time periods?"

"Or ahead! Or in the world of Tolkien. Hell, you could be a goddamned hobbit! Of course, it's simulated, and the people and places are still a blend of Alter-life and your memories. People, places, and things still exist in a time they wouldn't have normally been, but it would all seem perfectly normal to you."

"People? things?"

"Yes, so Alter-life creates the world, but it uses your memories to do so. So, even if you want to go back and live in the Wild West, your ex-wife could exist there, and you may have a revolver in one hand and a cell phone in the other," he says.

"I see…I think. I don't want to change much. A few tweaks but, for the most part, I just want to a do-over. I'd prefer to just live my life over again. Nothing crazy, just a second chance." I say.

Johan opens a folder with my name printed on it and pulls out a small stack of papers clipped together. "Alright, Mr. Grady, I need you to fill out these forms and, of course, we have to discuss the financials. I'll also need you to go home and read this booklet that will answer any additional questions on Alter-life. Once you complete the forms, we secure payment and assuming you pass your physical, we can enter you into our queue."

"Queue?"

"Oh, yes, there is a four to six week waiting list to enter Alter-life," he says.

"No, Johan, I have to go in today!"

Johan looks at me sharply. "No, I'm sorry, Mr. Grady, I'm afraid that just isn't possible."

"I'll pay you double," I insist.

"Mr. Grady, with all due respect, you haven't even heard how much it costs. Most people can't even afford to enter Alter-life once, let alone—"

"Double, Johan! Today. It has to be today."

Johan closes the folder, slides it across the table in front of me, and gives me a long stare, studying me again as he tugs at the small patch of hair below his lip. He gets up and walks over to the door and says, "Mr. Grady, please, look over the information and begin filling out the questionnaire. It's rather lengthy. Let me see if I can pull some strings, but don't get your hopes up. I'll be back shortly."

Johan exits the room with a wink, and I eagerly dig into the questionnaire. An informative pamphlet, basic health information, but mainly, from what I can see, a psychological profile with questions strategically geared to weed out the mentally ill, those running away from their families or people making rash decisions, in a bad place in their lives. Clearly, they fear being sued, but there are also firm warnings not to enter Alter-life unless you are in a place of mental clarity. I keep telling myself I'm doing the right thing and lie my way through the questionnaire. It's better this way.

The door creeks open, and I lift my head to see a light-skinned, slender African American gentlemen with salt and pepper hair and dimples you could see a mile away. I immediately recognize him from his pictures plastered all over the news.

He walks into the room and offers his hand to me. "Mr. Grady, I presume?"

"Yes, sir," I say, popping up from my chair.

"I'm Donald Morgan," he says with a firm grasp on my hand. "Please, have a seat and welcome to the first step in human immortality! Well, almost anyway. You could say I'm the father of Alter-life. This is my baby, and I love her. I want everyone who enters Alter-life to have an incredible experience. To live a life they would like to live over and over again."

He pauses, our eyes meet, and I feel as though he is studying me, searching into my soul. Perhaps he can see me for what I really am; broken.

"So, Johan tells me that you're willing to pay double to enter Alter-life today? Is that right?" he says.

"Yes, sir."

"What's the rush?"

"I just, I just…"

"It's just that, I have to warn you, Mr. Grady, people who enter Alter-life… in a dark place, they run the risk of creating a world that is quite dark and depressing. You see, your Alter-life world is created mostly by you. Our PR685 is just a referee of sorts. It governs and maintains your world. Human emotion is a very powerful thing. A little depression it can overcome, quite successfully in fact. However, darkness…darkness that comes from tragedy? The type that can change you from the inside out?"

"Mr. Morgan, I—"

"Doctor," he corrects me.

"I'm sorry?"

"It's Doctor Morgan. I've worked far too long, too hard throughout my life not to make good use of the title," he says.

"Of course, I'm sorry. Dr. Morgan, I assure you, I'm just eager to begin my new life, and I can afford it so, what the hell? What use would the money be to me in there anyway?"

I just don't care. The only thing that matters is ridding myself of this pain and saving everyone from years of mental torture. I could pay for Alter-life ten times over and still live comfortably. Stella and the kids will be well taken care of, and this is my chance to start over in a world without memory. It sounds like Heaven, regardless of my surroundings, and I'm willing to take the risk.

"I see. Well, I feel it is my duty to warn you. Of course, you'll have to be evaluated by Dr. Lattuga, our lead physician. Assuming you pass the physical and psychological exams, we can see about getting you into Alter-life by this evening. How's that sound?

"Great," I say.

The relief relaxes the muscles in my shoulders, and my spine eases. It will all be over soon.

"OK," he says and stands up, never removing his eyes from mine. "I'll have my staff begin preparing your chamber and assembling your program. Good luck, Mr. Grady, but please remember what I said. It's never too late, well, until it's too late." He laughs, slaps me on the shoulder, and says, "Catch my drift?"

I nod. My stomach is in knots, but I fight through the swarm of butterflies and manage to force a broad smile.

# PART II

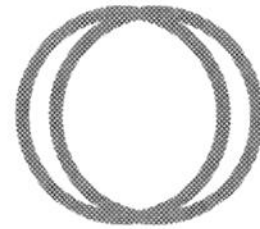

# CHAPTER 13

I shudder awake. A loud *bang* springs me upright in bed, and I am catapulted back to my reality. I was having another one of those dreams. I take in a deep breath and try to slow my racing heart. I have become a rather light sleeper since the Raxon infected our world, but this was loud enough to wake the dead. The building shook, and the dust from the rafters soiled my sheets.

I live in a one-bedroom suite on the top floor. The one on Sullivan Street with the plethora of artificial flowers, bushes, and the plastic trees to give the illusion of a world that once was. Since the day I moved in, I've obsessed about possible escape routes. I feel like a sitting duck, vulnerable to the elements.

I walk across my apartment and peer out of the dirt-laden window. It's dark, too dark to be morning, but since Raxon, most days are dark, gloomy, and filled with ash, how I would imagine purgatory to be. A world observed through Dante's looking glass, although there is no way out.

I see large golf ball-sized hail layer the street. Car alarms sound one by one, like dominoes, down the block. The thunder bellows, shaking the building once again, it's just another violent storm. It's Raxon winter. It's been ninety-three days since I last had the sun touch my skin. I look like death. We all do.

I dust off my bed, shake the covers, lie back into the hard cotton pillow, and try to go back to sleep, but I can't shake my dream. I dreamt of that day again.

It often visits me, replaying a vivid, distorted version of that day, over and over like a skipping record. I left her standing at the altar alone, angry, humiliated.

Usually, the world of my dreams grounds me. I see the world, another world, so clearly in them. A world where the sun still shines, the snow still gleams white, and people still smile. They often feel like someone else's memories, digitized as my own, but this, this one was different. A demon from the past, she haunts me. I tried to resist it! I wanted to go through with it, but the emotions were far too powerful. We recited our vows, and I was prepared to commit my life to her when, out of nowhere, I was overcome by wretchedness and like a switch, something flipped inside of me. My love was transformed into overwhelming, nonsensical hated.

To this day, I can vividly picture the look on her face, crushed, furious, and humiliated, but even as we recited our vows, I saw darkness in her eyes. A transfiguring darkness as though I peered into her soul and saw the demon hiding within her human flesh. I think I dodged a bullet that day, or perhaps I was the bullet, but either way, I believe I made the best choice for both of us.

I can't make sense of it, why I suddenly had no feelings for her. No, in actuality, I was flooded with feelings; I loathed her. It was surreal, unlike anything I had ever experienced. As if a higher power had intervened and poisoned my heart. I reason, however, that perhaps I was bestowed the power to see who she really was. At any rate, I know I made the right decision, though the guilt lingers, and it has emphatically followed me throughout the years.

I don't view myself as a heartless man. In fact, I often feel I am overly empathetic. I feel awful that I am responsible for such a negative event in someone's life but still, I'm not apologetic. We live one life and it should rarely be sacrificed for another's happiness.

Another series of crashes are heard, but these are different. More car alarms sound, and I hear a commotion in the street down below. I look out of the window and observe people looting and breaking into cars. I check my radiation meter and presume they must be transnukes. I don't see them wearing any gear, and my meter is in the red zone.

Several years after the Raxon were released, people with certain DNA markers develop mutations that allowed them to coexist. The media first branded them mutants, but human rights activists had a field day with that, deeming it a derogatory term. A new label, along with a new race of people was born, and they were to be tagged transnuclear.

Most of my officers still refer to them as roaches despite my attempts to rid the department of bias. They flood the streets at night, looting and stealing when the Raxon level is too high for *normal folk* to roam without their CoolAir masks.

I have a soft spot for the transnukes, and there are good reasons why I don't share the same sentiments as the majority. Quarantined to ghettos, where most remain unemployed, treated like nonhuman, savage beasts by the rest of society. People fear what they don't understand and shed their hatred onto those whom they are threatened. I saw neighbors who were quite successful, eradicated from society, left jobless, broke and, eventually, homeless.

They have been pushed to the corner of the city and left to fend for themselves. A world where fighting for survival is your job can make the most docile man hostile, ruthless beyond your wildest imagination. People will always do whatever it takes to survive because if you don't, you die; survival of the fittest.

Comparable to Nazi Germany, the government mandated that everyone get screened for mutations and marked those who tested positive with a mark reminiscent of a biohazard symbol behind their left ear. People returned to work the next day intent on moving forward with their lives. In fact, most were ecstatic when they discovered they could walk free in a Raxon-infected world. They could leave their masks and meters behind and breathe the air, fresh or not.

However, the world didn't welcome their gifts. Friends were reduced to acquaintances and, soon after, discarded like day-old donuts. Unemployable, with newfound anger and resentment in their hearts, they were forced to live on the street. If you are one of the lucky ones, you still have the funds to build yourself a shack in the ghetto, settled in the hills on the outskirts of the city. Sheltered from the vicious Raxon storms but forced to defend your newfound home against other transnuclears that weren't as fortunate.

The elements of Raxon winter would prove their ability to survive. After all, even though they were immune to the effects of Raxon, they could still freeze to death, die of hunger, thirst, or at the hands of another's determination for survival.

The ghettos naturally became a primary source for drug trafficking. As the lead detective, I took it upon myself to prevent the drugs from leaving the ghettos. I turned a blind eye when possible, and my kindness enabled me to make some friends, although most still viewed me as the enemy.

It was no longer black versus white. People devoid of the mutation were nearly unified in hatred of those who were branded by the state. Of course, they had their advocates, but soon, they, too, vanished. Some gave them jobs out of sympathy, but their charity was met with consequences. Their businesses were subjected to boycotts and many of them could no longer afford to stay open. After that, even sympathizers would turn them away out of the fear of joining them in their dissolution.

It wasn't only my empathy that drove my kindness. I have a secret and a secret I keep close to my heart.

*

Morning came, but you would never know it by looking outside. Raxon still curtains the sky, although the hazard levels have returned to the green zone. It's clear to walk the streets without my CoolAir mask, but I'd be suicidal if I left the house without it. Not because I'd be in any danger but because I would expose myself for what I really am. I leave it hanging from my belt to advertise my orthodoxy, and I make sure to check my meter often.

I wonder, are there others? Am I the only one who was able to escape the fate of a transnuke? I remember the day when I discovered I was one of them. It's branded in my memory, and she often still visits me in my dreams. Most transnukes celebrated joyfully that they had been gifted adaptation. They could breathe and walk without fear of Raxon poisoning, unbound to a mask or a meter.

I knew better than to flaunt my gift because it wasn't a gift at all, it was a mark. The mark of being different. A minority in a world that fears and trusts no one after the Raxon is not a blessing but rather a curse. Our quarantine is riddled with uncertainty and jealousy. I don't want to be divergent. I need to blend in because my life as I knew it greatly depends on my uniformity.

I was able to escape my fate with the help of a woman, a nurse. I suppose she, too, foresaw the fate of the transnukes. I don't know why she helped me. Perhaps she helped as many as she could. She risked her life to preserve my own, and I am eternally grateful. She imprinted on me, and even still, she resides with me in my dreams.

When she saw my lab results, her eyes quickly shifted to the corner of the room where I suspected *they* were watching. My eyes followed, and I spotted a camera pointed in our direction. Our eyes locked, and I was suddenly jolted with an overwhelming sense of familiarity. I sensed I knew her. I knew her intimately but not a bit, all the same. Is this what they mean by love at first sight? A charge of electricity awakened my body, and my heart quivered.

Skillfully, she positioned herself between the camera and the testing device, pricked her finger, and slyly smeared a droplet onto a test strip and, moments later, I was declared normal. She slipped the results into my chart, nodded, reddened, and promptly raised her index finger to her mouth.

"Shhhh," she said quietly, "trust me."

"I'm sorry, but…do we know each other?" I asked.

She shook her head without hardly moving an inch, raised a finger to her mouth again with her eyes opened wide.

I realize she was taking a huge risk. They may be watching, and I needed to be cool. I nodded, and our eyes met again and, for a moment, a fleeting moment, we were truly in love. It sounds absurd, but it was overwhelming. My heart raced, adrenaline gushed, leaving me weak in the knees. I'm not typically one to believe in love at first sight, but this was undeniably powerful. I loved this woman before I even knew her name. As instantaneous and irrational as I suddenly loathed Corina at the altar.

I scanned her hand for a ring and noticed she wasn't wearing one. Unable to resist the urge, I grabbed her arm before she walked out of my life forever.

"Excuse me, I know this may be…well…unconventional, but can we grab a drink sometime? Dinner maybe?"

Almost immediately, I detected the fear in her eyes, and my Adam's apple sunk deep into the catacombs of my belly. Noticeably uncomfortable, her eyes widened, body tensed, and her spine erected as she simultaneously took in a deep, hissing breath through her nose. The sign of rejection was blatant. Perhaps I'd misunderstood her signals?

We exited the room in awkward silence, and she, eager to get rid of me, tapped another nurse on the shoulder.

With an awkward stutter, she said, "Uh, nurse Emily, could you please show Mr. Grady to the front? Thank you, Mr. Grady. I'm sorry your results didn't yield you any superhuman powers today!" She chuckled and turned her back and walked towards the nurses' station.

Nurse Emily escorted me down the hall towards the patient waiting area, placed her hand on my arm, and guided me through the door. "Well, Mr. Grady, no tattoo for you today. You can go home early!" she says as if she were talking to a child waiting for his lollipop following a healthy visit with the pediatrician.

The door closed, and I savored a final glimpse of my angelic nightingale. I fell in love that day. I fell hard. I didn't realize that would be the last time I would see her outside of my dreams. I hoped fate would lead us to cross paths again, but it hasn't. She is my savior and, rather pathetically, my best friend.

We hadn't said more than a hundred words to one another, but she selflessly saved my life, and my heart is forever in her debt. The memory of her kindness, and even more prevalent, the emotion and unexplainable familiarity that overpowered me when our eyes met, remains embedded in me. It has led me to question everything; what is real and what is a figment of the imagination.

I think of her often, and she is very active in my dreams. In another world where the sun shines and our laughter echoes off the walls. Even when the sun sets and darkness settles in, our smiles illuminate our lives. Two realities clash and cleanse me in my sleep of a world clouded by Raxon. I often wonder if my recollection has distorted her face and if I would still recognize her if I saw her today.

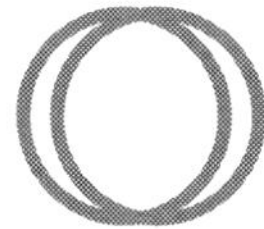

# CHAPTER 14

I enjoy walking to the station in the mornings, it clears my head of the haze my dreams leave behind like a hot-boxed car. They play tricks on me, and it's hard to shake. It takes me time, sometimes the entire day, to separate realms and reacclimatize to this one, the supposed real world. It's a rather brutal awakening and launches me into acute depression. I often daydream the world trapped within my dreams is the real world, but I remain imprisoned in a simulation.

I make a right down Broad Street and admire the progress made by the reconstruction team. Rebuilding our city has had its share of challenges, but when people come together, it's amazing what can be accomplished. Half of the eastern seaboard remains under quarantine, and it has been that way for the last eight years.

We are a country within a country, and other than the supply trains and the United States National Guard, no one is allowed in or out. It was nearly a year before the government acknowledged our plea for help and sent troops to support our efforts.

The first year was anarchistic. Chaos prevailed over reason while civilization embarked on total savagery. The first few weeks, however, were eerily quiet. So quiet in fact, a pin drop would echo in your eardrums. Nobody dared leave their home in fear of contamination. We were instructed not to. The streets were bare except for the occasional scientist decked out in hazmat gear, walking the streets, collecting Raxon and testing it with meters, probes, and test tubes with various solutions.

The restriction was finally lifted after the CoolAir masks and Raxon meters were distributed, but those who have survived this far would soon understand the capabilities of thy neighbor. Left abandoned and ungoverned, looters took to the streets and rioted. Vastly outnumbered, our police presence was ineffective, and the savage ferocity of the civilians was too fierce to overcome with reason. People were starving. We hadn't received any help from our government. We had been abandoned. Our food rations dwindled, and we had to assume that most of the food that wasn't in cans, containers, or in your home was contaminated.

You see, Raxon wasn't a bomb, at least not in the traditional sense. We didn't know what it was or who unleashed it. There weren't any explosions, it didn't destroy buildings or instantly incinerate the masses. No, our own people caused all the physical destruction. At a time when we needed to come together, sadly, we tore each other apart. People were left for dead in the streets, historic buildings were looted, burned, and brought crumbling down. City hall still lies mere rubble in the street. Essentially, a civil war ensued, but the only thing fought for was survival.

Most believe it was a biological weapon, released as an act of terrorism, but there are those who believe it was an act of God, punishing us for our sins. Whatever it is, we all agree on one thing, our government has answers, and they've left us in the dark.

The Raxon organisms on their own, cannot be seen by the human eye but when they bind together in packs, they are as dark as the night. They blanket the sky, where their colony lies, blocking out the sun, disrupting the atmosphere, and shifting the weather pattern. When there are storms, which is often, they travel in packs, ready to feed, like hordes of bees zipping through the breeze.

You need to directly inhale the organisms in order to become infected and display symptoms, but if you aren't wearing your mask, or it isn't tight enough, they will find a way in. At first, you present with a modest cough, but the Raxon feeds on your lungs, and in the most painful twenty minutes you can imagine, they link together and mate, igniting a thriving biome on the lining of your organs, multiplying, feeding, growing. It won't be long before your lungs are consumed by dark bloody mucus. Your breath shallows as your lungs are devoured from the inside out.

We have been provided very little information by the government, but they did tell us that the human body can tolerate a moderate amount of Raxon, and at low levels, a healthy adult can prevent the organisms from breeding. When your meter reads that the levels are in the green zone, it is safe to walk the streets without your mask. They say that we are all infected to a degree, but there is little danger at low levels. It's worth noting, however, that you never see a member of the Guard out of their protective biohazard suit regardless of the meter reading, prompting many of us to question the legitimacy of their facts. I for one, do not believe the quarantine will ever be lifted. We will never bathe in the bright warm sun or visit the beaches of Italy's Amalfi coast. This is our fate, and I have tried my best to accept it.

A Raxon death is an unimaginable way to go and, as a result, a simple cough can bring on utter hysteria. People have committed suicide at the first sign of a cough to spare themselves from a Raxon death. I can't blame them. I've seen many perish from Raxon, and if for no other reason, for this, I am thankful I am transnuclear.

It was July 15th, a treacherous, hot summer day, picturesque, without a cloud in the sky. I was at the beach, sunbathing and listening to my music, hypnotically watching the speaker bounce specs of sand, up and down like an equalizer. I recall being incredibly at peace and allowed myself to doze off. I woke shortly after, groggy and confused by the commotion stirring all around me.

I remember, astonishingly, how cold I suddenly was. I glanced up and down the beach, and as if God hit pause, everyone stood and gawked at the sky. I glanced up and watched in horror as the Raxon swarmed in, rapidly eclipsing the sun. About two hundred yards above, like a star, they diverted into five opposing directions, synchronized in song. The sound was deafening, a loud hiss like that of locust. Billons hovered and sang, preparing to feast on the masses.

They blanketed the sky in a flash, and a hot sunny day rapidly transformed into an eerily chilly night. The gaping and gasping quickly changed to terrified screams as small colonies, resembling a swarm of bees in the shape of cones, unified in movement and purpose, as if of the same mind, swooped down and fed on their first victim. She was just a girl. She couldn't have been more than seventeen. Her choking and terrified screams were deafening. As they devoured her, everyone fled the beach in terror. I don't know how many people died that day. Thousands? Millions? It was certainly a sight to see, but one I would like to soon forget.

My squad car was parked at the beach entrance, and I sprinted there faster than I had ever sprinted before, leaving all my belongings behind, my radio still playing the soothing sounds of the Beach Boys "Don't Worry, Baby."

Black Raxon clouds now cover most of the northeastern seaboard and have nearly blackened out the world as we know it. Initially, we were instructed to remain indoors, tune to FM 101.2, and await further instruction. A waiting game ensued as we sat by our radios, day and night with nothing but the white noise to fill the air.

Nearly six lonely weeks passed before we heard a word. People starved to death in their homes, abandoned and left to die. Apartment buildings became the first of many war zones. Neighbors ventured out of their flats in search of food and clean water, pillaging their way door to door. They took what they wanted: food, water, young girls. The strongest, most ruthless in the building became the underbosses. And so, it followed, one by one, building by building, gangs formed, and people joined the carnage or became the prey.

On a Sunday morning, at least I think it was Sunday, we finally received our first radio communication. An alarm sounded for five minutes, followed by an announcement issued by President Winslow. We all gathered around our radios and listened intently, praying for the good news.

"Good morning. It is with great sadness, but with renewed hope, I speak with you today. I, and your fellow American people, feel tremendous sorrow for the horrors and hardships you have been forced to endure these past few weeks. We can't imagine what you must be going through. We have been working diligently, and I assure you, we are utilizing all of the resources at our disposal to study the organism that appears to have been unleashed on our country as an act of terror.

"To date, no one has taken responsibility. However, we are confident our leads will bring answers. Answers that you so greatly deserve. We are calling the organism Raxon. It feeds on human tissue like a parasite, but this parasite will feed on you very rapidly, and the result is always death. We have developed, and will be distributing, CoolAir masks and Raxon meters. These will allow you to venture out of your homes and walk the streets.

"However, please, take great caution. I am being told that if the meter is in the green zone, it is free to walk without a mask, yet yellow and above, the mask must be worn. Do not leave home without them. Repeat, do not leave home without your equipment. I hope to have more for you in the coming days, but in the meantime, Godspeed, and good night."

That's it? That's all they have for us? What about food and clean water? How long do they expect us to be under quarantine? So many questions, so few answers.

The bittersweet news hit many differently. It was safe to go outside and, at first, there was peace, but the euphoric feeling of community pride only lasted a few measly days. The underbosses took their gangs to the streets and rioting and looting became rampant and widespread. Gangs quickly turned on each other, turf wars were declared, and a year of murder, mayhem, and destruction followed.

It was over a year of madness before the U.S. Government offered any assistance. We were quarantined, infected, and left to die or kill each other, whichever came first. They sent armed National Guard and transformed buildings into military compounds in every major city from D.C. to Boston.

As an officer, I welcomed their presence. We couldn't tame the gangs because, in a world where jobs have lost their value, our numbers were few.

Our police force was reduced to a rival gang with badges, and I, the elected underboss. We were often as ruthless as our counterparts; we had to be. In order to get the job done, it was often kill or be killed, but we attempted to restore peace in the midst of chaos.

When the National Guard came, the violence and mere destruction slowed, and gang violence, although still present, slid to underground operations. They didn't outwardly control the streets anymore, and people could finally leave their homes without the imminent threat of being mugged or killed. With their assistance, we now had the numbers to effectively patrol the streets.

The crime rate is still exponentially high, but life has somewhat normalized. A new norm, of course, but at least we have an economy again, and the United States government has begun to ship in food and goods we can purchase. Jobs have been created, and society has returned to a form of capitalism.

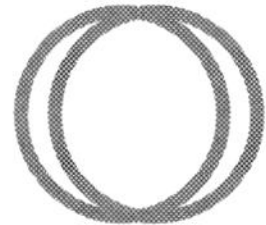

# CHAPTER 15

"Morning, Boss."

I hear his immediately recognizable voice behind me. The same one I have heard every day and grown quite fond of since he joined our cause.

"Morning, Darby. What do you have for me today?" I say.

"Coffee," he responds robotically but with a mild hint of humor.

"Not really what I meant, but thank you," I say, grabbing for the hot cup of government-issued instant coffee.

Officer Darby O'Sullivan has been my right-hand man ever since Raxon winter began. He didn't have any formal training, but he insisted on joining the *good guys*. We needed numbers, and he needed redemption. Darby lived in the Hamilton Building on the corner of Broadway and Ninth Street, in a two bedroom flat with his wife and two young daughters during the lockdown.

Lorenzo Bell, underboss of the Hamilton House gang, made a name for himself around the building. He was callous, merciless, inhuman and, to this day, he is still regarded as the most ruthless of all underbosses. A psychopath leading a band of thugs.

When Darby and I finally caught up with Lorenzo, he was cornered like a rat in a cage. I had no choice but to look the other way. It was the only time in my career where I felt that due process wouldn't be just punishment. Darby needed this. Fuck, he deserved it. The street war didn't take Darby's family, Raxon didn't either, Lorenzo did, and he did it savagely and without any regard for human life.

During a routine raid, Lorenzo discovered Darby was stashing food for his family. Darby knew they would certainly starve without it, so he hollowed out a mattress and crammed in as much non-perishable food as he could fit. He made the bed and covered it with his little girl's stuffed animals. Darby reasoned that if they didn't die by Lorenzo's hand, they would perish from starvation, anyway, so, what difference would it make?

He fully expected to be killed if it were discovered, but he hadn't anticipated a punishment so inhumane, so incredibly barbaric. A swift death to his wife and girls would have been torturous enough, but Lorenzo had other plans, plans so ghastly, so gnarly, I still cringe when I think about it. The guilt and anguish Darby carries with him every day is unimaginable.

Lorenzo dragged Darby by his ear into the family room, where he bound him to a support beam. He ordered his thugs to bring in his girls one by one and one by one, he forced Darby to watch in horror, as he raped and disemboweled them. He began with his youngest, Joanne, a mere six years old. He followed with nine-year-old Sadie and ended with his wife, Sharon, whom he anally raped using the blood of their children as a means of lubrication.

Darby, bound and gagged, was forced by two of his thugs to look into his wife's petrified eyes as Lorenzo slit Sharon's throat. Darby admits he still hears their bloodcurdling screams every night when he lies down to sleep. He has nearly overdosed on sleeping pills twice already, and I fear that, one day, I won't be around to save him.

On that evening, Darby recounted his story, tears flooded his cheeks, and he struggled to finish each word. I wanted to hold him like a child and tell him that everything would be alright. He is a rather large, burly man, and he stood before me, on several momentous occasions, wailing like a toddler. The image I paint is not intended to mock him. I don't think I could live with this memory at all, and the attempts on his own life are not out of weakness but a necessity for peace.

He continued to describe, in horrific detail, how he gasped and heaved, emptying out the contents of his stomach all over the shoes of his captors. His eyelids were held open, and he was forced to stare at his family's desecrated remains as they lie on the floor, gutted and profaned.

Trembling in disbelief, he pleaded to Lorenzo, "Kill me!"

Lorenzo would not, arguably showing the least mercy to Darby, mandating he remain alive. To be forced to live with this memory was the worst punishment of all. Lorenzo capped off his treachery, masturbating as he marveled over his bloody pornography. Darby described Lorenzo with vivid memory, as thoroughly aroused, grunting like an animal as he stroked his bloody, erect penis with pride.

It was his masterpiece, and he masturbated like a pubescent boy just discovering his first pornographic movie. Even Lorenzo's men had a hard time watching, but their fear motivated them to continue to hold Darby's head forward and upright while Lorenzo shamelessly ejaculated all over Darby's face.

Darby couldn't hold back his emotions. He screamed uproariously just as he did to Lorenzo. He taunted, mocked, and threatened him, but Lorenzo just smirked and giggled and lit a cigarette as one would after a satisfying sexual experience. Darby admitted to me that he wasn't sure if he was even making any sense or just barking like a rabid dog.

Shaking uncontrollably, he tasted the saltiness of Lorenzo's semen as it streamed down his face, creeping into the corners of his mouth as he growled and barked. His humiliation fueled his rage, and he prayed that if he threatened and mocked Lorenzo enough, he would kill him. He realized, however, that no matter what he did or said, no matter how hard he tried, Lorenzo would never kill him for he knew that killing him would be an act of mercy. Lorenzo just laughed and stroked his face while the remainder of his men gathered the contraband in the mattress.

Darby was left alive but hollow, bound to a support beam in the living room of his two-bedroom flat, physically unharmed but tortured beyond what any imagination could fathom.

Left with the desecrated remains of his family, sodomized and slaughtered before him, convulsing for nearly three days until his neighbors, John and Rita Slovski heard his whines and came to release him from his dungeon. Near death and unable to eat or drink, they managed to nurse him back to health by injecting liquid food and water into his mouth with a bulb syringe they used to remove mucus from their infant daughter's nose.

My mouth hung agape as I listened to his story. My heart aches for him, and I can't help but cringe and shiver when I think of it. It is the cruelest, most demoralizingly vile thing I have ever heard. After first hearing his story, I found myself tiptoeing around Darby as if he were a beaten animal but, truthfully, I think he is the strongest person I know, and he has always been there for me, a true friend.

*

"Boss, we just got a call about a body at Johnson square," Darby says.

"It's becoming our morning ritual, ain't it, Darbs?" I say, slapping him on the back.

Bodies have been piling up in the morgue. Rival gangs aim to take each other out and it feels like we start every day with another body found here or there. Cases often go cold because, in many cases, gang violence is unavoidable, and they collectively won't talk to the authorities, neither the police nor the Guard. To them, we are one and the same, nothing more than the enemy.

"Yeah, Cap, but this one is different. This is a little girl," Darby says.

I look up at him sharply from my desk and meet his eyes. "Little? How little?"

"Not sure, but the first responders said she's little, so..."

I grab my keys and toss them to Darby. "You drive."

Darby navigates to the scene in silence, and I use the time to flip through our folder of open case files. Suddenly, I'm distracted by a single ray of sunlight that breaks through the Raxon, beaming like a spotlight from the heavens and lands on the old Genovese building, highlighting the address, 551. I look over to Darby, and he seems to be unfazed, but how? How long has it been since we've seen the sun?

We continue down the street, and I notice that oddly, the next three buildings are also numbered 551. One after the next, and seemingly every building on Lexington Street is marked 551, 551, 551, 551. I rub my eyes and look again; 551, 551, 551…

"Hey, Darbs, ever notice that every building on this street has the same address?"

He shoots me a side-eyed glance. "How do you mean, Boss?" he says.

"They're all 551. How does that make any sense? Look!" I say, pointing as we pass the next three buildings. "5-5-1, 5-5-1, 5-5-1!"

Darby squints and decelerates, keeping his eyes fixated on the upcoming building number and stops the car. "Boss, are you fucking with me?"

"See!" I shout, exuberantly pointing at the next building.

"See what? That one says 6-9-7," Darby says flatly, narrowing his eyes.

"What? No, it's…it's 5-5-1!"

"Boss, you alright?" He stops the car after passing a few more buildings and slowly reads out the building number, one digit at a time, "It says 7-0-3."

I squint and rub my eyes. "No! It says…7-0-3? Wait, but the others? You didn't see them? What about the sunbeam that shined right on the Genovese building back there? It shined right on the address, 551!"

"Sunbeam? What sunbeam? Don't think I'd miss a thing like that, Boss. Hell, I'd give my left testicle for some sun. Sorry to say that there hasn't been any sun today. I'm driving with my high beams on. It's as dark as a fucken black hole out here."

Darby looks back and forth from me to the road several times, and I feel uneasy.

"Boss, you sure you're OK? Want to skip this one? We could just give it to Jerry and…"

A flash of light and a sharp pain blinds me, reminiscent of when I used to get migraines.

"Darbs! Dammit, I'm fine!" I snap. "Just get us there already!"

"What? Boss…we're here," he says, cocking his head to the side, following my eyes intently.

My cognitions, like a light bulb, build, click on, and I realize the car is no longer moving. Disoriented and confused, I try to recollect the rest of the ride after Lexington Street. Did I black out? The drive from Lexington to Johnson Square is at least six or seven minutes, but we arrived in the blink of an eye. I look over at Darby and notice he is still studying me. His eyes examine me, trying to meet my own, but I avert them out the window and scan the park.

I say, "OK then, let's go and see what we've got."

"Boss, looks like the Guard beat us to the punch," he says. "Look." He points out the window.

I look beyond Darby and into the dimly lit, decaying park, once full of foliage and life. I locate the crowd encircling what I presume to be the body and immediately identify Sergeant Rosario's large frame, shifting his weight and barking orders at my officers. It's easy to discern who the Guardsmen are because even though our meters read green, they are decked out in hazmat gear from head to toe. They look like giant penises dancing in the darkness, and Rosario, the largest dong in the pack. He's a domineering personality, pointing and ubiquitously shifting his weight from one side of the scene to the other. A big shot amongst his pack of dicks.

When the National Guard was deployed, they took ownership of the quarantined cities. I welcomed their presence, but Rosario and I immediately had tension. We needed numbers, but we didn't need to be micromanaged. We knew how to do our jobs, and it was clear right out of the gate they didn't know the first thing about real police work. We are both dominant personalities, and he tried to make me his bitch in front of my men. I made it clear I am nobody's bitch, least of all his. I view him as an equal with the same goal. He views me as part of the problem.

There is a rumor circulating that Rosario was sent here by his superior as a form of punishment. Apparently, King Dong couldn't keep it in his pants and foolishly slept with the Sergeant Major's wife. He and his men were banished, assigned to quarantine, and given his pomposity and lack of self-control, I have little doubt of its authenticity.

Many in the Guard believe they were sent here on a suicide mission and that they have their libidinous leader, the good Sergeant Rosario, to hold accountable, and based on the media reports they heard on the outside before entering quarantine, I can't say I blame them. The reports stated the quarantine will likely never be lifted, confirming my suspicion we will forever be imprisoned in darkness. The long-term effects of Raxon exposure and mutations are unknown, and all inhabitants are to be treated as contaminated, infected with a biological parasitic host until more is understood.

Record numbers of Guardsman have gone AWOL. In fact, the highest recorded number in the history of the United States military. Others who willfully accepted their fate wrote harrowing letters to loved ones, heralding their final goodbyes. One soldier I met in Sparrow's bar, Private John Berry, confided in me that he had attended his own funeral mass with his family the day before he was deployed. He had a flower petal from one of the flowers brought to his funeral, dipped in gold, which he wore on a chain around his neck in remembrance of a life left behind. "We are the walking dead," he'd tell me.

Many have relayed the sentiments of the outside world. They fear us. In fact, some are quite vocal about how the quarantine should never be lifted, and most doubt it ever will be. Political cartoons depict us as zombies with green skin, eyes depressed into our heads. We are infected and could unleash a virus that could wipe out all of humanity. It doesn't matter to them if we have the mark or not, we are all mutants, and we are a threat.

"Sergeant?" I say.

"Go home, Grady, and take these goons with you. We got this covered."

Rosario is a little man in big shoes. In reality, he's quite large, larger than me, but I believe he suffers from little dick syndrome. Those who like to abuse the power they are bestowed either have Mommy issues, Daddy issues, or little dick syndrome. Rosario is a unique case, and I suspect he checks all the boxes.

"This city is our responsibility, Sergeant, and unless you can explain to me how this young lady's unfortunate death falls under your jurisdiction, I suggest your men stand down and let me and my goons get to work."

I glance over at the body, so small, so delicate. Who would do such a thing to a little girl? Dainty, pure and innocuous, couldn't be any more than nine or ten years old. Her tiny body lies face down in what appears to be a purposely dug cradle in the dirt. The killer took great care, preparing and gently laying her to rest on a bed of red rose pedals. Her hair appears to be combed, and her nails, freshly painted.

Her bed was dug with precision and to depths that appear to match her anatomical curves, almost as if she lay face down in a mold, intended for her reproduction. He went to great lengths to assure she lay comfortably, outfitted in a beautiful white gown, and it's worth noting she doesn't appear to have any blood or as much as a speck of dirt on her. She is immaculately clean, resembling a porcelain doll. Is she even real?

I walk around the body, snapping pictures from every angle with my trusty old Polaroid. I want to document every angle of the scene because everything and anything, however insignificant, could be the clue that breaks this case wide open. When I reach her head, I stop, slip on rubber gloves, kneel beside her, and grab a clump of her long, wavy blonde hair. I lift her head high enough to get a good look at her face. I startle, stumble back, regain my footing using my hand to assist, and pop to my feet as a bolt shoots through me. Her lifeless head thumps back into its cradle, and I hear the officers behind me gasp, crying out in disgust.

"Oh, Jesus Christ!" Officer Jacobs yells, turns his back, and spews his breakfast at the base of the tree stump where he once sat.

"I know this girl!" I say, hysterical, on the verge of tears.

Rosario's eyes roll. He scrunches his face, all of the creases pruning, and with sickening insurgence, he says, "You know her? How could you possibly recognize this girl? Are we fucken sure it's even a goddamn girl?"

"I-I-I don't know. I know her! I know that face, but…"

"You know her face?" He chuckles. "Then, pray tell, who the fuck is she, Grady?"

"She's… I-I don't know?" I say, befuddled, staring off into space, trying to recall how and where I know this girl.

Rosario tosses me his handkerchief, and when it hits my chest, I'm suddenly aware of the tears that have begun to spill over my lids. This job has numbed me. The horrors I've seen since Raxon. The inhumanity, slaughter, downright anarchistic savagery. Yet, I sob for this girl? I know her...but I don't. Do I?

"Get a hold of yourself, Grady! How the fuck could you possibly recognize this girl?"

I pause and sniffle, drying the tears from my face, trying to regain my composure. "I don't know. I recognize her as clear as I recognize you, but I-I just can't place her."

Rosario walks over to the corpse, irritated, and with authority, grabs her hair, violently yanks her head up so high that he lifts her torso off the ground with it.

I brace myself for another emotional outburst. My eyes squint, and I look away.

"She has no face, Grady! How could you possibly identify this girl? Are you fucking with us or has the Raxon finally begun to eat away at your brain?"

I look over and see Darby's hand covers his eyes. I hesitantly turn to meet the corpse's gaze and notice she is, in fact, missing her face. Her eyes and skin have been removed with surgical precision, leaving only the flesh and raw musculature exposed.

"I don't understand, I-I..." I stammer disoriented, confused beyond what I ever believed to be possible.

"You're losing your shit, Grady!" Sergeant Rosario mocks.

He may be right. I can't explain it, but I saw her face. A little girl, and one so dear to me, so familiar, yet I stand here, her name escaping the prison in my mind. It's moments like these that have me questioning my sanity. Now and again, the world blurs, and the lines between what is real and what is simply another layer in the matrix wrestle, and I am left with a wavy line that leads me down a rabbit hole, searching for truth. Inevitably, things always normalize, and I move on with life as if that moment of mental distortion never occurred.

I meet the eyes of my men, disheartened, disjointed. Their once strong, unbreakable leader is losing his mind. They rumble and whisper, and it echoes, enclosing me within their bubble, amplifying around me. They're right. I've lost my fucking mind. As I always do, I now question whether the questions I ask myself are rational, a recurring cycle that always leads to the same place, denial.

There have been many instances that have led me to question my sanity, but It's been so long without recurrence I reasoned that it could be a vitamin D deficiency, or perhaps too much exposure to Raxon. It also occurred to me that I could have a brain tumor, but I'm still here, so, not likely.

One instance that stands out above the others. It was nearing my thirty-third birthday and the world kept, well, for lack of a better description, it just kept shutting off. No, I didn't black out. I could still think. I could still speak, but everything around me rang with white noise, amplifying in my ears along with a loud *beep* that rhythmically kept to the beat of my heart. I was consciously unconscious, frozen in time but existing in space. It felt like someone pressed pause on my life. I question my reality which, in turn, ignited inevitable questions of my mental health. After each episode, I awoke, and time appeared to stand still. People hadn't moved and conversations continued from the very syllable where they left off. A glitch in the universe, one that could remodel the physics of the realm.

I am catapulted out of my remembrance when I see movement in the distance. A stable, some one hundred yards off, beyond what was once a lush grassy field, now laden with dirt and debris. I see a black figure, and it appears to watch us from beyond the stable. It emerges in the doorway of an old rickety barn, dressed in all black, a cloak from head to toe. It seems to be remarkably large, taking up nearly the entirety of the opening.

Naturally, I question whether it's a figment of my imagination. I rub my eyes and look up again, and *poof*, it's gone. I scan the field, afore and beyond, and see no one, nothing. No sign of life, only dirt, decay and gloom. He couldn't have vanished into thin air.

Rosario jabs my shoulder with brute force, knocking me back, and I stagger step, awakening me from my illusion.

"Grady!" Rosario shouts, snapping his fingers in front of my eyes. "Anyone home, Grady, old boy? What the fuck is it?" He looks back and forth from me to the barn.

I look at him, my eyes filled with angst. “What is what, Sergeant?”

“What in the fuck are you staring at? Hello, Grady? You in there? I’ve been screaming your name, but you’ve been in God only knows where, la la land. For a second there, I thought you finally checked the fuck out! Jeeesus Chrrrrist almighty!”

I considered telling Rosario about the man in the black cloak, but as rapidly as my mouth gapes open, I reseal my lips. Frankly, I don’t trust my eyes right now, and the last thing I need is to appear more unstable than I already do, especially in front of my men. They need to think their leader is of sound mind and they can follow me anywhere. I have some ground to makeup, and clearly my mystery man in the black cloak wouldn’t afford me any progress.

“Nothing Sergeant, it’s nothing. Next steps, I was thinking about next steps. That’s all,” I say.

“Next steps? What, pray tell, would those be?” he asks.

“Well, Sergeant, we need to check our missing persons database, get a DNA test, and try to figure out what the significance of all this is,” I say, motioning my hand over the remains.

“Significance?” He jeers.

I take a step towards Rosario and square up to him confidently. “Well, yes, for starters, it’s likely our killer knew this girl.”

“And what makes you think that?” Rosario asks.

“Well, the killer took meticulous care of her body, dressed her in a gown, and…”

“How the fuck do you call removing her face meticulous care? Why would he do that, and how in God’s name would you know if he dressed her in this getup?” he snaps back.

“OK, I’m guessing he removed her face because…well…the most obvious answer would be that he wants to delay or prevent us from identifying her. Perhaps, and is most always the case, it was someone she knew intimately. Or perhaps, he loved this girl so much he couldn’t bear to look at her.”

“Loved her?”

“Listen, I’m not saying we aren’t dealing with a psychopath, but what I am saying is that our killer knew our victim intimately. Her dress is in pristine condition and appears to be freshly pressed. There isn't as much as a drop of blood, a speck of dirt, or even a single hair on her. Look at the time he took to prepare this bed for her. It must have taken hours to mold it, to cradle her like this, and I think the bed of red rose petals speaks for itself."

"So, what, he's taunting us then?" Rosario says.

"Could be, but more likely, he wanted us to find her. Maybe he wanted us to make sure she gets a proper burial. I don't know, but it was all done for a purpose, and I'd put money on it that he knew her. Darby, make sure the coroner checks for signs of sexual assault."

"Got it, Boss," Darby says, writing it in his small three by five notebook.

"Grady, the philosopher," Rosario scoffs.

"Alright, Sergeant, so, to be clear, you don't think there is any significance to any of this? Someone would take the time to mold an anatomical mold in the dirt, lay her in a bed of red rose petals, dress her in a pristine white gown, and leave her out in the open, presumably for us to find because why…they were bored?"

His face reddens, and he is noticeably humiliated, growing angrier by the second, and I fight the urge to stir the pot. These are clear observations for a trained eye, and he demonstrates how little knowledge he has. I look to my men and can see the gratification all over their faces. This was a win for Team Grady, and it felt rejuvenating. It didn't eliminate my temporary insanity, but it bought me some respect, and if nothing else, it validated my credentials.

"OK, Grady, you little pissant. You waste your time finding her killer, but if you ask me, whoever did this was doing us all a favor," he says.

"A favor?" I say. My voice cracks, and my brows simultaneously rise. "How do you figure that?"

"She bears the mark!"

I noticed she was transnuclear, but I don't share his bias, and I don't believe I would share his bias even if I wasn't one of them. I judge people based on their capability, decency, and merit, not on their appearance or abilities. Mutation or not, we're still human, and there is little difference among us to the world outside quarantine.

"She's likely one of them gang tricks," he says. "Don't waste your time."

It isn't uncommon for the gang bosses to take who and what they wanted from the ghettos. More often, young girls are purchased by gangs and used as sex toys for hire, but there isn't any evidence of that here. It's just another ignorant theory, one without any merit.

"A crime is a crime, Sergeant, and regardless of your prejudice, I will find and prosecute her killer," I say.

Rosario laughs. "Suit yourself, cowboy. Come on, boys, let's leave the officers here to play detective."

Rosario and his Guardsmen make their way to their vehicle. About halfway, he spins around and yells, "Don't you think you're wasting your time? I mean, shit, she was dead long before she died, anyway! You're all fucking zombies as far as I'm concerned!"

# CHAPTER 16

I find myself in the middle of a grassy field, tall, green, and unkept. The sun shines so brightly I must shield my eyes from it. Oh, how I've missed the sun. The world is so beautiful in color. I drop to my knees, spread open my arms, and bathe in its beauty. It's so gloriously warm and invigorating on my skin.

Suddenly, I hear a faint scream rousing me from my apex, and as if appearing out of thin air, I see a little girl in the distance, some forty yards ahead. She is positioned with her back to me. Her long blonde hair blows violently in the wind, and her body shakes as if she were pouting. Her screams are faint, and I can't quite make out what she is saying, but she is in distress. Her head darts left, then right. Is she is looking for someone? Is she lost?

I walk in her direction, but the wind picks up, violently pushing me back, so much so that it is difficult for me to keep my eyes open, and each step takes enormous effort. The closer I get, the seemingly harder it blows and the harder I must fight for progress. My legs flex, and I use my entire body with each grueling step. I'm close enough now to hear her calling out, "Daddy! Daddy!" Lost and petrified, I must help this girl.

I scan the field, but I don't see anyone, only green grass as far as my eyes can see. I continue to forge my way to her, but with each step, I notice my feet are sinking. They sink deeper and deeper into the spongy, marshy grass, and I walk harder, faster, sinking further and further. In no time at all, it has swallowed my knees, and all progress has ceased.

I hear her cry out in an inhuman decibel, a pitch that could shatter glass, "Daddy! Daddy! Where are you?"

Her voice echoes, reverberating in my head, and I feel immense pressure build as it unyieldingly bounces off the corners of my skull. I place both of my hands on the sides of my head and squeeze, fearing that if I don't, it will certainly implode.

"Arrrgg!" I shriek.

My cry follows suit, echoing, carried by the wind. It is its own soulless entity, screaming back at me, "Arrrgg! Arrrgg! Arrrgg!"

I wince and turn red, shuddering from the harrowing pain, whilst I refrain from making a peep, fearful of an ongoing vicious cycle. My body trembles, shimmying me deeper still. I remember the girl, and my eyes pop open, and as if teleported, my surroundings are reset. I am no longer in that grassy field but stand in a long, dark, wet tunnel. Still knees deep, but in murky water that flows between my legs. The girl remains motionless, her back to me but closer now. Perhaps only ten to fifteen feet remain between us.

"Hello?" I call out to her.

She doesn't move an inch, still and silent. All that can be heard is that of dripping water; *drip...drip...drip.*

I call out to her again, "Hello? Little girl? Are you alright?" But, this time, my voice does not make a sound. Inaudible, although I feel it reverberate in the back of my throat, which I grab a hold of in shock.

I try again. "Hello?" But again, my voice fails me. *Drip...drip...drip* is all that penetrates the sound barrier. Eeriness envelopes us in a cloud of depersonalized phantasm.

I have an overwhelming desire to go to her, to help her, but when I try to take my first step, I'm met with resistance. Peering down at my feet, I notice what was once water is now wet concrete. I gasp in disbelief as it rapidly dries, bonding me in place.

I screech, terrified, and shout, "What in the fuck?"

Inaudible still, taunted by the *drip…drip…drip.*

Without warning, the sound is muted by a loud ringing behind me. Chimes of church bells vibrato, banging the drums within my ears. I twist my torso as far as I can, timidly look back, and what I see baffles me. A tree, although a tree unlike any I have ever seen. Six exposed roots meet at the base, spiraling up and intertwining to form the stump. They wind up the trunk until each extends outward in opposing directions, collectively forming the limbs. Each branch sprouts leaves reminiscent of an omega. They shake violently with every ring, blaring so loudly that my body oscillates in response.

Confused, I spin back around, and my heart sinks into my stomach. Caught off guard, the girl now stands inches away, her head down, her long blonde hair covering her face. When she looks up, I realize it is my sleeping beauty. The young victim from the park. Still gowned, faceless, with tears streaming down the raw, exposed musculature on her face.

"Pick up the phone," she says.

My eye twitches, and I ask, "What?"

*Drip…drip…drip.*

"Pick up the phone," she says louder.

"Who are you?"

"Daddy! Pick up the phone!"

I launch myself upright, gasping for air as if I were just re-birthed. Disoriented, I reach for the phone on my bedside table, clumsily knock it off the receiver, where it swings like a pendulum, banging between the nightstand and my bed frame.

"Hold on!" I say. "Give me a second." I reach down, grab a hold of the receiver, and put it to my ear. "Hello?" I say, morning rasp still holding its tune.

"Morning, Boss. Sorry to wake you."

"Darby?" I say. "Uh, no, that's alright. I was just having the strangest dream. Glad you woke me actually. What's up?"

"I searched the DNA database. I got a hit!"

Suddenly wide awake, I spring to my feet. "Well? Who is she?"

"I just have a surname. Oddly, the file was locked, but I was able to get enough to start looking. A Ms. Mousakis. Her DNA puts her as our victim's mother. That's all I was able to get, no address, but she is listed as transnuclear so, where better to start than the ghettos?"

"OK, well, it's something. Pick me up in fifteen?"

"Wear your bio-suit, it's snowing pretty good out here, and the meter is a solid red."

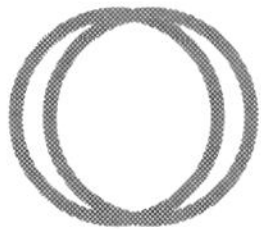

# CHAPTER 17

The snow is falling hard, blowing in all directions. A blizzard in July, not unusual for Raxon winter. It isn't sticking yet, but that doesn't make it any less dangerous. The flurries glow a faint lime green, lighting up the night like glowing embers falling from the sky.

The Raxon clouds block out the sun, but they also prohibit anything from leaving our atmosphere. The result is our pollution remains trapped within the bubble, recycled and sent back upon us like tiny missiles that destroy all that was once beautiful. The melt is equally dangerous, and civilians are only seen sparingly until all has completely melted.

The economy, if you choose to call it that, stands still, and the transnuclear raid the stores like kids with their hands stuck in a cookie jar. After all, shelter is sparse, and they have nothing to lose. Their lifespans are already projected to be cut in half, and many will perish from various forms of cancer before their thirtieth birthdays.

Following a storm, the Raxon parts and releases the imprisoned sun for a few short hours. Temperatures return to their seasonal norms and could reach a stifling ninety degrees in a matter of minutes. The rapid temperature shift is so extreme, windshields crack and streetlamps shatter, leaving much in disrepair.

I watch as we close in on the distant Trans Ghetto, now only a mere mile away. They are positioned on the side of a large hill, referred to by most as Fire Mountain. They only have fires to keep them warm and to provide lighting and, from a distance, the small mountain looks as though it were set ablaze.

In a matter of minutes, we are at the gates, the entrance greets its visitors with four steel drums on either side, lit with fires burning like massive torches. Those who couldn't obtain prime real estate, have made camp here to huddle by the warm fires. They don't pay us any mind as we creep past, careful not to hit the children who build their luminous snowman on the side of the path.

Further down the road, however, we are met by four thugs straddling their motocross dirt bikes, blocking the road, presumably searching for an easy target. A welcoming party for the not so welcome. The one in the middle wears a worn out, red and white hockey mask, dismounts, unties a baseball bat that is harnessed to the side of his bike, and slowly makes his way over to us, slapping the bat into his hand in a threatening manner.

Darby reaches for his gun, strapped to his hip, but when the boy lifts his mask to expose his pimply, freckled face, lined with a patchy adolescent beard, I reach out my hand and signal for Darby to keep it holstered.

"I know this kid. Zip up your suit and roll down the window," I say.

Darby shoots me a concerned look. "What about you, Boss?"

"I'm good over here, don't worry about me," I say. "I got this, trust me."

Darby rolls down his window, and I observe Jared tightening up his grip on the bat. He winds his arm back, preparing to swing.

"Jared!" I shout, halting him mid-swing.

Jared lowers the bat, bends down, and studies both of us.

"Long time, old friend," I say.

He meets my gaze with a crooked smile. "Oh shit! Rooster? That you? What da fuck you doin' here, dog?" He cups his hands around his mouth and calls out, "Cock-a-doodle-doo!"

Darby glances over at me perplexed, more than a little curious I'd say.

"Jared, we're looking for a woman, a Ms. or Mrs. Mousakis. Do you know her?"

He answers me with a blank, hardened stare.

"Jared, do you know her?" I ask again, reaching into my pocket.

"Whoa, whoa there, cowboy!" he says, winding up, threatening to swing his bat.

"Relax, Jared," I say, removing my hand with a twenty curled in between my fingers.

"Why are you looking for this woman, Roost? You all don't come round here for no other reason than to make trouble," Jared says, taking a step backward and slapping his bat into his hand again.

"No trouble. We came here to let her know her daughter was murdered, and we're trying to..."

"Ms. Mousakis ain't got no kids," Jared interjects.

Darby and I look at each other perplexed.

"Are you sure?" I say.

He settles back down, leans in, and folds his arms, resting them on the driver's side window. "Never seen her with any. Never spoke of them, neither."

"Well, we have DNA results that say otherwise. Listen, we aren't here for trouble, we just need to speak with her and see if she can help us figure out who our girl is," I say.

"Nah, don't think I know 'er," he says without budging an inch from the window.

"You trying to shake me down, Jared?" I unzip the torso of my bio-suit, take another twenty out and offer it to him, and he reaches out and snatches it.

"You gotta do better den dat, bro!" he says.

I smile. "Consider it a gift. You still running with Lin's crew?"

"Who?"

"Oh, you know Jerry! Come on now. Now, you know I know. It isn't as big of a secret as you may have thought."

"Know what?" he says.

"You stash his shit in the crawlspace under your crib, and he takes care of you and your mom. Yeah, I know all about that. Have for years, but I've been doing you a solid. How about you return the favor, huh?"

Jared turns pale, and I see the scared little prick I met years ago. He looks down at the ground and considers his options, but he knows his hands are tied. He meets my gaze, tips his hat, and nods.

"Give me a sec," he says, humbly making his way back to his crew.

He huddles them together and, moments later, they scuffle, and for a moment, they contest him, but it's clear Jared is their leader. He pushes and shoves several of them, and they fall back in line, straddling their bikes like outlaws mounting their horses.

In unison, they kick their starters, and their engines fire off a cloud of exhaust, and I see Jared's hand, signaling for us to follow. Darby fights to keep pace, careful not to lose their agile cycles, whipping in between and around the debris in the dirt roads, now laden with mud and luminous slush. He knows very little about my operations in the Trans Ghettos, and I know he must have plenty of questions, but this isn't the time to ask.

We turn up a steep road and maneuver up the winding, slippery path. The old Lincoln struggles to gain traction but finds a footing in the tracks made by the children's homemade sleds, built out of plastic bottles, cardboard boxes, and other common household trash. We gasp in disbelief, observing people, by the dozens, huddled around bonfires. Many of them are set in large, steel oil drums, like the ones we saw lining the entrance. Many others wait in lines to get close enough to the fire to warm their hands and heat up their breakfast scraps.

Their homes are stacked side by side, and many are merely large branches stacked against each other in order to form a teepee. Trash is used to fill in the open spaces to reduce the airflow and toxic precipitation. Some of the more lavish homes are small wooden or tin shacks, but many are missing entire walls, endlessly under construction.

I'm distraught and ashamed, for I am one of them and have escaped this life only because of the kindness of a stranger. I am a fraud. I was given the gift of life, and I shouldn't take it for granted. Rather, I should pay it forward, dedicate my life to helping them, regardless of the cost. It's about time I make a difference, and I'm going to start by solving this poor girl's murder. No one else thinks she's worth the hassle, but I refuse to let her death be in vain.

We make a sharp right, continue further up the hill, and enter the *affluent section*, where most of the shacks are well built for Trans Ghetto standards. Some even have hearths for cooking and heat inside, with chimneys made from clay. You can tell who'd likely been carpenters by trade. Their homes are solidly built. Some even have a decorative flair, although, despite the nicer appearance, dumpsters still spill over, littering the streets. Strays cunningly dive into the dumpsters in search of food while trying to avoid becoming meals themselves.

Trash has value here. It's fuel for their fires and building material for their dwellings. However, the toxic smoke remains entrapped under the Raxon clouds, and a permanent smog engulfs the hill. It is so thick that you can't see more than fifteen to twenty feet in front of you, and it has vastly contributed to our pollution problem, which further contributed to the cyclical blame game. Banishing them from society had unexpected consequences, and their unavoidable pollution rains down on us as a reminder of our sins, fueling resentment from both sides.

Darby skillfully keeps a close distance behind Jared and his misfits, weaving around curious onlookers and hugging the tight windy turns up the slippery hill. We eventually reach a clearing near the top and enter what appears to be a long driveway encased in bare, needle-less pine trees. The driveway, hardly wide enough for our car to fit, is so steep I question if the car will make it up. Darby backs up, shifts the car into drive, and slams on the gas. Our wheels spin as the car struggles to make it to the top, but it appears that the pine trees, though bare, have provided enough cover for us to gain traction.

A well-built log cabin, quite large and luxurious when compared to the other structures we saw below, sits perched at the top of the hill overlooking the mayhem. Jared and his crew stop and point at the cabin.

"I guess this must be it," I say.

They punch their bikes and spin in a circle, kicking up the contaminated snow all over our windshield, and speed down the hill, out of sight. Darby activates the wipers and smears the green slushy mess across the windshield with a sigh.

"Zip up, Darbs. It's even nastier up here." The wind howls, bobbing the car back and forth. We check each other's suit closures and exit the vehicle.

Darby approaches and knocks on the door while I walk around and inspect the sides of the cabin to ensure we are free from an ambush. I peer around the right side and notice a flickering light in the window and observe smoke billow from the chimney. Someone is home, despite Darby's multiple unanswered knocks.

"Keep on knocking, Darbs, someone's here. A fire's lit," I say.

I see a silhouette pass by the window, momentarily blocking out the light, and I'm suddenly uneasy.

"Perhaps we should have kept our guns accessible?" I say.

How could I be so careless? What if Jared set us up? We are sitting ducks with our holsters locked inside of our bio-suits. Perhaps contamination is better than death.

Suddenly, I hear a loud bang from inside the house. I drop to my knees and scurry to open my enclosure for access to my gun. As I grab for the zipper, the door opens as far as the chain guard will allow.

"Yes? Who is it?" a soft female voice says. "What do you want?"

"Ma'am, we're looking for a Mrs. Mousakis?" Darby says.

"Yes? What do you want?" she says.

"Ma'am, we're terribly sorry to bother you, but we have some rather unfortunate news about your daughter. Can we come—"

"I'm sorry, you must be mistaken. I don't have any children. Bye now," she says and swiftly shuts and locks the door.

I knock on her door…no answer. I knock again…still, nothing. We stand in silence, unsure of what to do next, but I refuse to leave without at least a conversation. I knock again, harder this time.

"Mrs. Mousakis, please? If we could just speak with you for a few minutes? Your DNA puts you as the girl's mother, and whether it's an error or not, the smallest detail that could link you to this little girl could help us find her killer. We mean you no harm!" I say.

I pause and listen but hear nothing. Our attempts continue to be ignored. Darby looks to me, defeat in his eyes, but I decided long ago I will not give up.

I will make camp on her porch if I must. I will wait her out. She has to come out eventually, right?

"Ma'am, please, this was a young girl, couldn't have been older than nine or ten maybe. The perpetrator removed her face, for Christ's sake! Even if you're not her mother, someone is, and I'm sure she is worried sick about her little girl. If you could please just…"

The door squeaks open, and a woman appears before us. Her long brown hair is tied back into a ponytail with a CoolAir mask strapped tightly to her face. Her arms remain folded under her chest, closed off, likely skeptical of our intent. I'm baffled. A CoolAir mask? Why would a non-transnuclear be living in the ghetto?

"Well…come on in then," she says. "But for God's sake, remove your gear. Hang them up here in the mudroom and make sure you use those sanitary disinfectant wipes! Don't drag any of that crap into my house." She points her finger at us and says, "Wait! Identification please."

We step into the mudroom, remove our hoods, unzip the torso of our suits, and reach for our badges, handing them over nearly simultaneously. She gives Darby a quick once over and hands it back, but when she looks at mine, she hesitates. Her eyes spring open, and dubiously glances to me and my ID, studying it closely.

Her tone softens. "Uh, come in when you're clean. I'll be by the fire."

*

We enter the cabin, and I scan her living quarters. Although it is a far cry from lavish, it's suitable quarters for most anyone. There is a great room, if you can call it that. It's rather small but includes an open kitchenette with running water and two additional rooms, which I assume to be bedrooms. This cabin must predate the days of Raxon. It is a mansion in comparison to the structures built below.

How did she get a place like this? Why is she here? Why is a non-mutant living in the ghetto and how does she have the nicest property nestled at the top of the hill, away from the mayhem.

I spot her standing, her back to us, warming herself in front of the blazing fire.

"Ma'am?" Darby pauses. "Well, I… Why are you here?"

"Pardon?" she says, turning to face us. The fire casts a shadow over her face, and although I can't see her clearly, I can still see the irritable look in her brow.

"I'm sorry, Mrs. Mousakis…" I begin.

"Ms. It's *Ms.* Mousakis," she says.

"Of course, my mistake. Ms. Mousakis, I think what Darby means is…"

"What is a single, non-mutant female doing living in the ghetto among the transnuclears?" she says, stepping into the light.

My heart flutters. I am aghast. A rush of adrenaline surges through my veins, blasted with unconscionable affection. I try to speak but, suddenly, I'm mute. My mouth opens and closes like a puppet without a ventriloquist, rapidly red, hot and flush. Is my mind playing tricks on me again? I rub my eyes and hope that when I reopen them, they will behold the truth.

"Boss?" Darby says setting his hand on my shoulder.

"Oh, uh…well," I stammer.

I clumsily look to Darby for help, struggling to regain my composure. He looks at me, befuddled, and I presume he must think I'm having another psychotic break. My sudden, erratic behavior prompts him to take the lead.

"Ms. Mousakis, as we mentioned before, your DNA puts you as our victim's mother. Now, although I understand you say you don't have any children, DNA doesn't typically lie," Darby says.

"Call me, Stella, please," she says.

Stella? I look up and internally combust. My eyes widen, my heart pounds within my chest, and I have been reduced to a pile of mush. There is so much I've wanted to say to her. I've yearned for this day to come, and now that it presents itself, albeit, not how I pictured, two strangers in a very real world. Here, I'm a blundering fool and not the Don Juan that exists in the world of my dreams.

"There is really no other option. This has to be an error, I have never had any children," she says.

"Are you sure that—"

"Am I sure I've never had any children, Officer? Quite certain," she says, growing irritated.

I look to Darby, lay my hand on his shoulder. “Stella, do you mind if Darby takes a look around your home? Standard procedure, of course,” I say, hands raised in surrender.

She glares at me irritably. “Oh…fine,” she says, “but please, please don’t touch anything.”

Darby nods and walks slowly to the far bedroom, adjacent from the kitchen. He stops and turns around to observe our silence, and I wait until he is out of sight and sound.

“I owe you my life!” I blurt out. “What are you doing here?”

“I’m sorry. Do we know each other?” she asks, squinting her eyes, appearing to search for recollect.

“You’re a nurse, aren’t you?” I ask.

“I am. Well, yes, I was.”

I study her face as she studies mine. She’s puzzled, trying to place me within a long list of patients and colleagues. She doesn’t remember me. I’m crushed. She has played such a large role in my life, and although I know it sounds insane, we have a life together. A glorious life, albeit it exists only in my dreams, but she has become an integral part of me, but perhaps it’s time I accept she is simply an imaginary friend. A compensatory delusion to help me cope with my dark, lonesome world. I know it’s extraordinarily peculiar, but I never thought of her in that way; imaginary, that is. It…we…everything seemed… real. However important she may be to me, I appear to be no more than a fleeting moment in her life.

I dream of her often and our connection is validated within magnificent glimpses of a reality that still represents part of my existence, for it has molded me, much the same as this one has. Her voice and even her face are exactly the same. Every crevice, even the tiny beauty mark above her lip is the same. How could I possibly remember details so minute years after a single meeting?

We still have a life together, even though it plays out cinematically in my REM, and when morning comes, I reflect on what happened the night before, the sweet things we said to one another or an argument we had. I realize how crazy this all sounds, and what’s crazier still, is that I talk to her as if she were still with me, here, throughout the day.

I understand it isn't real, but that doesn't take away from the fact she is the sole reason I remain single. Admittedly, I would feel overwhelming guilt if I laid with another woman. I haven't given my heart to anyone since Corina because nurse Stella is the only person who could fill that role. She fills the void in my dreams, in a world where I escape the darkness and have a family that provides meaning and purpose. I am loved and needed by all of them.

Suddenly, I'm tangled and distraught, interwoven within two worlds. They link together like nuclear fusion, and that which was already insane becomes downright madness, blasting me deeper into my fiction. I know now who our victim is. Our poor, sweet little...

"Are you alright, Detective?" Stella says, waking me from my phantasm.

Her voice bounces me back to reality and suddenly, I recognize how incredibly insane I must be. I can't allow the crazy to take over. Besides, I reason, if she were my daughter, well, then wouldn't my DNA have been a hit also? I need help, I'm losing my grip on reality.

"Boss, can you come take a look at this?" Darby yells from the bedroom door.

I meet Stella's eyes and see a hint of concern. I hesitate to move, afraid of what Darby may have uncovered. I may be crazy, but that doesn't change the fact I owe this woman my life. I refuse to let anything happen to her, no matter what she may have done. We walk to the bedroom, side by side, and I feel the tension build with each step. We enter the doorway much too rapidly. I am unprepared, befuddled as Darby stands tall in the middle of the room, gripping a small black and white teddy bear.

"What's up, Darbs?" I say.

He holds the teddy bear out, rattling it in front of my face. A black and white panda, about twelve inches in length, looking rather worn and crusty. I grab the bear and immediately notice that much of the fur has been matted together, glued from what I presume to be mucus and tears.

"Stella? Who does this belong to?" I ask, sounding more incriminating than I intended.

"It's mine!" she barks.

Clearly a lie. Her lip always quivers slightly when she does so. It's one of her many tells…but wait…how the hell would I know that?

"Yours?" I ask. I hardly think a grown woman is cuddling with a teddy bear, but I must admit I have seen far stranger things throughout the years.

"Uh, yes! It's very lonely out here and…and…I don't have to explain myself to you!" Her face hardens, and I can tell that our welcome has rapidly come to a close.

"Would you mind if we borrowed the bear?" I ask.

Her mouth drops open, and she gasps. "No, you certainly may not! Now, I have answered all the questions that I'm prepared to answer tonight. Please, hand over the bear and find your way out," she says.

She slings her arm out and snatches hold of the bear but before she rips it out of my hands, I grab a piece of its crusty fur and hang on tightly. When she rips the bear from my grip, a small sample of fur remains, crimped between my fingers. I will not let anything happen to Stella, but I know she is hiding something, and I have to find out what it is.

"Sorry if we've been a bother, ma'am. Please, accept my apology. Darbs, why don't you get the car started while I finish up here."

"I have nothing left to say to you so you might as well go with him!" she contends.

I nod to Darby for him to go.

"Boss, I really think we should—"

"Darby, it's alright, please?" I say.

Darby uncomfortably complies and heads cautiously towards the mudroom, where our suits hang, presumably still dripping with toxicity. When the door finally closes, I look Stella in the eyes. Hers remain stern and hard, her lips pursed, and her brow scrunched into a V.

"Stella," I say softly. She turns her head, refusing to look at me, staring angrily into the corner of the room. "Stella, please?"

I don't know if it was the soft tone or the empathy in my voice, but her eyes finally meet mine. I stare into them longingly, overcome with affection. My heart skips a beat, finally face to face in the physical world. I have so much I want to say to her. It takes enormous effort not to throw my arms around her and tell her I love her. Tell her…everything, but I know everything is utter insanity.

"Listen, I don't know if you remember me, but I remember you, and I owe you my life, and trust me when I say, I will never let anything happen to you. But," I say with my finger raised, "we need to find out what happened to our little girl," I say.

"Our?" she says.

"What?"

"I keep telling you I don't know anything about any missing girl," she says.

"I know you have nothing to do with her disappearance, but the DNA does show you to be the girl's mother. It could be an error, of course, and I assure you, I will run it again. Just, please know you mean the world to me, and I know that sounds crazy but—"

"Yeah, I'd say that's about right," she says.

"You saved me, Stella. You spared me from that life," I say, pointing out of the window and down the hill.

Her lips soften, and she says, "I think you may have me confused with someone else, Officer. I hope that you catch this girl's killer, but you're wasting your time with me."

Her eyes are cold but loaded with conflict. There is something that occupies her mind, something she isn't telling me.

"Very well. I'm sorry to have bothered you, Ms. Mousakis." I reach into my pocket and grab one of my business cards. "Here, please, if there is anything I can ever do for you, anything at all, please, call me."

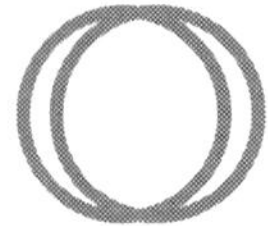

# CHAPTER 18

I see happiness there within all their drama. Through all the temptation and grief, they are happy, *we* are happy. Perhaps that's why they call it a dream? A vision occurring in my mind when I sleep, but is that really all this is? They seem different from other dreams. Real even, like memories replaying themselves over and over, taunting me with their beauty. Showing me not what could have been but rather what was. Another life, and it's filled with glory and meaning.

I am a spectator, a peeping Tom, a voyeur, but I am here and, for now, they are mine. I view them as I would a movie. A film starring myself, but one in which I was never cast. A wife? Children? I watch them, I love them, I envy them.

The way Stella looks at him, me, us…I'm jealous. I wish to be this man and to have all that he has because this man is rich beyond what his pockets could hold. The sun shines as brightly as their love for him, illuminating their lives with precious moments, though strangely, the strain is evident on his face. Something plagues him in a world near perfection. I hate this me…I hate this me…I hate this me.

A gorgeous home, a beautiful wife and four happy children. He decorates their tree with their young boy. The carols blare, and the lad is consumed with holiday cheer. Stella and the girls follow suit, baking holiday cookies, and the aroma is downright intoxicating. They are creating wonderful memories together, ones that strengthen the fibers of your childhood.

Is this my future? He is considerably older than I am. Everyone looks to be so happy, everyone, that is, except me. I appear irritated, in a hurry to get it over with, quickly placing ornaments on the tree and growing agitated with the boy's careful consideration as he tries to find the perfect spot for each decoration. Why are we rushing through this beautiful moment? He's ruining our boy's memory! He's ruining my memory!

He hurries to the living room, turns on the television, and tunes to a football game. The New York Giants are playing the Dallas Cowboys, but the uniforms are not how I remember them to be. He dials up the volume so loud it drowns out the Christmas music and instantly drains the holiday cheer. His son desperately tugs at his pant leg, making every effort to re-capture his attention. The excitement of the festivities is overwhelming, and the little guy can't get enough. He couldn't be more than three or four at the most.

I watch in disbelief as I, the other me, chooses a game over a beautiful memory. I want to smack myself in the back of the head and point out his obvious shortsightedness. The anger stirs inside of me while I observe the selfish diorama unfold. I hate thoughtlessness, and I loathe selfishness. This man is blind. This man is not me.

"Wake up, you idiot!" I holler, and he instantly turns and glares in my direction.

Our eyes meet, and we stare at one another. His eyes darken, and the pupils expand until the whites in his eyes have disappeared. He growls like a rabid animal, frothing at the mouth.

Can he see me? I look behind and am bewildered when I realize it is only him and I, me and me. We are alone, and he is alerted, like a wolf to his prey.

"Don't you see what you have?" I say, but my voice breaks like a pubescent boy.

"What I have is what you abandoned!" He snarls.

His face grimaces, back arched, hunched and kyphotic, reminiscent of a werewolf morphing under a full moon. His muscles flex and remain inflated like hard, vascular balloons while the veins in his neck protrude and can be seen quivering from some thirty feet away. His lips are spread wide and thin, exposing his clenched, grinding teeth, salivating like a rabid dog. It streams from the corners of his mouth, running like a faucet and forming a foaming puddle on the floor. His growl deepens, and the bass rumbles the floor beneath my feet.

Suddenly, the world obscures around us. The light dims, and the sun, which I once had to shield my eyes from, no longer gleams through the windows. Darkness envelops us, and I see Raxon eating up the blue sky.

"No!" I scream, running to the window and watch as they swoop down and surround the house in a bubble. "No! You can't have this world. Not here! You don't belong here!" I shout.

The house rapidly transforms in front of my eyes and becomes worn and shabby. The freshly painted green walls age rapidly, changing from green to gray, dark and weathered as if it were abandoned for many lonely years. Ashes fall in front of my eyes like snow flurries and settle into the space around us. Large, thick, tree-like vines, hastily grow in between the floorboards, splitting them like tissue paper while winding and slithering their way throughout the house like a den of anaconda.

I waft the ashes away from my face and discover that our house, once beautiful and filled with love and laughter, is now a dark, decrepit vineland. The loud hiss of the Raxon amplifies, and I fall to my knees and clamp my hands over my ears. I look back to the other me and realize the furious hiss of the Raxon rumbles from his core. His mouth lay propped open, and his gullet rolls to the tempo of the Raxon.

"Do you see?" he growls, sending a wave of shivers up my spine.

"What?" I ask, cowardly covering my eyes with my forearm.

"What you have done!"

"What I have done?" I say.

"How dare you judge me!" he roars.

The house trembles, shaking so violently that my knees bounce in vibrato on the floor.

I grab onto the counter for support and, simultaneously, as my hand hits the countertop, I hear a loud *crack*. The wood has begun to split beneath me, dividing and threatening to swallow me whole. The world has torn at his feet and extends hastily in my direction. I widen my gate and straddle the opening but feel myself lose my balance.

He crouches into a four-point stance, howls and kicks his feet behind him, as a bull would, preparing to charge, and it gyrates a cloud of dust behind him, making it difficult for me to see his movements. I prepare for an attack and take a step backward and search the kitchen for something, anything to protect myself.

I see a knife set on the counter and reach for one, but as soon as I do, a vine shoots from the wall and grabs a hold of my wrist. I sling my free hand over and grasp hold of a knife, but I return with only the smallest of steak knives. In one clean swoop, I stab the vine and turn the knife within the flesh. A high-pitched scream echoes from the gash, however, it wasn't enough for it to release me. It bleeds darkness. A thick, black, viscous venom with a violent stench that burns my nostrils. I move to strike again, but another vine sprouts up from the beneath the floorboards, lassoing my free wrist and binding me.

I watch in horror as the black venom slithers up my sleeve, curling around my neck, and outlining my cervical spine. I clamp my mouth shut and avert my head, but that doesn't prevent it from entering me. It creeps into my nose, slinking its way down my throat and travels deep into my chest, where it intends to consume my heart. Within seconds, I feel utter hatred, paranoia, distrust, and confusion. I realize, however, that it isn't directed at him, it's reflected inward, unraveling deep-seated animosity for myself.

Without warning, he is upon me, and his face is inches away from mine. The reek of his breath is pungent, and his teeth are sharp like fangs and grow larger before my eyes. His mouth opens wider, and I can't help but fixate on the back of his throat as he lets out a boisterously wicked laugh. His uvula dances, hypnotizing me as it gyrates.

And this is when things get really strange, if they weren't strange enough already. His mouth expands, and his head balloons. It grows larger by the second until it grows so massive that it consumes his body entirely and all that is left is a massive head with his mouth propped open. I stare in disbelief, gaping down the cavernous orifice, outfitted with sharp, pointed teeth, jagged like stalactites, and the urge to walk in and explore it is overwhelming.

My restraints release, and just as I'm about to take my first step, his tongue rolls out of his mouth like a red carpet, and I am magnetized, unable to resist the urge. I take a step onto his spongy tongue and voyage into the abyss, but it's dark, too dark to go very far. I'm about to turn back when I hear a voice muttering gibberish in the distance, and I follow it like beacon, roaming deeper and deeper into the murky darkness. Suddenly, there is a spark, a flicker of light. The strike of a single match that illuminates the cavern like a torch.

Corina stands alone, dressed in the same wedding gown she wore on the day I left her standing at the altar but as if she never took it off, it is worn and shabby. The flowers in her hair have wilted and makeup runs down her face, mapping her tears.

I walk closer and see she is pregnant, and she is rubbing her belly like a genie's lamp and grimacing at me.

"You erased them! How could you?" she says, tears welling up in her eyes.

"Who?" I ask.

"Who?" she says, clutching her hands over her heart. "Who?" she says again, louder and grits her teeth.

"I-I-I don't..."

Her voice deepens and, with tremendous force, she shrieks, "Get out!"

"What?" I say, trembling as if I am a frightened child.

"Get out!" she roars like a god. Her voice propels me off my feet and hurls me out of the mouth like pneumatic mucus.

*

"And then what happened?" Dr. Chowdry asks, peering over the glasses that sit perched on the tip of his nose. He reverts back and forth between me and my chart, pen in hand.

"Well...then I woke up," I say.

"I see," he says, continuing to write his notes. "So..." he clears his throat, "you've been having a lot of these dreams? Dreams about being someone else?"

"Yes, sort of. But this one was different," I say.

"Oh? How so?"

"Well, I'm usually him…me. I mean, I'm not a spectator. He and I are the same. This felt real, too, but it was more of a nightmare. We were like two separate people. Enemies."

"And the people you see in these dreams, they're always the same?" he asks.

"Yes, always, but ever since…" The picture of her, faceless and mutilated, darts across my conscience like a knife.

"Ever since what, Dylan?"

"Ever since I saw the mutilated girl in the park," I say.

Feverishly writing, he says, "I see, and why do you think that is?"

I consider not telling him, but what good would that do? If I can't be honest with my therapist, how can he help me? I need to tell someone.

"The girl…" I pause, trying to think about how to say it and sound slightly less committable.

"Yes? The girl what?" he says, motioning his hand for me to continue, leading me down his analytical path.

Releasing my inhibitions, I blurt out, "The girl is my daughter!"

Dr. Chowdry remains motionless but oddly doesn't appear to be surprised, or even a little disturbed by what I have just disclosed. He continues to stare at me with his elbow resting on his knee and his index and pointer fingers pressed firmly against his face, indenting his cheek.

"Her name is Elena or Eileen…no, it's Ileana!" I blurt out excitedly. "Her name is Ileana, and she is my daughter! I mean, our daughter, uh…in the dream."

"I thought you said the killer had removed her face?" he says calmly.

"He did," I say, suddenly remembering how completely insane it all sounds.

He observes me silently, and I feel increasingly more uncomfortable, and I fidget and pick at the dry skin around my fingernails. I hate not knowing what he's thinking. I mean, give me something. Tell me I'm bat shit crazy, anything!

Calm, emotionless, and robotic, he says, "Then how could you identify the girl as this…this Ileana? A moment ago, you could hardly remember her name, but you can identify this faceless girl from a dream?"

I think about what he said and recognize how incredibly preposterous it is. I know he's right, I'm mad. I glance up at him, embarrassed and confused, although, more than anything, I'm afraid. I fear I may no longer have the ability to decipher what is real.

"Listen, Doc, I realize how this all must sound, but I saw her…I swear. I saw her face! Fuck! Help me, Doc! I think I might be losing my damn mind! I mean, I've even half-convinced myself that my dream world is the real world and this…" I say, turning my palms up, "this is a simulation." I pause and our eyes lock. He remains motionless, expressionless, and stares through me, great and all-knowing. "I know! Before you say anything… I know."

I bury my face in my hands and tug at my hair in frustration when, unexpectedly, his desk phone rings, startling me in my chair. Dr. Chowdry answers it, calmly, almost as if he were expecting the call, never lifting his eyes from me.

"Hello," he says, and without even a second to hear a response, he immediately extends the phone to me with a nod.

"For me?" I ask, placing my hand over my chest.

"Yes, it's for you. Go ahead, take it. Remembering is a curse, Mr. Grady. I'm here to help you forget."

Confused but riddled with curiosity, I grab the phone and hesitantly put it up to my ear. "Hell…uh, Hello?"

A loud, high-pitched squeal sends me into an epileptic fit…blackness.

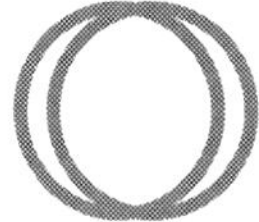

# CHAPTER 19

I lie awake in bed, weightless. The harmonious hum of violins, a symphony reciting a masterpiece, peacefully serenades my soul. I feel incredibly rested, unloaded of the burdens that weigh on me and, for the first time in a long while, I am content with the world. I am…happy.

My lips curl into a smile, but in the midst of my blissful sedation, it suddenly occurs to me that I don't remember how I got home. In fact, I can hardly remember anything from yesterday. Was there a yesterday, or is today yesterday? Does that even make any sense?

What do I remember? I remember making the coffee, listening to the static and crackle of the emergency broadcasting station, and marking an X on the calendar, representing the number of days since I had last seen the sun. This has been my morning ritual and the only way to keep organization in a world of disorder.

I walk over to the calendar and confirm it wasn't a dream. Yup, July 23rd, X. I let out a sigh, power on the radio, and white noise rattles off the walls of my apartment. The same dead air that has looped continually for the last seven years since they announced that the National Guard had been deployed. Perhaps I'm nostalgic, or maybe I'm just one of the few who still hold onto hope that the outside world hasn't completely abandoned us.

I don't recall dreaming last night, either. Perhaps that's why I feel so incredibly rested. After all, it's exhausting living two lives, day and night. Do I ever really sleep?

I miss them, my family. They nestle within my dreams, though, if I'm being honest, they torment me. In their world I am at peace, only to awaken imprisoned in tragedy. My days often begin in a state of depression because, deep down, I know this is my reality, dark and lonesome.

I refocus and search deeper, scouring the tiny crevasses in my brain, but I still can't recall even the smallest detail. It's as if the day were erased or even skipped over entirely. What began with confusion quickly transitions to paranoia, and the euphoria I woke up with fades away.

It's about time I admit I have a problem. My brain isn't working right, and I'm losing my grip on reality. I need to speak with someone. I need to call Dr. Chowdry. Chowdry! I saw Dr. Chowdry yesterday! Wait, didn't I? I recall having a ten o'clock appointment, and I think I remember shaking his hand but then…nothing. If I blacked out, wouldn't I be in a hospital? Was it a dream? I just can't decipher what's real anymore.

I have to get to the station. Maybe Darby can fill in some of the blanks. My morning routine is riddled with bedlam but the ritual for my sanity must go on. Coffee, white noise, exercise, white noise, shower, white noise, get dressed, walk to work.

As soon as I walk into the station, I hear a commotion. The boys huddle around Darby's desk, feverishly debating whether or not we should be celebrating Thanksgiving. The holiday is months away, but when the boys grow bored, they love a good fight.

Johnny stands in a huff, and using his inflated belly like a wrecking ball, he collides with Darby. Darby reaches for him in retaliation, grabs ahold of his shirt, and lifts him off his feet like a pubescent child.

"Boys, boys, boys! Relax, it isn't that serious," I say, placing my hands between them.

Darby releases Johnny, returning his feet to the ground, and Johnny stumbles away, face flush and loaded with regret. Darby is strong and often silent, but don't ever fuck with him. We hit it off immediately, but there are reasons beyond our friendship I keep him by my side.

"Well, shit, Cap, what do we have to be thankful for?" Johnny says, tucking the jolly back under his shirt. "I mean, we've been left in this shit hole to die! Why should we celebrate a holiday specific to our country when our country has deserted us?"

"Well, actually, Johnny, Thanksgiving is celebrated in a number of countries and is about giving thanks for the blessing of the harvest with a feast," I say throwing a jab into his arm.

"Boss, with all due respect, that's bullshit! Thanksgiving is as American as Apple pie!"

"Johnny, even if that were true, we celebrate Thanksgiving because we have each other to be thankful for. We are a family, goddamnit, and I better see you at that table this year!" I say, slinging my arm around his shoulder.

"Oh, I wouldn't miss a feast like that," he says with a chuckle, patting his belly.

"Well, then what the fuck are we arguing about?" I pick up a donut and shove it into his mouth. "If your jaw needs a workout, chew on this."

The station phone rings, everyone disperses, and Johnny waddles back over to the front to answer it. His belly is still half-exposed, and crumbs tumble out of his mouth, leaving a well-marked trail.

"Dello?" Cough, cough. "Mmm…hello, Station 34," he says, fumbling over his words.

I can't help but roll my eyes at the sloppy bastard but, truthfully, I love him. I love all my guys. We are a family, and as good as a family as anyone can ask for in a post-Raxon world. Most of us are our sole survivors, and we fight every day for our family's memory.

I nudge Darby with my elbow and pull him aside. If anyone will know where I was yesterday, it's Darby. Hopefully, he can jog my memory. After all, when we aren't sleeping, we are often together.

"Hey, Darbs. That was interesting yesterday, wasn't it?" I probe.

"What's that?" he asks.

"You know, the thing with our faceless girl," I say.

"Boss, I didn't see you yesterday. You said you had something to take care of in the morning, but you never came in. Never called or nothing. Weren't pickin' up the phone, neither. Was starting to worry about you. Was pretty relieved when you walked in this morning."

Swing and a miss. What now? I thought for sure Darby would have been able to fill in a few blanks. Hell, I can't remember the last day where we didn't see or speak to one another. Well, at least I know I wasn't with Darby.

"Right!" I say simultaneously slapping the table. "Never mind. Guess I must be getting my days mixed up."

"Oh! But that reminds me, Boss. Our sketch came back from the forensic artist. We have a face!"

"A face?" I say excited, but then again, terrified as to what or rather, who, I might see.

"Yeah, to our faceless girl!"

"Yeah, right."

Will it be Ileana, or will it just be some random girl, confirming my suspicions that I've lost my damn mind. Either way, I lose because each outcome presents with conflict.

Darby rolls opens his desk drawer, rifles through the files, and after a few laps, he becomes frantic. He pops up, scratches his head, and says, "Boss, did you grab the file?"

"Did I? No," I say innocently and rather shocked he would think I would enter his drawer uninvited.

Confusion rapidly shifts to fury. He marches over and snatches a megaphone off the storage rack, climbs onto his desk, and hurls his voice across the station, "OK, which one of you fucks has been in my desk? Where's my Jane Doe file?"

He paces back and forth on top of his desk and kicks his pen holder, full of utensils across the room, spraying them like arrows. "No one? Someone has been in my damn desk! I'm going to give you until I'm done with my coffee to return it without consequence!"

The room has grown quiet, and the boys look to one another for answers, but no one budges. Darby gets down from his desk and returns to his drawer and wildly flips through the files once again, but like before, he returns empty handed, defeated, and furious.

"I'll ask again! Where the fuck is my Jane Doe file, and which one of you sorry sons-a-bitches has been in my desk?"

Getting ready to throw a tantrum, Darby holds his index finger in the air and takes a deep hearty breath about to blow his top when suddenly Johnny interjects, "Boss, we got another homicide. A boy, seventeen to twenty years of age. He's at 551 Grove Street. Oh, and, Boss, no face."

Another faceless victim? Do we have a serial killer on our hands? What are the chances we would have two faceless victims not connected by the same killer?

*

When we arrive at the scene, the first responding officers encircle the body as if they're performing a cult ritual. I feel overwhelming relief when I realize Sergeant Rosario and his Guard haven't arrived. They hinder our investigations, but I expect that they will grace us with their presence sooner or later, but it would be nice to be given an opportunity to survey the crime scene without his sarcastic condemnation.

Darby and I approach the victim and are blasted with a foul, wretched odor. One so rancid, I question how my men were able to stand so close to the body.

"Let's put our masks on to minimize the stench," I say.

Upon first observation, I note that our victim is male, late teens to mid-thirties, although as with our Jane Doe, his face has been removed, making it nearly impossible to approximate his age with any real accuracy. Times like this, I wish people had rings like trees.

The victim has red hair and bears the mark of a transnuke however, unlike our last victim, this boy was not treated with the same level of care. There is no cradle carved for his head, nor is there a bed of flowers for the victim to rest on. The evidence suggests he was brutally beaten, tortured, and discarded. I'd wager that most of his bones have been broken and disjointed.

He lies in the dirt, limbs postured in impossible positions for the human body to bend. Like a rag doll tossed aside, Raggedy Andy lays with his legs and arms sprawled to unreachable lengths. His spine has been broken, extending sharply backward, nearly forming a right angle, somewhere around his L5, S1 segment. The right elbow has been disjointed, and there is visually a separation between the bones where the flesh has been twisted and wound like a child's toy, awaiting release.

His ankles and wrists have bruising and abrasions, providing evidence they were bound. His feet angle erect as a ballerina with point shoes. The multitude of bruising and lacerations leads me to believe that much of the desecration was done while our victim was still very much alive. I only pray this boy was dead long before our killer got creative.

"Is this the same killer?" Darby asks with his nose drawn up and wrinkled. "Jesus, Boss, what the fuck kind of monster—"

"I don't know, Darbs. Probably, but we can't rule out a copycat," I say.

I break off a long brittle stick from one of the dead trees and poke his body at various points. The corpse is stiff in places, yet like Jell-O in others. Rigor mortice has set in, but his bones are shattered and disjointed, allowing the flesh to jiggle without resistance in some areas.

"Copycat?" Darby contests. "We didn't release anything to the media."

"Precisely. At least it narrows our search," I say, standing tall.

His head whips around. "Wait, you think one of our guys could have done this?"

"I don't know what to think. It's either the same killer, the Guard, or one of our own. I know one thing for sure, Rosario would be my first person of interest. Guilty or not, I'd love to tear into that sick fuck's past. I can only imagine the shit I'd find!"

Just as the words leave my mouth, I hear rustling in the leaves behind me, and a spotlight illuminates the park to our right, tracking its way like lightning to our position. I spring my left arm up to shield my eyes and see my adversary marching confidently towards me, encased in his band of lemmings.

"Well, well, boys, look what we have here. Officers Tweedle Dumb and Tweedle Dee," Rosario mocks.

I'm hardly a stranger to his insults. I ignore it and remain squatted by our victim, making notes in my pad. Rosario and his Guardsmen huddle behind us like a steroid-enraged football team, suited up and crossing their arms like little plastic army men.

"So, Grady, how in the hell is the search for your killer going?" he says with a hearty, patronizing laugh.

I look up at his giant silhouette and bare my teeth, smiling. "Well, although likely, we're not positive our last guy did this."

Rosario laughs. "No face, Grady! What, you think there is a band of killers out there removing kids' faces and ditching them in the middle of the city parks for us to find?" He raises his hands in the air, glances over at his men for approval, and makes his way over to me with a cocky swagger.

"No, what I think is both murders have similarities, but we have to at least consider the differences."

"Pray tell, Grady."

"OK..." I walk around the body. "Yes, both victims' faces have been removed, but our first was done with surgical precision. This? This is jagged and sloppy. I hate to think it, but it's feasible our victim was still alive and struggling while his face was literally being torn off."

"Sucks for him," he says.

"Yes, I'm sure it did Sergeant. Our killer or killers likely knew both of the victims and yes both were left in city parks but—"

"And how do you know he knew 'em?"

"This is a brutal act. An act of passion," I say.

"Passion? So, what, our perp is a...a twinkle toes?"

I'm dealing with a buffoon and a bigot, so I must speak to him as I would a child. "I have no idea of his sexual orientation, Sergeant. I mean passion in the sense that it was done with intense emotion."

"You can't know that for sure, Grady," Rosario says, snickering.

"No, nothing in this line of work is a sure thing, but we work with what we're given. It also appears both victims are transnuclear."

"OK, so what's different then?" He snarls impatiently.

"Well…look at the way this body was left when compared to the other? This boy was mangled and discarded. Tossed here like a rag doll. Our Jane Doe was dressed, manicured, and laid to rest on a bed of flowers. She was flawless. Great care was taken to assure she was meticulously clean and there wasn't any sign of physical harm. In fact, the coroner indicated the face was removed postmortem and her cause of death is undetectable."

I turn around and see Rosario place his foot onto the corpse and attempt to turn him. With his heel dug into the victim's ribs, he bolsters his weight and pushes the victim over. The victim's spine has been severed at the sacrum and internally decapitated at the cervical/thoracic junction, so the torso flips over rather quickly, while both the legs and the head follow only by the energy generated by the torso. The body settles into its new position, and I see something so incredibly recognizable to me that our victim couldn't possibly be anyone else.

"Wait! I know this boy!" I say.

"Oh, Jesus Christ. Here we go again. Another faceless identification? I mean, really, Grady? What in the fuck?"

"No, I can't mistake that tattoo, the red hair. It couldn't be anyone else." I lean in and examine it more closely. It is a poorly-drawn, faded tattoo of a rooster, positioned off-center on the victim's deltoid.

"It's a fucking rooster, Grady." Rosario grunts.

"Yes, I know, Sergeant. His name is Jared Boone. I used to joke with him that I'd recognize his cock anywhere," I say with a chuckle.

Darby's eyes shoot up and meet mine, and I nod, confirming this is the same Jared who led us to Stella's house. The same Jared I have a history with, and one I still owe him an explanation.

Sergeant Rosario eyes me accusingly and flutters his fingers in the air, making insinuations about my sexuality. A wicked smile takes control of his face, and he slowly removes his foot from Jared's mangled corpse. The weight of his foot has left an indentation in Jared's ribs, and I hear a *crack* as he releases it.

"One more thing both our victims share, Grady," Rosario says.

"Yeah, what's that, Sergeant?"

Rosario heartily slaps me on the back and slings his arm around me. "They both knew you, pal. Don't you think that's quite the coincidence?" he says, massaging my shoulders.

"You can't seriously think I had something to do with this?" I sling back.

"Well, I'm just saying, Grady, I mean, you are another commonality our victims share. We can't reasonably rule you out as a suspect, can we?"

"I mean…I don't really know them. I-I-I…I mean, I know Jared but…"

"Grady, where were you yesterday?"

"You're serious?" I ask.

"Dead," he says, snickering. "Pardon the pun."

I frantically search for an answer, but I have no idea where I was. I have little recollection of the day before, but one thing I know for sure is I didn't kill anyone.

"I was with Darby," I blurt out as casually as I can manage. "We were with each other all day."

I look to Darby, pleading with him with my eyes for his alibi.

Rosario looks to Darby. "Well?"

Darby pauses. Only for a mere second but long enough to make my heart race and my adrenaline soar.

"Yes, yes of course," he affirms. "We we're together all day."

Rosario studies Darby for what feels like an eternity, but Darby stands strong and still. Silence fills the park, and everyone stands motionless, waiting for Rosario to deliberate. My left eyebrow twitches, and I feel like the guilt is written all over my face. Could he really think I'm a killer? Could anyone think I am capable of this? Capable of murder?

My blood pressure soars, and I hear my heart beating in my ears. I have an intense urge to take deep, penetrating breaths, but I remain cool and appear calm. I'm about to buckle under the pressure and unleash my fury when, suddenly, my attention is drawn to movement at the edge of the park.

I see a figure, the man dressed in the black cloak, unmistakably the same man I saw at our Jane Doe. It has to be! He's closer this time, standing only fifty or so yards away but still not close enough to identify any distinguishable features. He stands confident and unwavering, legs spread with his arms crossed in front of his chest. He is dressed in all black, with his hood drawn so I can't see his face, but he appears to be staring directly at me…through me… into me.

I feel myself being drawn to him as if my soul is being sucked from my body. I try to alert Rosario and my men of his presence, but I find I'm unable to move, I'm incapacitated. My hands stiffen, my face goes numb, and my vision flickers. Flashes of light followed by electromagnetic noise, reminiscent of when I had my blackout episodes, years ago. I am a prisoner within myself. My soul marches deeper and deeper into his trance. Rosario snaps his fingers in front of my eyes, and just as he does, everything goes black.

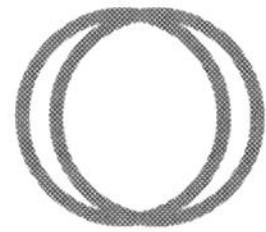

# CHAPTER 20

Where am I? Is this Heaven or Hell, or am I having another one of those episodes? The ones where everything just, shuts off? Perhaps this is something new entirely. I turn my head all around and inspect my surroundings, but all I see is darkness. I put my hand out in front of my face, waft it back and forth, but still, I see nothing.

The movement, however, did stir up a cool breeze, and it gloriously collides with my face, prompting me to think, *Ah, I must be alive.* If I were dead, would I still feel? If I were dead, would I still think? If I were dead, would I still remember? I remember Jared's mangled corpse and the crack of Rosario's fingers as they snapped before my eyes.

If my mind is here, then where is my body? Is this what a coma feels like? No structure, no landscape, no shape and, presumably, for that matter, no end, and I suppose no beginning. There is just…me.

A bout of déjà vu strikes me. I can't help feeling as though I have had those thoughts before. I feel sudden uncontrollable sadness. My heart pounds within my absent chest as though I am going to cry, but why, how? If my mind is disconnected from my body, how can it beat so hard? I see flashes of a girl in a hospital bed. Wires and tubes allow her to breathe. I feel incredible sorrow. I feel more hopeless with every *beep* registered on the monitor.

Suddenly, as if appearing out of nowhere, my attention is drawn to a dot, and within that dot, I see light, and within that light, I see hope. It's remarkably small, couldn't be larger than a pencil eraser, but it is the only thing illuminated, so it blares like a beacon and is remarkably captivating. So captivating I realize my legs are already moving, propelling me towards it. I march, as a wooden soldier would, and as I advance, I notice the light growing larger. Larger and larger, the wormhole sucks me forward until the light in front of me expands, reminiscent of an old projected movie screen. The picture distorts, and static appears momentarily until I see a countdown begin in black and white: 10, 9, 8, 7, 6, 5, 4, 3, 2, 1…

I see a baby. I see…is that? Mom! Dad! The baby is me. Seconds later, it flashes and, suddenly, I'm three years old. It's my birthday party, and I'm blowing out a giant candle shaped in the number three on my cake. I see my childhood friends I grew up with from the neighborhood. They were my first friends, the ones I first explored the world with. It's John and Pat, Sue and Paul. We were so close, and I often regret losing touch.

Friends were endless back then, and one by one, I shut them out until I was left with just a few. Then the Raxon came, and they took the rest, along with Mom, Dad, and Cheryl, too. My sweet baby sister Cheryl, I miss you so much. Mom, Dad, and all the friends who have come and gone. All gone, all laid to rest. Perhaps they were the lucky ones? Perhaps the survivors should be mourned, especially those unfortunate enough to have been cursed with being *gifted* transnuclear.

The screen flashes again, and now, I am around six. The sun shines so brightly I dip my head back to take in its glow. I miss the sun terribly, and I remember how revitalizing and colorful the world used to be. It was so incredibly beautiful, so alive, and we took it for granted.

The pictures flash, and a million memories rapidly pass before my eyes. Faster, faster, and faster, they cycle, and I am entranced. I see them, I feel them. Fuck, I can really feel them! All the emotions, the hopes and dreams, the love and hate, flow through me as the reel rolls on like a Rolodex, one day at a time. My whole life flashes before my eyes.

Perhaps I was wrong, maybe I *am* dead? Is this it? Is this judgment day? Waves of emotions crash through me, a pendulum bouncing from one extreme to the other. Happiness, sadness, regret, jealousy, depression, nervousness, shyness, apprehension, love, pain, loss.

Corina? Wait, no, this isn't right! I didn't…no, I didn't marry her! A life unbeknownst to me unravels before my eyes. I see our 'I do's', I see laughter, depression, and conflict. I feel ugly. I feel…but then I see *her*, and nothing else matters. She is so beautiful, and even in the midst of her wailing, she is the most precious thing on Earth. My baby girl has been born. The nurse weighs her, eight pounds, four ounces of perfection. I feel instant love, devotion, and utter adoration. A shiver is sent up and down my spine, igniting a tear to roll down my cheek. I see the tag on her bassinet, and it reads: Haley Grady.

The pictures roll on and on as an alternate life unfolds like a bout of déjà vu. A movie I once saw but grips me to the edge of my seat because I can't remember how it ends.

I see Stella, and the years roll by, through love and tragedy, and I notice I'm crying. I shut my eyes tightly and fight the urge to look any further. The pain is too great, I can't bear to watch any longer. I resist to open them until I can't resist any longer, the temptation to see what happens next is too overwhelming.

I reopen my eyes, but I'm too late. The final few pictures steamroll by, leaving me utterly confused.

"Welcome to Alter-life, where your life is our dream…"

*

As if I were raised from the dead, I slingshot upright and gasp for air. It fills my lungs with air so fresh that it feels, just how I imagine a baby's first breath to be. I open my eyes to piercing light and shut them rapidly, echoing pain in my head, front to back, and I ease my body back into the hard, lumpy pillow. There is a crick in my neck and a continuous *beep, beep, beep* that rings in my ears, but it takes a few moments for it to register.

I reach down and discover there are wires mounted all over me. There is also a pinch in my penis, along with an obvious swelling in my prostate. I lift the sheets and see a tube entering me, and it's much larger than what I imagined could ever fit. Catheterized and in the hospital? How did I get here? How long have I been out? I feel a little disoriented, but other than a tremendous headache, I think I'm OK.

My heart sinks, and I feel a pit swell in my throat, and as it did then, my imagination runs wild, recalling the pictures that flashed in my head. It was just a dream. Wasn't it? Strangely though, it still feels like déjà vu, and unlike a dream's segmented memory, I remember everything. The shame lingers, and I can't seem to shake the horrible emptiness that looms. I feel…different.

I hear footsteps, squint my eyes, and see a nurse walk in, dressed in green scrubs and holding a basin filled with a bag of IV fluids and a change of sheets.

"Oh, hello there! Welcome back, Mr. Grady. Nice to see you awake again."

I open my eyes hesitantly to allow them time to adjust to the light. "Do we know each other?"

"Not exactly but…well, I did put in your Foley catheter, so perhaps I know a little more about you than you do about me," she says with a wink.

"Foley? Uh, what happened? Why am I here?" I ask groggily.

"Well, the doctor will be in shortly to speak with you about it, but I believe they think you experienced some sort of panic attack. Just blacked right out! Never seen anything like it. They said it was like you just well…turned off!" she says.

"Turned off?"

"Yeah, like a robot or a TV or something. Just shut down. Doc said he hasn't ever seen anything quite like it, but now you're all cozy in good old room 551. Just relax, it'll all be over soon."

"Did you say 551? What will be over?" That number haunts me. It has imprinted on me. I see it everywhere, teasing me, a subliminal message I am supposed to decode.

"Yup, we'll have you back to normal in a shake of a lamb's tail."

"How long have I been here?"

"Oh, not long. Four or five hours or so. You were in a coma, but not. Like I said, Doc said never seen nothing quite like it. Didn't know if you were a long term or short-term resident."

Her accent reminds me of someone from the Midwest, Minnesota perhaps. Like Frances Mcdormand's character in the movie Fargo, wholesome and oddly comforting. I bet she wishes she stayed in the Midwest. She may have a tan, lounging at the Great Lakes instead of a prisoner in quarantine.

"No, no that can't be right," I say.

"Well, all's well that ends well. Did you see your visitor?"

"Visitor?" I say.

"Oh ya, she's been here ever since they brought you in. Well, at least an hour after you were brought to the floor."

"She?" I scan the room, but the only evidence that anyone has been here is an ancient magazine and a cup of coffee resting on the arm of the green visitor's chair.

"Oh, she will be so upset she missed you. Is she your wife?" she asks with a glimmer in her eye.

I feel my face flush. "Wife? No, no, I'm not married," I say.

A question I should be able to answer without hesitation suddenly bewilders me. Was I? Fantastic, just what I need, more riddles, more reasons to question my sanity. I close my eyes and focus on breathing deeply, in and out through my nose. I have always had an unhealthy distaste for hospitals. I get overwhelming nausea every time I smell the iodoform, the smell particularly unique to hospitals.

A code blue is announced over the loudspeaker, and she urgently exits.

"Gotta go, hon. I'll be back."

I'm relieved to see her go. She's quite pleasant, but I need some peace and quiet until this ache in my head subsides.

Moments later, and just as I'm about to fall asleep, I hear a soft voice. "Detective Grady?"

My eyes spring open, and my heart trembles when I see her. Stella? What is she doing here? She stands in the doorway, holding a stuffed brown bear with a white belly gripping a balloon that says: Get Well Soon.

She smiles at me. "This is room 551, isn't it? Glad to see you're awake, Detective. I was beginning to worry about you."

Did she say she was worried about me? Why would she worry about me? Suddenly at a loss for words, I just stare at her speechless and dumbfounded.

"Sorry to bother you... it's Ms. Mousakis, uh... Stella. Stella Mousakis, that is."

I clear the hoarse from my throat. "Ms. Mousakis? What are you doing here?"

She grabs the arm of the green chair by the door and drags it across the room. It lets out a loud *screech*, and I can't help but cover my ears and wince in pain.

"Oops, sorry!" she says, covering her hand over her mouth.

She positions the chair next to my bed, sits down, and places her hand on my shoulder. I feel two worlds intersect once again, and I'm having trouble stabilizing my emotions. I can't help but feel remarkably uncomfortable. My eyes twitch, and my complexion shifts to a dark red. I try my best to maintain a straight face, but I can't counter the irresistible urge to smile. Even as I smile, my right eyebrow continues to uncontrollably twitch. I force myself to make eye contact and immediately notice there is conflict in her eyes. My smile dissipates and my lips neutralize flat.

"What's wrong?" I say.

"Someone is trying to kill me," she says quietly, staring down at her clasped hands, resting in her lap.

"Kill you? Stella, who's trying to kill you?"

She looks at me and studies my eyes as if she were searching for something. Perhaps she doesn't find the answer within them because she averts her eyes and says, "I don't know."

"Stella, why are you here? If someone is trying to kill you, why not go to the station?"

"Aren't you the police?" she says quietly, looking up at me with puppy dog eyes.

"Well, yes but…"

"It's a man. He dresses in a black cloak. He wants to erase us. That's all I know."

"Us?" I ask narrowing my eyes.

"Me...Detective Grady...me. He wants to take me out of this world, and he won't stop until he's done it," she says.

So, there is a man in a black cloak, and he isn't just some figment of my imagination. He's our guy! But wait, why would he want to kill Stella, and what are the chances she hits as our Jane Doe's mother and the killer is trying to kill her also? That would be one hell of a coincidence. Clearly, there is a lot she isn't telling me.

"Why?" I ask again.

"Dylan, that doesn't matter—"

"Doesn't matter?" I say. "If someone were trying to kill me, I'd certainly think the *why* would be important."

"Listen, we can talk about that later, but for now, you need to trust me. I've saved your life once, and I'm about to do it again! You need to follow my lead. You need to trust me, Dylan!"

She caresses my face with her hand, and I lean into it longingly, intoxicated by her touch.

"Wait!" I say, shaking my head. "What lead? Saving my life, again? Stella, what the hell are you talking about?"

She looks intensely into my eyes. "Yes, I lied to you, and I'm very sorry about that. I will explain everything but, for now, we need to get you out of here."

"No, I'm not going anywhere. Let's clear it up now! Lied about what, and for God's sake, why do I need to get out of here? Listen, Stella, you need to come clean with it."

"That night you came to my house, I remembered you." She sighs. "I remember everything, but we need to stop him before your—"

The door swings open, and Darby stands in the doorway with two six-shooters strapped to his belt like an old western cowboy. Stella's demeanor immediately changes, and I can tell she has grown uncomfortable. She yanks her hand away from me and places it in her lap, sits up, tall and rigid in her chair.

"Remember what I said, Dylan, follow my lead," she mutters under her breath.

"Glad to see you're awake, Boss," Darby says, tilting his head to the side. "Ms. Mousakis, what are you doing here? When we spoke at the station, I turned my back for a second, and when I turned back around, you were gone. How did you know Detective Grady was here?"

My attention shifts to Stella, anxious to hear her response. This all just seems so strange to me. I can't make sense of any of it. I'm beginning to think that perhaps my dreams are less confusing than my reality. I see her struggling, searching for an explanation. Her mouth opens to speak, but nothing comes out.

I can't bear to see her struggle, so I interject, "Never mind that for now, Darbs, what's up? Everything OK?"

He looks back at me, his expression stern.

"Boss, where were you?" he says. His eyes plead with me, forming a frown underneath his brow.

"Where was I when?" I say.

He hesitates, takes a deep breath, and looks at his hands.

"Darbs, what is it?"

"Boss, Rosario has it out for you. After they took you to the hospital, he came back to the station. Began asking around as to your whereabouts yesterday."

"OK, so?"

"So? So, where the hell were you? Boss, he knew you were lying, he knew *I* was lying. I didn't know what to do!"

He looks up to the corner of the room, and I can see the guilt written all over his face. I suspect he caved under Rosario's pressure.

"Darbs, it's OK. I understand."

"Boss, I tried! Please?" he pleads. "Tell me you can explain all this? I mean, things aren't looking too good for you right now."

"Darby, the truth is..."

"He was with me, Officer," Stella asserts. She was very convincing. So convincing in fact that, for a moment, I entertain the possibility that perhaps we were together.

I raise my brow to Stella but try my best not to blow her cover. Darby looks to Stella, and if I know Darby, he isn't buying what she is selling.

He cocks his head to the side and says, "Come again?"

"You see, Officer, Dylan and I have a somewhat…well, a convoluted past, and when we saw each other, something sparked."

"Then why didn't you just say that when Rosario asked you? It would have been better to—"

Stella cuts him off before I have a chance to answer, "We spoke about it at length and decided no one could know about us. You see, it wouldn't look very good for the lead detective, the captain of the force, to be sleeping with a…a person of interest in an ongoing murder case, would it?"

Darby pauses and scratches his head, just as he does whenever he thinks about things from multiple angles.

"I-I-I don't know what to say. Do you have any proof of this? I mean Rosario…"

"What? I'm sorry, Officer, do you want to swab my vagina for traces of his DNA?" She chuckles and kisses me on the corner of my mouth.

I turn bright red and unsure as to whether her story is fact or fiction, I remain silent. Was this a risky gamble or an honest divulgence? Clearly, she is being sarcastic, but you shouldn't offer DNA to an officer unless you're certain you will come out on top.

"Perhaps I'll take you up on that, Ms. Mousakis. After all, it would certainly clear detective Grady and validate your story," Darby says.

Clearly not the response she was expecting. Follow her lead, she says? Her lead could land me in prison, and then I really would be Rosario's bitch. Unless…we did have sex? I mean, clearly, I don't have anything to hide… right?

"Well, Darbs, wow. This is embarrassing. You know I always wear a condom. What are the chances that any DNA would be there, what, two days later? You're just going to have to take our word for it on this one."

I reach my hand out and take her hand into mine. We interweave our fingers together, and she pulls my hand under her chin and places her lips upon it, kissing the back of my hand. Our eyes meet, and I feel it; I feel *us*. The us that is so wonderful and so incredibly familiar it forces me to question my reality once again.

"OK, Boss, but there's something else."

"What? What something else?"

"When we got back to the station earlier, a girl was there with Rosario, giving a statement. Her name was Haley."

"Haley?" My eyes widen, and my heart pounds, nearly jumping out of my chest. The lines between my two realities continue to blur, and the boundaries I've set up in my mind have faded even more. All the while, for the life of me, I still can't remember anything significant from yesterday.

"Yes, Haley something or other. Why? Know 'er?" Darby says.

"No…no, sorry, go on," I say as blasé as possible.

"Apparently, she was in the closet while her boyfriend, Mr. Jared Boone, was taken."

"OK, great. Did she get a good look at him?"

Darby sighs. "Well, Boss, she kept pointing at it over and over. It was rather eerie. Made the hair on my head stand right up."

"What, Darby? What was she pointing at?" I say and suddenly realized Stella's grip has tightened enormously around my fingers.

"Rosario just kept pressing her and, at first, she said she couldn't be sure 'cause the guy was dressed in all black, but after a while…"

"For Christ's sake, Darbs, what?"

"She pointed to your picture on the wall. She kept saying he looked a lot like you."

"What? That's impossible!" I say.

Darby looks divided, uncertain of what to believe. I can feel his tension, and it cuts into my heart like a knife.

"Oh, Darbs. Have you ever, for a minute, thought I was capable of murder? Murdering a child, no less?"

Darby looks away, ashamed but struggling with what to believe. The evidence is rather damning. He takes a deep breath and lets out a long, hissing exhale.

"Of course, I don't want to believe you did it. I mean…I don't think you did, but fuck, Boss, it really doesn't look good, and you know Rosario would love to…"

"To what?" I say.

"To end you, Boss. He would take great pleasure in that, and he has you dead center in his sights."

As if Rosario just read his mind, Darby's radio goes off. "All officers be advised, Sergeant Rosario of the National Guard is in route to Burnsville Regional Hospital to take Captain Grady into custody. Repeat, The National Guard is in route to take Captain Grady into custody."

"I was hoping I had more time. That's what I was coming to tell you. Boss! You know how this works. You're guilty if he says you are!"

"Well, then you two better get the hell out of here before he gets here and locks us all up," I say.

"But, Dylan…" Stella starts.

"It's OK, go! Please? I'll be alright, now go!

*

Darby and Stella leave, and I search within myself for answers. I need to clear this fog that muddies my consciousness. *Think, think, think!* I can't waste any more time. I must get out of here, but equally important, I have to remember where the fuck I was yesterday! My future greatly relies on those details to clear myself.

Stella's story, implausible at best, is the only thing I have to work with. We never had any past, only a fleeting moment in a government testing lab. There wasn't any relationship per se, at least not in this reality, and I don't suppose Darby bought much of it, either. There hasn't been a woman in my life, not a one-night stand or even a wink I hadn't boasted to him about.

Not to say I haven't had my share of secrets over the years. After all, I never entrusted him with my biggest secret of all. I am transnuclear, and it is a secret that, I have little doubt, would shatter his faith in me. His disgust for the transnuclear has never been a secret, but still, that isn't why I kept it from him. It wasn't to protect myself, it was to protect her. Stella would have been crucified if anyone were to find out what she had done for me, and I vowed not to allow that happen.

I have lived this double life as long as I can remember, both literally and figuratively. There is my alternate, dream universe where Stella and I have a family, a home, a life together, and there is *this* reality where I'm lonely, dark, and without a fulfilling purpose. I don't blame Darby for questioning my sanity over the years. How could I when I question it myself?

I hear a nurse outside of my room say, "Darling, the only thing sending you home early is a code black! We got an all-nighter here, Sue my dear. Better saddle on up!"

Suddenly, I remember what Stella had said. The man in the black cloak is trying to erase us. An interesting choice in words. I must find this man in black before any more of them get hurt.

Rosario's coming for me. I have to go! I flail my arms up and tear the electrodes off in one clean swoop, hastily remove the intravenous line, and watch the blood stream down my forearm and pool into the palm of my hand. I sling my legs over to the side of the bed and hop to my feet when, suddenly, I feel a tug. A tug where an uninvited tug shouldn't ever be felt. The catheter!

Shit, I can't go anywhere with this thing hanging from me but…but how the hell do you remove it? I have no choice. I take a deep breath and muster up as much courage as I can. On the count of three I tell myself and as if getting prepared for a game of tug of war. One…two…three, I rip the catheter from my member with one swift and mighty tug.

The pain is indescribable. I pick up the pillow, press it against my face, and shout into it, every combination of profanity you can imagine. Biting and tearing it with my teeth, the pain shudders down my legs. I peer down at my member and, to my horror, I see blood and urine gush from my urethra. It splashes onto the floor, forming a red, bloody, urine-filled puddle. I become weak in the knees, nearly losing consciousness, and allow the weight of my torso to crash onto the bed. Clearly not how to correctly remove it, but what choice did I have? Certainly, Rosario has notified the hospital, so I can't imagine they would have removed it voluntarily.

When I remove the pulse ox from my finger, the patient monitoring alarm sounds, and I realize I have mere seconds to get out of here before a nurse rushes in to check on me. I spot my clothes in a clear plastic bag, hanging from an IV pole and stumble over to grab them. I open the bag, but as soon as I do, my nurse appears in the doorway, accompanied by a rather large orderly.

"Mr. Grady! What are you? You can't just—"

"I'm sorry, but I have to go!" I say, wincing. I lower my shoulder and plow through the orderly, knocking him back a few feet. His hand reaches out and grabs hold of the string enclosure on my gown and rips it off as he falls backward.

"But all you have to do is sign out AMA!" she yells after me.

No time to waste, I continue my long strides to the elevator and feel an indistinguishable draft. My gown hangs open in the back, with my derrière and testicles exposed, bouncing, thigh to thigh, while leaving a trail of bodily fluids that gravitate down my leg.

I stop in front of the elevators. One is out of order, and the other ticks like a slug from the twentieth floor. I see a door to the stairwell across the hall and make a run for it. I open the door. It bangs hard against the door jam and echoes down the stairwell. I glide down the U-Shaped stairwell as fast as I can, 'round and 'round and 'round I go until I am too dizzy to go on. I stop about two-thirds of the way down, put my clothes on, and regain control of my body.

When I finally reach the ground floor, I peek my head out of the stairwell door. Scanning to my right yields the lobby, all clear, but when I look to my left, down the long, dimly lit corridor, I spot Rosario and his men standing by the elevator. They unmistakably stand in unison, like seven monkeys grooming each other at a zoo.

Rosario confidently pats one of his men on the back, and they embrace in hearty laughter. I've never seen him look so jolly. I suppose my arrest would be equivalent to celebrating Christmas in July. His face shield hangs by his back like a hoodie, his gun and cuffs are exposed, clipped to a holster at his hip, ready for me to give him a reason to use them.

I consider remaining tucked in the stairwell, but I hear footsteps from above, rapidly descending, and I think that perhaps it is the orderly I knocked to the ground seeking redemption. I must slip out unnoticed. I must go now! I estimate it couldn't be more than a hundred paces to the door. I casually exit the stairwell and walk towards my freedom, with my hands nonchalantly tucked away in my jacket pockets.

Just as I'm about to pass through undetected, a heavy, red-headed woman, with long dangly earrings and far too much makeup, screeches and reaches out and grabs ahold of my arm.

The woman shrieks, "Where's your suit? That's suicide! What, are you crazy or something?"

I stop in my tracks, turn around, and look down the hall. Rosario snaps his head up and locks onto me. His broad nose flares, and I can see his rage building in his posture.

"Grady! Goddammit, you stop right there!" Rosario hollers.

Instinctively, I freeze, raising my arms in surrender.

"Stop him!" he yells again.

It occurs to me, however, I have no other choice but to run for it. Leaving my fate in the hands of ignorance, without compromise, determined to destroy me, is suicide all the same. I would become his prisoner, and Stella and the kids would be left to die. I can't live with knowing I didn't try to save them.

While I stand and watch Rosario and his men run down the hallway, reaching to unholster their weapons, the muscles on my face flex into a broad smile because, in this moment, as I watch them charge like medieval warriors, I realize that in a world of decrepit solidarity, I have them. Real or not, they are real to me, and they are my purpose.

I start to back through the doorway, and the meter above flashes red, and the safety alarms sound.

"Fuck it, shoot! Shoot him, Goddammit!" Rosario barks.

I don't have my suit, my CoolAir mask, or my meter. I don't need them. Either they'll think I've committed suicide, or they will finally know what I really am. Either way, my life as I know it is over, but none of that matters because this life isn't worth living without the ones I love in it. The ones who give me purpose. Stella, Ileana, Jay, Haley, and Annabel bear. They are a part of me, and they live in my heart, and I know that, somehow, they are real. This man in the black cloak is trying to erase them, trying to erase my happiness.

# CHAPTER 21

The wind fiercely blows, momentarily knocking me off balance. Toxic green slush glows under my feet and illuminates the night. I scan the streets and notice they are eerily vacant. All that can be heard is the howling wind and the buzz of the Raxon in search of their next meal.

I hear a bang on the glass. I turn and meet Rosario's eyes, mere inches from mine. His breath fogs the window, glaring at me with a sinister smile spread wide across his face. Determined to destroy me, for he has waited patiently for his moment since the very day we met. His Guardsman rush to zip on their hoods and cock their Glocks, and I realize that whether he believes I will die from Raxon or not, he has clearly given the order to bring me to him, dead or alive.

I take off running, in a race for my life. Trials and tribulations lie ahead, although I realize my psyche is my real enemy. Perhaps it always has been. I huff and puff, sprinting down the street and am suddenly slowed by a weight in my chest. I have never dared to walk the streets during a storm without proper protection, and this is the first time I have truly felt what it is to be transnuclear. I watched the Raxon enter me as weightless, black sludge but in my lungs, they feel like concrete, filling up the empty space. I continue to run through the discomfort because if I stop, I'll surely die. They latch onto to my lungs and vibrate my core with their hum. I am their transporter. A taxi to their final destination.

I look behind me and see I have a healthy lead, so I stop and let out a hacking cough, trying to clear enough space in my lungs to continue. A small cloud releases, but it still feels like bricks are stacked against my ribs. The lack of a bio-suit enables me to run faster, but the Raxon burn in my lungs, and I can feel them crawl and cling to the base of my esophagus like a cluster of spiders. Though they can't harm me, I feel like I'm a participant in their carnage, and I refuse to play a part in genocide.

I hear the guard's hazmat suits rubbing together as they run. They are close. I have to move! I pick up my pace and scan for an escape route. There is nowhere to go, and I don't know how much longer I can keep up this pace.

I hear a car zipping up behind me. Time is up. I look back over my shoulder and see an old yellow station wagon fly by the Guardsmen and pull up alongside me.

"Get in!" a voice yells from the driver's seat.

I look to my right and see someone in a hazmat suit driving the car and signaling for me to get into the back seat. The rear window lowers, and I squint to see who it is.

"Dylan! Get in!" the voice cries out again.

As we pass the streetlamp, it shines into the car and illuminates Stella's face behind the shield.

In one fell swoop, I duck my head and dive into the back seat. I hit the window mid-abdomen and feel my solar plexus tighten and my esophagus burn as the Raxon are drawn closer to my mouth. A small cloud is ejected, screaming like a swarm of mosquitos in my ear, and I reach to grab a hold of the seatbelt, slithering my way in when, out of nowhere, a hand grabs a hold of my ankle.

A Guardsman grits his teeth and holds on tight and Stella instinctively accelerates, but in doing so, his weight releases onto my legs, and as his feet drag on the concrete, gravity pulls me slowly back out of the window. I grab a hold of Stella's head rest, hugging it tightly.

"Go! Go! Go!" I holler, hoping he won't be able to hold on much longer.

She punches the gas, though he tightens his grip, grappling my legs and using me as a ladder. Within seconds, he grabs hold of the door and pops his head and shoulders through.

"Close the window!" I shout.

"I tried! It's too much weight! It won't budge," Stella shouts, nearly hyperventilating while continuing to slam her finger on the window's trigger.

I twist and wiggle my way onto my back. My rear falls to the seat, and I am able to shake one of my legs free, but in doing so, he is able to inch a little further inside. I take my free leg, wind it back, and his expression shifts from determined to terror.

"No! No! Please," he begs, but I kick and stomp his face shield until I see that it has broken open at the seam, exposing his face. He draws in a deep breath, holding it like an Olympic swimmer, but his panic works against him and, already, only mere seconds later, he has become red in the face. We both know his time is running out, but he, still determined, reaches out to grab a hold of my throat.

Like a smoker trying to clear his lungs, I push deep within and expel a cloud of Raxon like dragon's breath. He releases his grip, covers his face shield, trying to seal the gaps, but it's useless. A stream of the demonic plague flutter, entering him through his nose and attacks his virgin tissue.

A muffled scream followed by a creaking, eerie groan as they devour him. Reaching for his throat, he begins to claw at his chest. With a final stroke, I place my foot on his forehead and push him out of the window and watch him tumble down the street, gripping his throat and gyrating.

I see a spark.

A bullet ricochets off the trunk. Sparks fly, and I duck my head, throwing myself into the back seat. Stella pushes the pedal to the floor, and the car accelerates with a hiccup, pulling us quickly out of reach.

"I thought I told you to leave," I say.

"Uh, you're welcome? Besides, I couldn't just leave you," she says, concentrating on the road, hands gripping the wheel tightly at ten and two. "I would've been here earlier, but I wanted to make sure Darby bought our story."

So, it *was* a story. Although I knew in my heart that it was, I still can't help feeling disappointed.

"Got lucky, too! Man, that Darby sure likes to talk. Didn't think I'd make it, but when I pulled up in front of the hospital…it was like God willed it. There you were, running down the damn street!"

"Why?" I ask.

"Why what?"

I meet her eyes in the rearview mirror. "Don't get me wrong. I'm eternally grateful…again, but why are you risking your life for me?"

I watch her eyes harden through the mirror, and we enter the ghetto in silence. She loops through the dirt roads, climbing and weaving in and out of the districts. She passes people on the street and, collectively, they put their hands together in prayer and bow. Many blow kisses, and Stella nods and waves as a princess would in her carriage. They appear to worship her in some way, and I can't help but think shit just keeps getting stranger and stranger.

We climb her steep driveway, and I see a large cavernous hole dug into the ground, with branches surrounding it.

"Get out and wait for me here," she says.

I watch from the side of her porch as she navigates the car down into the manmade tunnel. She gets out, covers it with the large branches scattered about, and both the car and the tunnel disappear under what now looks like fallen debris.

She escorts me into the mudroom and asks me to remove my clothing. Thoroughly contaminated, soaked from head to toe, my clothes and even my skin are tainted with a greenish hue. I remove them one by one and toss the filth onto the porch and spray myself down with the hose.

I awkwardly enter the house, exposing myself with as much confidence as I can muster, fidgeting and trying to figure out what to do with my hands. Stella creeps out of her bedroom with a dry set of clothes, and I rest my fists foolishly on my hips as if I were Superman. She quickly averts her eyes, but I catch her sneak a quick peek, and her cheeks flush instantly, compelling her to look away. I reach out and take the clothing and casually dress slowly, yearning for her to look again.

"Where'd you get the duds? Old boyfriend?" I laugh, admiring and showcasing the floral printed Hawaiian shirt.

She cautiously turns to face me, eyes squinting, and she verifies I'm decent before opening them fully. My trousers are safely in place, and I work to button the shirt.

"Well, it's all I had." She laughs. "It's the best I could do."

"I think I'd prefer to be naked," I say with a chuckle.

She returns my quip with a wink. "Suit yourself." Instantaneously, her face flushes again.

Overridden with pubescent excitement, my body uncontrollably responds. I become stiff and immediately take a seat at the dining table to hide the blooming tent in my pants. Beet red and suddenly incredibly hot, beads of sweat accumulate at my hairline.

"Uh, where did you get these, anyway? You don't see many people wearing brown baggy trousers, Hawaiian shirts, and suspenders anymore? I mean, green suspenders? Ouch!"

"They belonged to the man who brought me here," she says solemnly.

Suddenly struck by jealousy, I shrug. "Oh, I see."

"No, it wasn't like that," she says. "The people asked them to shelter me."

"What people?" I say.

"Those people," she says, pointing down the hill.

"Yeah, what was that all about, anyway?"

"What?" she asks.

"The people, they bowed to you, blew you kisses, held their hands in prayer. What are you, like the leader of the transnukes? Should I be kneeling?"

She turns her back to me and walks over to the counter, grabs a bottle of red wine, along with two pieces of crystal stemware, and decants a healthy pour into each.

"I was brought here… No, I was banished here by our government for helping people, people like you."

"There are more then? Like me?" I say.

"A few...only the ones I knew from there."

"There?"

She closes her eyes and shakes her head violently as if her mind were an Etch a Sketch and the memory would be erased.

"The people here, they've kind of declared me a saint of sorts."

"A saint?" I ask raising my brow.

"When the government left me here, an older couple took me in. This was their home. I told them my story, and the news spread down the hill. The people vowed to protect me, and they honor me for making sacrifices to save their people, but trust me, I'm no saint!"

I grab her hand and caress it. "You are."

"No, Dylan, I'm not! I am ashamed!"

She pulls her hand away, walks towards the hearth, and sets logs in place to prepare a fire.

"How could you be ashamed?" I ask.

She faces me, and I see a single, glistening tear run down her cheek. "You'll think I'm crazy," she says.

"Darling, you could never be crazier than me," I reply softly.

She takes in a deep breath and sighs. "I didn't help them because... I wasn't trying to be a savior. I wasn't fighting a grand injustice, Dylan. I saved them... I saved them because..."

"Stella, it's alright. What is it?"

"I saved them because I knew them. I knew you from my dreams. I know it's fucking insane, but I see you in my dreams all the time. I see them all in my dreams. In another world, a beautiful world where...where the sun still shines and fruit still grows on trees and, and, and...we are in love. We have children, Dylan. A family!"

I gawk at her in disbelief. My jaw hangs open, and my eyes are pinned wide. I'm speechless. It's as if she read my mind. Like she is playing a trick on me, and I'm waiting for her to yell gotcha!

"See! Before you say anything, I know how fucking insane it is. Oh, I'm well fucking aware," she says.

"Oh, no, no, you aren't crazy at all!"

"Dylan, please don't patronize me!"

"No, really! Well, yes, it's fucking out of this world insane..."

"Gee thanks, that's more like it," she says.

"No, Stella." I place my hand on her shoulder. "Since that day, the day you saved my life...I have had the same dreams about you and Ileana, Jay, Haley, and..."

"Annabel!" she screams. A smile instantly spreads across her face, and a gleam of hope overshadows her tear-filled eyes.

"Yes, Annabel!" I say, matching her enthusiasm.

We stare into each other's eyes, and my heart pounds. I'm incredibly excited, though, like a schoolboy, I'm terrified of making the wrong move. I summon the courage and lean in and kiss her. Our lips meet, soft and supple, and with every moment, the intensity builds. We connect, and our energy intertwines. A charge of electricity jolts through my body, and our lips magnetize, and no matter how hard we try, the bond cannot be severed. Static electricity sends our hair northward like a compass.

Images dart in front of my eyes just as they did when I blacked out. However, with this newfound revelation, I pay closer attention. I no longer view them as bouts of crazy but rather as one would a series of projected home videos.

Her eyes rapidly dash hastily in every direction and, clearly, she sees what I see. Lives unfolding before us from a different world. A panoramic picture show guiding us on a journey through a parallel life, lived beyond our years, and with each image, the events that unfold become more and more foreign, though strangely familiar all the same.

A fierce shock as our lips disconnect. I cover my mouth and rub my lip from the burning pain. I look up to her but quickly realize she is crying. I reach out to wipe away her tears, but she smacks my hand away.

"How could you?" she says.

"What? I don't know. I..."

Confused, I step back and examine her when, suddenly, there is a loud knock at the door. Silence pries us from our moment, and we freeze in place. My heart pounds and adrenaline surges.

"Were we followed?" I whisper.

Stella shrugs her shoulders and wipes away her tears on her sleeve and moves casually towards the door.

"Wait!" I say in a loud whisper. I creep over to the window on my hands and knees and peek through the corner of her poorly homemade, red curtains.

"It's Darby," I say.

"What should I do?" Stella mouths.

I take a moment to think it over when another loud bang at the door is followed by, "I know you're in there! I see the fire flickering in the window, and your damn clothes are on the porch! Answer the door!"

"He sounds upset," Stella says.

"What choice do we have? Go ahead and open it," I say.

"Are you sure?" she says in a rush.

I shrug my shoulders and hesitantly nod.

The door creeks open, followed by the unmistakable *click*, the hammer from Darby's revolver being cocked. It echoes throughout the cabin and bounces from ear to ear. Stella backs up, her arms raised in surrender.

"Darby, what in the hell are you doing," I snap.

Still wearing his hazmat suit and dripping toxic sludge all over the floor, he quickly turns the gun on me. I never thought I'd see a scenario that would have me staring down the barrel of my best friend's gun.

"You two, over there!" He flips the gun, motioning us over to the couch.

"Darby, listen to me…"

"No more lies, Dylan!"

"Listen, Darby, I can explain—"

"Save it, Dylan! Ms. Mousakis, you think you have everyone fooled, don't you?" He turns the gun on her. "Our DNA results came back on your stuffed bear, and what do you know, it's a match to our Jane Doe."

My focus promptly shifts to Stella. "She was here?"

Stella breaks down and howls, crying reminiscently of a mother who truly has lost a child. She tries to speak, but her words are indiscernible, wailing gibberish.

Darby slings his revolver back to me. "And you, you're hardly innocent here. You've left me no choice but to bring you both in."

"Darby, if you just give me a minute to explain. You have it all wrong."

He maintains his gun pointed at me in his right hand, reaches his left hand awkwardly across his body, and fishes out a folded-up piece of paper from his right jeans pocket. He shakes it, unfolding it from its creases, and shows me the missing forensic sketch. It is unmistakably our Ileana.

"Remember this?" Darby says.

Fighting the urge to cry, I bite down on my lip and fixate on the sketch of her beautiful, innocent face. She is very much alive on that piece of paper.

"This is the first I'm seeing it! Darby, I know it's gonna sound crazy, but—"

"First? You're first seeing it now? Really? I found it in your desk, Dylan! You've been sabotaging this case from the beginning, and you've been taking advantage of my love for you to do it!"

"What? No, Darby, I've never seen that before," I say.

He shakes his head in disgust and taps the gun against his head. "You know, I didn't want to admit it to myself, but you're the only other one with a key to my desk drawer. I keep it locked at all times. You're the only one, Dylan! No one else could have taken it! It broke my heart to see it in your desk, but if I'm being honest, I knew it was there long before I ever looked."

Still weeping into her hands but trying to regain her composure, Stella rips the sketch out of Darby's hands, and he wildly points his gun at her. I surge my body in front of Stella to shield her, fearful he may react volatilely in the midst of his grief.

"No, Darby! Don't!" I shout.

Stella studies the sketch, and her face involuntarily scrunches up. "She was here! I tried to save her, but they saw. They took us, tattooed her, and banished us to…to…this place. We made the best of it. We made a life together. She was so sweet. It was so natural to be…her mother. I know now she was mine, not in this world but another. I loved her."

Darby scowls at her. "Another world? What in the fuck is that supposed to mean?"

Darby's bubble bursts. He feels hurt and betrayed by his best friend, and it likely drives the animus. I was all the family he had left in the world, and now he questions my authenticity. His life has been permeated with pain, and I am inadvertently responsible for more. I understand his suspicion. I certainly look guilty, but I'm innocent, and I need him to believe me.

Darby maintains his gun on us, and his hands tremble. I wrap my arms around Stella, prepared to surrender myself to him when, unexpectedly, we hear rustling leaves and a sinister laugh followed quickly by the sound of metal striking metal. Voices overlap voices until it is clear that a mob of people have gathered in the front of the cabin.

Darby, keeping his gun pointed at us, sidesteps over to the window to have a look at what is going on outside. The thought of charging, overpowering, and disarming him had entered my mind, but even if that were possible, Darby is not my enemy. He is my friend, my brother, and my partner, and despite his incertitude, he is a good man and a good friend.

I cringe when I hear glass shattering and the high-pitched screech of metal being scraped.

"What in the fuck?" he hollers. "They're hitting my car with fucking bats. These fucking animals!"

"Darby, take us in," I say, placing my hands out in front of me. Stella sourly crosses her arms across her chest, but I return her haste with a reassuring nod.

"I only have one set of cuffs," Darby says.

I grab Stella's hand and lift our hands up. "Then cuff us together."

"And leave your hands free?" Darby scoffs.

"You have my word, Darby, and in time, you will see we're innocent. Besides, what choice do you have? If you don't trust me, they will eat you alive."

Darby realizes he doesn't have a choice and proceeds to cuff my right wrist with her left and guides us to the door.

"Point the gun to her head."

"Excuse me?" Stella barks.

"Darbs, they're here to protect her. She's like saint to them. They won't risk harming her. Just keep your safety on, for Christ sake. We can't afford to have an accident." I look to Stella. "Trust me. Darby is the most honorable man I know. He won't hurt you."

The storm has subsided, and the meter strapped to Darby's hip flashes yellow. I help Stella strap on her CoolAir mask and drape her coat around her shoulders like a shawl.

"Where's your mask?" Darby asks me.

"I don't need one," I say. "I—"

"What do you mean you don't need one?"

I take in a deep breath and release a long sigh. "Darby, I'm transnuclear. I'm sorry I didn't tell you sooner, but please understand..."

He shoots me a woeful look. "Since when?" He shakes his head in disgust. "Wow, you think you know someone..."

We reach the outer door, and I see hordes of people, men, women, and even children gather on the front lawn, surrounding Darby's car. They're rabid and hungry to punish. This isn't only about Stella. Darby is a representative of their exile. Today, he will stand trial, held solely responsible for their pain, suffering, and expulsion from society. Perhaps this wasn't the grand plan I thought it was. Darby may be in real danger. Outside of an old movie, I've never seen people hold bats and pitchforks nearly foaming at the mouth quite like this.

Starved for justice, judge and jury they stand, and Darby is guilty upon sight. His CoolAir mask and badge have sealed his fate. His unguided squad car ignited them to rally their posse, and they crave blood.

"Stella, please? Calm them down. Let them know you are alright, and that Darby isn't their enemy."

Stella turns her nose up and scowls at me, grumbling, "Put the gun to her head you say? You'd rot in jail to save your friend?"

I look into her eyes and plead, "Yes, Stella. Unequivocally, yes! Please, trust me?"

She rolls her eyes, irritated, and though reluctant, she yells out to her people, "Listen, I know you want to help me, but I'm not in any danger. These men are not our enemy! Now, please, go home. I will return later this evening."

"Then why does he have a gun to your head?" a woman yells from the crowd.

"Yeah!" another hollers in agreement.

"Only for his protection," Stella explains.

The crowd looks hesitant, still intent on making Darby pay for non-transnuclears' crimes on humanity. His CoolAir mask is symbolic of their segregation, pain, suffering, and torturous living conditions.

The crowd encircles and closes in around us. We are mere steps away from Darby's car door, but the driver's side window has been shattered, and glass litters the driver's seat. A plethora of dents blanket the hood, the result of repeated hammering with numerous bats and metal pipes. It is nearly unrecognizable.

Darby looks down and realizes all his tires have been slashed, deeming the car un-drivable, and lets out a loud, bellowing, "Fuck!"

We start to panic, and I'm clear out of ideas. I think, *This is it. This is how it ends.* Whether I'm a target or not, I will fight with Darby to the death, his prisoner or not.

The crowd is now within striking distance, and hope is all but lost until Stella yells, "Have I not given my life for your people? Have I not loved and sacrificed everything? My comfort, my food, my family, my livelihood? If you have ever loved me, appreciated me, trusted me, trust in me now! Repay my kindness and let these people go! This man. This man is the love of my life, and he…he is Darby. He is his brother! Now, go home! He is not our enemy!"

The people stop in their tracks, and silence transcends the mob. The moment of our deliberation is upon us, and every second of stillness is more harrowing than the last. Our fate rests in the love and trust in their Saint. But is their love for her stronger than their hate for their oppressors?

"We owe this to Stella!" a man yells from the back.

"Let them pass," another says in the middle of the pack.

One by one, grumbling and grunting, they clear a path, and Darby's car, however un-drivable, has been relinquished to us.

"Let's take my car," Stella says.

"Good idea," I concur.

Darby releases a breath of relief and holsters his revolver.

"I drive," he commands and motions his hand out to permit Stella to lead the way. Stella drags me behind her, walking through the crowd, thanking them, and returns their bows graciously.

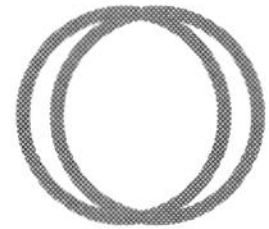

# CHAPTER 22

We pull away from the ghetto with a roar of the engine. I lean back into the seat, look over to Stella, and mouth, 'Thank you.' I view Darby in the rearview mirror, and although strong and silent, he appears to have softened. Much of the tension is no longer evident on his face, nearly in a catatonic trance.

A loud *beep*, followed by the muffled voice of Sal Gentile, one of my youngest officers, blares over Darby's police radio, "*Pshhhhht*...we have a one-eight-seven. Young girl, and guess what, folks...*pshhhht*, no face. *Pshhhhht*...at the State park, 551 Briar Rd. Right by Boilers Point, *Pshhhht*...over.

Darby proceeds to drive, silent and motionless, neither removing his hands from the wheel nor his eyes from the road. Not even a blink.

"Uh, you going to answer that, Darbs?" I ask.

He remains silent and still.

"Darby?" I call out again a little louder. "Darby?" I raise my voice even louder, but still, he only responds by nonchalantly lighting a cigarette. I've never allowed him to smoke in the car, and he knows I loathe the smell.

"Darby, can I ask you something?" I say, becoming agitated.

Darby turns and blows smoke directly into my face, adding insult to injury. I tilt my head back and struggle to remain calm.

"Darby! If there is another victim, how could I be the killer? When would I have had the time to kill anyone?"

I think I can see the wheels turn, but even still, he says nothing.

"Darby, you know me, and you, of all people, know I'm incapable of these crimes. You have to believe me! But, besides, it would be physically, humanly impossible for me to have killed this girl, remove her face, and dump her body. When? How? The state park is right around the corner. Go see for yourself! Stop this nonsense! Let's go!"

I slump back into the seat with a *thump* and take Stella's hand back with me. I look over at her, frustrated and growing weary. She returns my look with one of her own. One that cries, 'I told you so!'

I lean back and settle into my fate and consider maybe Stella was right, Darby is too far gone. He's too convinced of my guilt. Our years of partnership, of brotherhood, have been flushed away in a matter of days.

Without warning, Darby slams on the brakes, sending Stella and I crashing into the seats in front of us. The tires skid, and the car fishtails back and forth, bringing us to a screeching halt. He closes his eyes, still and reticent, and I study him through the rearview mirror, trying to predict his next move. He reaches for his police radio and pauses as he presses it to his lips, and we sit and listen to the *tick, tick, tick* of the hot engine, anxiously waiting.

"*Pshhhht*...ten-four, I'm about two minutes out, Sal...*pshhht*...over."

"*Pshhht*...ten-four, Darbs," Sal says.

Darby cuts the wheel, slams on the gas and the G-force pushes us back into the seat. The car whirls around, and Stella slides across the seat into me and wraps her free arm tightly around my waist. The wheels chirp, and the engine races to our new destination; the state park.

We enter the parks winding roads, and I take in the scenery that was once a beautiful lush park, loaded with flowers, green grass, and vibrant trees, and is now dark and desert-like. Flowers no longer exist in quarantine, trees are leaf-less and dead, and grass is a fond memory of a world that once had color and life.

Off in the distance, but rapidly approaching, I see a picnic area with four steel tables, and all but one is rusted and forgotten. The lone dressed table is decorated with a red and green tablecloth and it appears to have items scattered about. In the middle of the four tables, I see a white lump on the ground, but as we close in on the scene, I realize the lump is not a lump at all, it is our victim.

I point. "There!"

"I see it," Darby says.

Not surprisingly, we are the first to arrive on the scene. We were only three or four blocks from the park entrance when Darby received the call. The state park is located only a few miles outside of the ghetto, bordering the outer edge of the city limits on one side and the Trans Ghetto on the other. As a result, it is largely recognized as neutral territory and is how a lot of the drugs cross over from the ghetto.

I am certain Rosario will show, and when he does, he will unquestionably arrest me on sight. A rather unfortunate, although likely, conclusion to our journey. I have solid alibi this time, but I can't imagine he will believe anyone in this vehicle. I can only hope that, in the little time we have, I can find some undeniable evidence that clears my name.

We walk over to the scene, and my attention is drawn to the picnic bench, decked out with a tablecloth and a fancy medieval candelabra in the center. A feast, relatively untouched, is set out upon it, loaded with artisanal bread, a partially carved roasted turkey, stuffing, cranberry sauce, and a green bean casserole, just like the one my mother used to make. A Thanksgiving feast laid out on a table set for two. Real silverware, folded embroidered napkins and gold-rimmed Lennox china without any remnants on them. Was the victim killed here? I note there isn't any blood or any evidence of a struggle, but if she wasn't killed here, then who was the meal for?

"There is a smudge on that plate. We have to dust it," I say.

We walk over to the body and immediately note the victim lies in the identical position as Ileana, and it appears the same level of meticulous care was taken. She is gowned in white, and atop her head lies a golden tiara.

I look over at Stella. Her hand covers her mouth, and her eyes well up with tears. I feel her body stiffen, and she lets out a quick bark of laughter under her breath.

In shock, she asks, "Is this what happened to our Ileana?"

"I'm afraid so," I say, running my hand through her wavy hair.

She snorts and whimpers, trying to refrain from crying, but the tears uncontrollably stream down her face in a fury. I turn her to face me, pull her in, and hug her with my free arm.

"We can mourn later. We have work to do, and we don't have much time," I say.

I bend down, lift the victim's hand, and inspect under her fingernails for blood or foreign tissue. When a woman is killed, it is always the first place I search for DNA because, oftentimes, they scratch their attacker in self-defense.

"Nothing here. Fingernails are clean, as with Ileana." I clear my throat. "As with our Jane Doe, it appears she was given a manicure, so it's entirely possible he took great care to remove any evidence. We should see if we can recover anything, anyway."

Darby proceeds to walk around the body and removes the note pad from his pocket and details his observations.

"Shit!" Darby says. "My camera is in my car."

"Radio it in. One of the boys can bring one," I say.

I give Stella a gentle tug and move to approach the victim's head. I brace myself and try to find strength. I need to remain strong for Stella.

"This corpse is warm and stiff," I say, looking up at Darby. "Deceased anywhere from three to five hours, I'd guess."

Darby glances over at me and nods. Relief spreads across his face, and a smile creeps its way into the corner of his lips. He recognizes the timeline would make it impossible for me to be the killer. After all, the science doesn't lie, and I was in a coma-like state in the hospital, for God's sake. I suddenly feel reinvigorated. I feel immense relief. I sit down on the ground and take a moment to enjoy the solace, but as they say, all good things must come to an end.

Darby lifts and holds her head high, and all I can do is stare. A seesaw of emotion and a flash of our victim's face strikes me like a bolt of lightning, leaving me breathless. I hear a man's voice far in the corner of my mind say, "I'm sorry, sir, we did everything we could for her." Oh, no, not my Haley...

I look to Stella, eyes wide, gulping back tears. It isn't clear to either of us how we are connected and how all this could be happening, but we are, and it is. In some unexplained way, we are a family. We take some comfort knowing we are in this together, but it doesn't make it any less preposterous.

In some way, we are all connected, and this other world exists in lieu of elucidation. Like me, I imagine Stella must be questioning her reality. Which of these worlds is real, and how can we separate fact from fiction?

"You know her...don't you?" Darby asks. He looks timidly at me, and I suppose he is fearful of my reply, but I suspect he already knows the answer.

Doing my best to hold it together, I glance up at him, but all I manage to do is shrug my shoulders and shake my head as if to say, I don't know how, but yes, I do. He looks back at me, closes his eyes, and sighs.

"We have to tell him," I say to Stella.

"What?" she says. "He'll never believe us! Shit, we can hardly make any sense of it ourselves!"

Darby looks at us sharply, and his eyes rapidly dart back and forth, eagerly waiting for one of us to fess up.

"Tell me!" he demands. "No more secrets, Dylan!"

Our story hovers at about a two on the plausibility scale, and I presume he will finally throw in the towel and have us committed, but Darby's right, no more lies. He deserves the truth, regardless of the outcome.

"Darby," I begin hesitantly. "I...we...we know this is going to sound crazy, but please, just hear us out. Keep an open mind."

But just as I'm about to unravel our marvelous tale of science fiction, love and tragedy like the one before our eyes, I see a fleet of car lights approaching and picking up speed.

"Shit! It's Rosario!" I say, slamming my fist to the ground.

"Well, you knew he'd show," Darby says, extending me his hand. "Come on, get up."

"I know, but I guess I thought I'd have more time. Anyway, it was worth it. At least you can see we're innocent," I say.

"Well, I guess that depends on what you were about to tell me," he says.

Wrists bound, Stella and I prepare to be taken into Rosario's custody.

All of a sudden, Darby's Police radio blares at his hip, "*Pssssht*...please be advised that Captain Rosario has elevated Captain Grady to shoot on sight. Repeat...*pssssht*, shoot on sight. Grady is said to be armed and dangerous. *Psssht*...May God be with him. *Psssht*...over.

"What the fuck?" Darby says perplexed. He picks up his radio. "*Psssht*... Captain Grady is in my custody and is not armed. Repeat...*psssht*...Grady is in custody and is not armed! *Psssht*...over!"

Their vehicles hop the curb and drive up onto the grass to the tree line about fifty yards away. I see Rosario's large frame exit the first vehicle, followed by six Guardsmen with their weapons already drawn. Rosario hollers, "Go, go, go, go, go!" And one by one, in military combat formation, they race towards us.

"They're coming in strong Boss!" Darby says with his hand to his holster.

"Let's raise our arms to show him that we are cuffed," I say.

I whip our arms up in surrender when, without warning, one of his men opens fire. I hear a bullet whiz by my ear and, in a panic, I dive to the ground. Stella's impulses follow suit. However, she dove in the opposite direction. Our wrists snap, and our body's pause, suspended in midair, and we flop to the ground, hard and unforgiving. Stella gasps for air. She may have knocked the wind out of herself. I look over to her and hear another shot, and it lands a mere foot in front of my head, kicking up dirt into my face.

"What the fuck!" I yell.

"Stand down! I repeat, stand down!" Darby orders.

"We are unarmed! We surrender!" I scream as loudly as I can, but that doesn't stop the shots from being fired. Bullets fly, and I impulsively roll on top of Stella to protect her.

Another shot, and then another.

Rosario has given the order to shoot to kill, and we are sitting ducks. We have to run. We must run for the trees and never stop. I hop to my feet, grab Stella, and fling her over my shoulder. About to make a run for it, I see Darby on the ground, grasping violently for his throat. He's been hit! His throat spurts blood and it uncontrollably seeps through his fingers, pooling at his chest. A fatal shot.

I drop to my knees, release Stella to the ground, and we scurry to Darby's side.

"No, no, no, no, no!" I cry out.

The firing ceases, and the Guard slow to a walk but maintain their pistols pointed in our direction. I lift and hurl one of the picnic tables onto its side to shield us from their fire, but as expected, my movement instigates another cluster of shots. Stella and I duck behind the cascade of bullets that ricochet off the table.

I need to pull Darby to safety. Attempting to keep Stella shielded, I scamper on my knees, reach my free arm out, and grab a hold of Darby's suit behind the neck and pull his large frame with all my might.

A shot buzzes past my ear, and I duck, but only seconds later, their next bullet is fired, and it finds its target, entering my deltoid and knocking me onto my back. I squirm and wiggle, release my grip, and curl onto my side.

"Ahhhh, fucking shit!" I cry out and instinctively reach for my burning shoulder.

"Yeah! Got 'em!" I hear one of them celebrate.

"Are you OK?" Stella shrieks in terror.

*It's only pain,* I tell myself. I need to make another attempt to pull Darby to cover. I take a deep breath and stretch my hand out, grab a hold of his suit, and with a scream that could undoubtedly be heard echoing throughout the park, I heave and launch his torso to safety. More shots rain onto the table, and Stella and I duck and throw our hands over our heads.

Darby releases his hand from his throat and reaches out, unplugging the drain. Blood gushes as he struggles to speak. He places his free hand into mine, and I feel something hard and cold touch the inside of my palm. His eyes strain to remain open as he holds on a moment longer. My heart beats heavily, the way a heart aches when it knows it's lost something dear to it. Someone that fills your every day with a little more joy just knowing they are a part of it. This is our last moment together.

"It's OK, Darbs, go…be with them."

I see a smile begin to arch, but before he goes, he wheezes, "Run…"

He lets out a final gurgling breath, and my partner, my brother, is gone. I want to sit and mourn, but if we don't run now, we both will die. Rosario's men are gaining ground and only seconds away from close range. I grab Darby's revolver from its holster and hold it to my chest and close my eyes tightly.

"We have to run for the trees."

"No! We'll never make it!" Stella screams.

"We have no choice! We'll die here. Now, let's go! We need to zigzag! Don't run straight," I shout. "Follow my lead!"

I lift Darby's gun and fire over the table at the guard, and when I see them duck and dive for cover, we sprint for the tree line. One foot in front of the other, unified in mind and body, we glide in harmony, moving as if we were one. Our feet strike the dirt in stride. I zig, she zigs, I zag, she zigs. Bullets fly by us but, so far, we've been able to evade them.

My arm pulsates. The pain is agonizing, although the adrenaline has kicked in like a shot of morphine, so I am able to bear it. We approach the tree line, and I hear bullets hit the trees, one after another with deep and penetrating *thuds*. Our heads bounce as the branches shatter, and they rain down on us like confetti. We're going to make it! We pick up a little more speed and continue our slalom through the trees, and then, out of nowhere, I hear a deafening shriek.

Stella cries out, "Ahhhhhhhhh!"

We both know that if we stop now, we're as good as dead, so we continue to run, and she continues to keep pace, so I think, perhaps, it isn't anything serious. Once we've gained some distance, I stop and push her against a large tree to inspect her. I frantically pat her down, scanning every inch of her body. Blood? Where's the blood? No blood! Thank God, she's OK! I release a deep relieving sigh but when I look up, I see her, whining and afraid, and my soul shutters when I see that her mask has been hit, shattered at the beak.

I feel the Raxon stir in my lungs and, uncontrollably, they force my mouth open, flutter out, and funnel like a tornado between us. I desperately suck in air, trying to draw them back in. However, as soon as they enter my mouth, they immediately shoot back out of my nasal passages. In a stream, they enter her and attack her virgin tissue, and I watch, helpless, as she gurgles, coughs, and chokes. Her terrified eyes meet mine, and I can't help but cringe, listening to her heave and wheeze.

I was finally able to touch her, to hold her, to kiss and love her with these hands, these lips and in this life, and now, I must sit here and watch her die? My body releases, fists unclench, and I see a shiny set of keys drop to the ground. Within all the chaos, I had forgotten that, in Darby's final moment, he had given me something, and what he had given me was my freedom. I quickly remove the cuffs from both of our wrists and toss them aside.

Stella panics, violently grabs for her throat, and falls to her knees. She tears at her chest and bucks against the tree. I grab her, pull her in, and embrace her, kiss her head, and gently ease her onto her back. Her breathing slows, and she wheezes as she meets my helpless gawp.

"Shhhh, shhhh, shhhh," I say, trying to calm her.

"Go! Just go! I'm dead, anyway!" she whimpers.

Out of nowhere, as if they were transported to our position, we hear cracking leaves and branches, and we know that, although we are hidden, they are close. We can no longer sit here. We have to move.

"Go, Dylan!"

"No! I won't leave you!" I say and pound my fist into the tree beside me.

I take her hand and pull her to her feet, bend down, and sling her over my shoulders.

"If we die, we die together!"

I peer behind the tree and see two lone soldiers tracking us, but they are a good distance off and heading in the wrong direction. I move cautiously through the trees, carefully considering where to place each foot to minimize drawing attention to our position.

I always imagined that, in any scenario, I would fight to the death, but now? Now, I'm not so sure. The man in the black cloak has taken everything and everyone who matters from me. I wonder, will they still be there…in my dreams? If they die in this world, are they still able to exist in the other?

"Dylan, I can't. Just leave me," Stella says in my ear, no louder than a whisper.

I slow to a stop and look for a place to lay her down safely. I see a large stump that abuts a shallow ditch and remove my coat and lay her down gently upon it.

"Then…I'm ready to surrender, too," I say.

"No! Go Dylan, run, God damn you!"

I sit next to her and let my body crash back into the stump, close my eyes, but then, suddenly, her fist lands in the middle of my chest. My eyes pop open, and she looks at me, crying and furious.

"Stop pitying yourself! Just go," she says.

I lean in and embrace her, resting my chin on her shoulder. I close my eyes and think how nice it would be to stay here forever. I wipe my tears on her coat and try to refrain from having a total meltdown.

"Dylan, I would die a thousand times over if it meant it would keep you alive. Please, don't let my death be for nothing."

My eyes open, and as if appearing out of thin air, I see him. He stands alone, in a clearing that appears as if it were prepared for him for this very moment. The branches of two trees meet and intertwine, arched above him like an altar. He stands confident, robed in black from head to toe, challenging me with his arms crossed, legs mounted, and firmly shoulder-width apart. My core is set ablaze, teeth grind together, and panting like a rabid dog. I don't care if I die, but please, God, give me the satisfaction of killing him first.

"I'll be back. Don't…just don't… Please, just hold on for me?"

She nods, and I kiss her. As I pull away, it occurs to me that our second kiss could also, very well be, our last.

"I love you," I say.

Stella nods, but the pain is too great for her to respond.

I shift my feet to face him, and as if he were waiting for me, he remains immovable, taunting me. I hear him laugh, and it tickles my ears as if it were the whispering wind. My adrenal glands fire like ballistic missiles, pumping blood to my heart in tremendous powerful bursts, and with the ferocity of ten men, all six hundred and fifty of my muscles flex simultaneously, and I charge, swatting away branches that enter my path. I rapidly close the gap between us, but he remains unchanged, unaffected, and not in the least intimidated.

I close within six feet, lower my shoulder and prepare for contact. I lunge with my arms out, ready to tackle him to the ground, but I come up empty, falling to the sludge and skidding to a stop, laid out on my stomach. I pop back to my feet prepared for a fight, but like a ghost, he vanished into the dimly lit woods.

I spin around, scanning the trees. Got 'em! Two o'clock, thirty yards away. He remains in the same cocky stance as if he were transported there. My feet react before my brain can even tell them to go, and I run at an inhuman pace, rabid and gasping for breath. I push harder to move even faster and close my eyes to conjure the necessary energy. It was just for a second, but when I reopen them, he's gone again. How could this be?

"What the fuck!" I holler.

I scan all around me again, but he's nowhere and has seemingly vanished into thin air. I fall to my knees, clamp my hands to my head, and think I must be fucking insane. Is he really just a figment of my fucked-up imagination? Enough of this cat and mouse bullshit! I stand and retrace my steps back to Stella when, out of nowhere, a voice, whispers into my ear, tickling my eardrums as if he were standing right next to me.

"You're welcome," he says.

I shiver as his breath tickles the cilia within my ear, and I grit my teeth when I see him standing beside a large tree that differs from all the others. It blooms, a wonderful lustrous green, and a beam of sunlight is released and shines upon him like a spotlight. With every ounce of energy, I fire myself at him like a bullet, lift Darby's revolver, and with two bullets remaining, I fire my first shot, hitting my intended target. However, extraordinarily, he parts down the center of his body like a curtain, enveloping, and then disappearing around the massive trunk.

I reach the tree, searching behind and around it, but once again, I come up empty. Have I imagined this? Is the man in black a figment of my imagination? Surely, he can't just vanish into thin air. I hear a laugh echo from behind me, and I frantically spin in circles, but no one is there.

A whining cry breaks the silence. I whip around and point the revolver, about to fire when I see that it's Stella. She holds a branch like a cane, leaning most of her weight upon it, moving, with barely enough strength to keep herself upright.

"What are you doing? I Almost… I told you to wait. Save your strength," I say.

I run over, and she releases her weight into my arms. I lay her on the ground, wheezing and gurgling. She coughs violently, spewing up bloody mucus, and a small colony of Raxon depart with it.

"I heard a shot and…" she says, struggling to speak.

"Don't, it's OK. Don't talk," I say, stroking my hand through her hair.

I look around and listen intently for the man in the black cloak, the Guard, anyone, but I no longer hear voices or the sound of the leaves and branches breaking beneath their feet. It appears, at least for now, whether he is a figment of my imagination or not, the man in the black cloak has led us out of the Guard's reach. However, the gunshot will surely lead them to us sooner rather than later.

I look at Stella, struggling to breathe, and quickly remove her shattered mask. There's no use keeping it on. It no longer offers her any protection. Her breath is shallow, and her eyes are dark and sunken as though she were looking out through a mask.

"Try and expel them," I say. "Like I did in the car."

"I don't know how."

"Close your mouth and push with your diaphragm, then open and push them out."

Stella closes her mouth, and with all her might, she pushes. Her face turns red, and her eyes dilate. My eyes widen in anticipation, but instead of a colony of Raxon, she lets out a hideous cough. She leans over and vomits blood and mucus onto the ground, sending another small colony out, but as quickly as they came out, they re-enter her.

She looks up to me helpless, with blood covering her mouth, and although I am not ready to accept it, I know the Raxon are in their final feeding stage.

"I can't," she says weak and forlorn, clutching ahold of her chest.

"Please, one more time. Like this," I say, demonstrating.

I push from the base of my throat, using my diaphragm, and release the Raxon from my lungs with a puff of breath. A small cloud buzz out of my mouth, hover in the air in front of us, but before they can enter Stella, I suck them back in.

"I have an idea!" I say.

"Dylan, no. It's too late."

I lean in and whisper, "Trust me."

Our foreheads touch, and my heart sinks. I know she's right. Even if I were to remove all the Raxon, she would die, anyway. Far too much damage has already been done, but I'm still in denial and have to try. I move my mouth to meet hers, and I kiss her bloody lips. A tear rolls down her nose and drips onto the crease of our lips, pooling within our philtrum's.

"I have to try. Please?"

With my fingers on her chin, I prop her mouth open, and I suck the air out of her, attempting to siphon the Raxon from her lungs. Her throat oscillates, but the Raxon fight and cling to her tissue, refusing to release their deadly grip.

I release my suction and gasp for air and see I was only able to trap a small colony. I try again, but this time, I take a deeper, more robust initial breath in hopes the initial force will catch them off guard, sweeping them into my lungs. Moments later, I release, out of breath and unsuccessful. They don't want me. I am simply their carrier, not a host.

It occurs to me in this moment I was the transporter who brought them to their meal. I brought them to Stella, and I am responsible. It's true that, without a functioning mask, the same fate would have likely fallen upon her, but the thought I had played a role in her torturous pain and, ultimately, her death, is unimaginable.

I lean in to make a third and final attempt, but she halts me, placing her hand firmly onto my chest.

"No more," she says. "Just be with me. Let's just be together here, like we always were, there. Hold me one last time, my love. I hope you will see me in your dreams 'cause I'll be there waiting for you."

My eyes squint, mouth quivers, and I weep. My voice cracks. "No, don't give up. I…"

"Dylan, it's over, my love."

A tear streams down her cheek, and my heart reduces from racing to a slow thumping pain, taking my breath away. I press my cheek up against hers, and my lashes collide with her tear. It enters my eye, and her tear has seeded my own.

"Oh, honey mou, it's OK."

Honey mou? Like a wave of explosions in my head, I see a flash of images, but I now, understand them to be memories. I fight the urge to get sucked into the trance, to return to Stella in her final moments, but the power of hypnosis is too great.

It unravels like an old movie reel, and this time, it picks up right where I refused to continue the last time. However, as with many harrowing things, I can't look away. I need to see, to feel, to experience how our story ends. A viewfinder flipping through tragedy, I watch in horror, a beautiful life sink. I feel what he feels, and I suddenly remember. We are one, we are the same. Parallels imprisoned in opposing worlds. Yin and yang, interconnected, though independent of one another, we collide in our conscience.

I watch his world implode, beginning with the notorious Cunt Log, which, bizarrely, I remember writing at my desk, on my beloved red leather swivel chair. I loved that chair. All the events that led to my sweet Annabel's accident and Haley's ensuing guilt and inner conflict pierces my heart.

She has been forced to harness so much pain throughout the years. More than any child should have to endure since the divorce, and it led her to climactic agony, distrust, and mental distortion. She couldn't live with the weight of Annabel's accident, and she placed the blame squarely upon her shoulders. Sisters until the end of time, and time cannot exist for one without the other because each other is the only true and unconditional affection they had ever known.

I see our love and adoration for Ileana and how shattered we are by Stella's betrayal. The grief that accompanies the realization that Ileana isn't of his own making, and the uncertainty of whether anything he has ever loved has ever been real. Mountainous lies, cheating, abuse, and deceit hardened him instantly.

Our children were weapons in a war they should have never been made a part of. A war that should have never been a war in the first place, and it was our job to raise them into happy, healthy, well-adjusted adults. We failed them, Corina. Was it really worth it? Did it really have to be this way? Our children's mental health should've been more important than your scorn.

We didn't see this coming although we should have. The signs were there, and our ignorance was fueled by our resentment for one another.

Haley harbored so much conflict and at an age of innocence, she was tainted with the weight of her parents' conflict. We continued to build upon her burden, one block after another until she couldn't bear the weight any longer.

So much had happened so quickly, extinguishing all the light that was left in his world. Now he lives with the darkness in his heart.

A slogan stands out in front of my eyes and remains long enough for it to be read over and over and over again.

(ALTER-LIFE WHERE YOUR DREAMS CAN BE YOUR REALITY)

Suddenly, I am overcome with hopelessness. I am alone. I am selfish. I am ashamed.

"Sweet dreams, Mr. Grady," I hear a man say, and a glass chamber encloses around me.

Suddenly, like a computer, the window closes, and I am mirrored back to my reality.

I lay with Stella, curled up in my arms, and as if I never left, I hear her continue to wheeze and gasp for breath. She convulses, and when I look at her,

I only see the whites of her eyes, and I know. I know what I must do.

I grab hold of the gun's grip, and my hand trembles violently as I lift it up. I lean in and kiss her cold lips one last time, and my tears fall and glisten on her lips, and I listen to what would be her last breath. I force myself to squeeze the trigger, and with a loud *bang* that echoes throughout the dead forest, I watch her go into the darkness. Her lifeless body releases a haunting rattle as the Raxon scurry to feed one last time before the tissue is exhausted of life.

My act of mercy has forfeited my position, but I love her, and I couldn't watch her suffer. The Raxon swarm out of her mouth and nose like a shadow. They stop and hover in front of my face, and I open my mouth, allowing them to enter, just so I can have a piece of her with me.

I recall the memories, sifting through the painful images from my other life. An emotional journey to…to…ALTER-LIFE, WHERE YOUR DREAMS CAN BE YOUR REALITY.

This is my Alter-life.

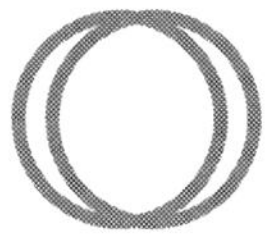

# CHAPTER 23

I look around and take in this dark, lifeless world with newfound understanding.

"I did this?" I ask aloud. "I want to wake up now! Get me out of here!"

My voice echoes through the bare woods, transmitting my coordinates like a beacon to my assailants.

I hear them now. They're close. I lean down, lift Stella's head off the dirt, and cradle her lifelessness in my arms. I hold her, still feeling her warmth as if she never left me and kiss her one last time.

"I love you, my sweet angel. I'm so sorry. I have so many regrets, but you should have never been one of them."

I hear steps marching closer. The crackle of the dead foliage reverberates in my ears. I press my back against the giant tree base, and when I peek around it, I see two men moving rapidly, hunting as if I were their quarry. Their guns are drawn, fingers anxiously gripping the trigger.

I mute my soul and desperately search for a way out. I have to create a diversion. I pick up the blood-spattered revolver and fling it as far as I can to my left. It sails through the air, snapping branches in its path and hits a tree with a *thud*. The trigger-happy Guardsmen simultaneously open fire, and I take off running in the opposite direction. With blazing speed, I sail through the maze of trees.

"There! He's there!" I hear them shout behind me.

I dart in and out of the trees and dance around the fallen branches when, out of the blue, a train whistle blares nearby. It nearly startles me out of my boots, and I slow to hone in on the *chug, chug, chug* and try to determine from which direction it travels. It must be a supply train from one of the neighboring Raxon free states. They are the only transportation allowed in or out of quarantine.

I hasten towards it, sprinting until I reach a clearing. An open field of dead grass and weeds that stretches about fifty yards is all that lies between me and my escape; life and death. What happens if I die in here? If I die in Alter-life, do I die everywhere? Suddenly, a bullet whizzes by my ear, and I decide it isn't the time to find out. I hear another shot and duck, slamming my foot down into the soft ground. It sinks into the sludge and sends me tumbling and rolling.

No longer shielded by the trees, I know I must react quickly. I hop to my feet and take off running for the train. I huff and puff and small bursts of Raxon heave out of my lungs. My heart rate rapidly escalates, reaching its full capacity, and the Raxon buzz, looming in my ears like nagging house flies.

I scan down the line of train cars and spot a flatcar at the end, carrying goods covered by a large gray tarp. There is a steel ladder to the rear of the car, and it is my only chance to hitch a ride. I've reached the train about ten cars too soon. Bullets spray the side of the large, metal shipping containers, prompting me to race down the line, against the direction of travel. My head bobs uncontrollably as the bullets scatter. My life has been left in the hands of Lady Luck to guide me to safety.

I reach the car in seconds flat, remarkably unscathed, and double back to keep pace. I struggle to run faster and see the ladder approaching rapidly. I will only have one chance to grab a hold of it as it passes. I reach my hand out and snatch the bottom rung. My feet drag on the dirt and rocks below, kicking up a cloud of dust as I struggle to hoist myself up. My muscles flex, but the sharp pain, where I'd been shot in my shoulder throbs immensely. The excruciating pain makes it increasingly difficult to hold on.

I strain, kipping my feet, trying to pull myself up when, out of nowhere a bullet strikes the car, inches from my ear. Metal sparks send my body recoiling, but the bullet ricochets and finds a new home, lodged into my right foot.

I screech in pain.

My body goes limp, and I hook my elbow onto the ladder. Dangling like a rag doll, my feet drop back to the ground and drag, pulling me down.

"I think I got 'em!" I hear a Guardsman celebrate.

They continue to discharge ammunition, and round after round, miraculously, they miss their mark. One more shot will certainly be the end, but with each bullet fired, again and again, they come up empty, and with each miss, I am reinvigorated with newfound determination to survive.

I grunt, managing to grab the second rung, and with all my vigor, I scream, cry, and pull myself up, utilizing almost entirely the left side of my body. With another scream, I swing my injured foot up and onto the car, squeeze my core, and with all my might, I launch myself up onto the bed.

I roll onto my back, wincing in pain, panting as my heart palpitates. My wounded limbs ache, and I'm rapidly losing blood. I feel the color leave my face, and I weep, and I realize I am responsible. I've created a world devoid of happiness and divest of meaning, and I'm being hunted by the very things my mind has spun to imprison me.

I close my eyes tightly and listen to the trains *chug, chug, chug* outrunning my adversaries. Their shots become distant and faint, no longer posing an immediate threat, and I reach for my wounds to inspect them. My sleeve is sealed to my arm with blood, and my foot throbs as it sloshes in a pool collecting in my shoe. I don't have much time.

Like missing pieces to a puzzle, it has all come back to me in waves, and I am flooded with a new appreciation for the life I once had, all that is real, and all that is of my own creation. This can't be how our story ends, can it?

Though, it is true, that worse things have happened to better people. Perhaps this is exactly what I deserve. I abandoned them, and no ending seems truer than for me to die alone on this train at the end of the line.

*

My eyes open, but all I see is darkness. Day shifts to night in a matter of seconds. Did I pass out? I blink and attempt to refocus them, but the blackness remains, hovering over me like a cloud. I rub my eyes, but blood from my hand smears into the crevasses, obscuring my vision. I grab my dry shirt and clear them as best I can, and when I reopen them, I see a face appear before me. One veiled in darkness, one all too familiar, a face I have known all my life.

He is aged beyond my years, bitterness written in the rhytids on his face, and I could trace maps of disappointment within them. His eyes have yellowed, and his teeth have sharpened, but above his ghastly physical appearance, I see fear, the ugliest of emotions. He couldn't move on from tragedy, and perhaps that is the greatest tragedy of them all. It put into motion a cluster of events that birthed a monster, and the turmoil enriched his blood until it boiled over and poisoned his soul. He let his weakness control him, and it manifested into anger and hatred.

Divorce littered his perfect life with provocation, and he allowed the shrewd witch to infect him and their children. She led them down a path, paved meticulously with her nefariousness. She had always been miserable and toxic, in marriage and in divorce. He shouldn't have ever allowed her myopic perpetual scorn to infect him because a diseased mind is hard to cure.

"You created this world, and then you destroyed all that was good in it!" I shout.

I unleash my fury upon him. However, I now understand I had a hand in creating this nightmare. I helped kill Ileana, Haley, and Jared. The man in the black cloak is me, I am him and, together, we are the two opposing forces that make up Dylan Grady, the light and the dark.

He stands massive, towering above me, and his voice bellows, a roar so deafening and powerful his breath punches me, rippling the tissue away from my face.

"I've paved the way for us to forget. To live free of pain and torment. To start anew in this world where we can be who we were always meant to be!"

I struggle to rise to my feet, determined to confront him face to face, but the wind from the moving train makes it hard to gain my footing. I grab ahold of the tarp and hoist myself up, finally free to see him for what he is. Composed entirely of Raxon, a lone face in a black cloud.

We did this. We are the darkness, and we are responsible for the misery because we are Raxon.

"Meant to be? Look at this place! This world is not a haven, it's a wasteland, filled with death and loneliness!" I say.

"This place has given you a home and is all you have ever known! Don't lecture me about death, loneliness, and loss. You don't know the first thing about it, runt!" His voice deepens, and he grumbles malevolently.

"Oh, no? You have shown me all I need to know. You have taken them from me and now...now, we are both hollow shells!"

The cloud shifts, and the Raxon comes together, embodying the man in the black cloak. A human form, though still devoid of humanity.

"I am nearly done, and then you will soon forget," he says maliciously. "We can then live out our life in ignorant bliss."

"Nearly done?" I ask.

"In order for you to forget them, I have to delete them all. Annabel and Jay still remain, but don't worry, you won't even remember they existed. We have our good Doctor Chowdry for that!"

"Chowdry?" I ask.

"Chowdry, our antivirus. He was installed to keep your memories at bay. He's failed us until now, but once everyone has been deleted, there will be no memories left to trigger. They simply won't exist."

"I don't want to forget them! What is a life if it's devoid of the people you love? If you don't have love? Or, or memories? Or even the pain you feel when you lose them. Well...then you aren't alive at all!"

"Nonsense!" His voice echoes a gust of air, and it pushes me back.

Seemingly all at once, I recall all the memories from the world we left. They are a part of me, and even with all the pain, deceit, and torture, I'd rather be there. I don't want to forget them. The good and the bad, the love and the hate. I know his pain, and I've felt his anger. However, without them, we divest ourselves of our humanity. A barren soul in a vacuous world.

"I won't let you erase them!"

He laughs boisterously with his hand over his chest, layered with ridicule.

"You don't get to choose! I created this world, and I alone can alter it!"

"Well…what if I choose not to live in your world?"

"You still seem to think you have free will. You haven't grasped the fact that, although we may be one, I and I alone am in control," he says.

We approach the beltway bridge, which crosses over the Harold River to enter the city. The bridge towers two hundred and thirty feet high and spans a little over a mile long. Countless souls have come here and leapt to their deaths to escape the Raxon.

I personally responded to many of the calls and rushed to the bridge, hoping to save them, but I now recognize they were dead long before they jumped. Dylan Grady killed them. Our mind poisoned this world and filled it with the darkness that had consumed our heart. A world created by a man who's forgotten what it meant to be alive.

We quarantined our soul, deleted everything that made us human, and hid within its boundaries an innocent. We are not innocent. I am the Alpha and the Omega, the beginning and the end.

I created this world, and now I must put an end to it! I won't be a lemming, controlled by the darkness that poisons my mind. I must destroy it, and the only way to do that is to terminate that which gives it life.

"You need me!" I shout. "This world does not exist without me. *You* do not exist without me!"

Raxon shoots from his limbs, surging to grow, sprouting like a tree. He is god of this world.

"I am this world!" he yells with a powerful echo. "And you are but one instrument in my orchestra! You will obey me once they no longer poke at your conscience. They are a virus! They make you weak! They will soon be gone, and then you will see how free you are. Only then can we rule this world as one!"

The train whistle blows as we enter the bridge, and I see ahead that our final destination rapidly approaches. I look at the vast river below, deep and rough. Raxon winter has changed the tides, and the river is choppy like the seas. Waves ferociously crash onto the shoreline.

It isn't suicide. On the contrary, it's an attempt to live. This world isn't real, and I won't be an accomplice to this nightmare. A world without their memory, without free will, love or consequence, isn't a world at all. With a gush of overwhelming euphoria, I release my grip from the tarp and dive backwards off the platform.

"Noooooo!" the man in black shrieks.

I free myself from his control, and as I fall to my death, I am finally at peace. I stare into his bitter eyes and see panic. I was right. This world cannot exist for one without the other.

I see the Raxon swarm and spiral together to form a massive ball, and without warning, he launches it towards me. A growing appendage sprawls and manifests into a massive fist, catching me and clenching my torso as if I were no more than a bottle of beer.

I swat and battle with them, struggling to break free, but it's no use. The harder I fight, the more Raxon swoons in to reinforce his grip. Hovering several hundred feet above the water, several hundred feet above our freedom, he detains me, trying to preserve the fate of his world.

Pain strikes my forearm hot, burning as though it were on fire. I peer down and see the veins in my forearm running black, like intravenous fluids tracing the branches of my circulatory system. I feel his darkness infecting me; ugly, sullen, and broken.

I'm whisked away into his misery, devastated with feelings of despair. I feel just as he did when he stood over Annabel in her hospital bed, and when he howled on the hospital floor as Haley received chest compressions. Hopelessness overcomes me, staring at the wires and tubes that sustain their lives. Breathless, my heart pumps blood throughout my body in powerful bursts, but I am drawn to the overwhelmingness that has hollowed my core.

I turn and see Corina. Her face, more wicked and sinister than I remember and lacking any empathy. She absolves herself of any responsibility for her part in all of this. She is always a victim.

"You did this!" she says.

Her words cut through me, and I am met with acrimony. She feeds negativity and breeds hatred.

Entombed in his grip, paralyzed, forced to confront these emotions. The pain is unyielding, but I fight the power of negativity and think back to all our wonderful memories. The beauty that fills our souls with warmth and happiness. I think about the laughter, the kisses, and the hugs. I hear them. Oh, I can really hear them!

"Daddy! I love you!"

Haley's face lights up when she saw me at her first science fair. I cheered her on as if it were a sport. I was so proud of her.

Annabel crawls into bed with me at every overnight, cuddling into the nook of my armpit. She wraps her little arms around me and refuses to let go until morning. Those were the best nights of my life.

I can almost feel Stella's touch and see the twinkle in her eye when she looks at me as though I were her Superman. She always made me blush, and my heart still flutters when I think of her. Our lips, magnetic, would meet often. I remember how true and deep our love was for one another. She was the one. She has always been the one. Two bodies with one intertwined soul.

I realize the man in the black cloak is struggling. Once all-powerful, resilient, and impenetrable, he now labors to hold on. His face is full of strain, and with each loving memory, the warmth in my heart rises, and the Raxon fades, combusting around him like shooting stars. As their numbers dwindle, so does the forsaken world around him.

I think back to when Haley and Annabel were young, and I took them to the park. We spent hours making jewelry out of wildflowers. Haley made a tiara and crowned Annabel Princess of Daddy's house. I remember with fondness how Annabel's smile warmed my soul. Oh, how Annabel idolized her big sister. I smile and let out a chuckle, and as soon as I do, the beast's grip loosens.

Ileana was born, and a second chance was birthed with her. Her little body lay upon the scale, and the hair stands upright on my head. A tear falls from my right eye, a tear of joy. A healthy eight-pound, ten-ounce baby girl. First crawl, first steps, and her first word: Daddy. She may not have been of my loins, but she is, and always will be, my daughter.

"It's a boy!" Little Jay, finally a boy to model after myself. It seemed like he took off running right out of the womb. He would always take off after a bath and his wet, naked little body scurries all over the house to avoid capture. A few more minutes before bed to release his ferociously boyish energy.

Finally, I am free! Free from the darkness that has riddled my mind. Free from Corina's narcissism, and free at last from my mind that has imprisoned me. I am as free as I allow myself to be. I have confronted my demons and defeated them with overpowering love.

My shirt flaps in the wind, and I realize I am falling. I set my arms out like wings on a bird and take in my last few moments. I'm not scared. I'm not sad. I am at peace. The Raxon clouds part, and the sun shines through like a laser beam. It hits my eyes, and I take in all its glow. I am no longer his prisoner. I have released this world from my affliction, and he no longer has authority over it. We are released, we are free, we are weightless, and I am me.

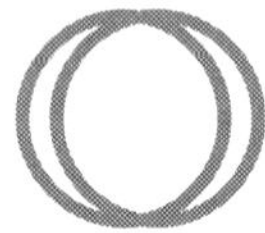

# CHAPTER 24

"Clear!"

Commotion creeps into the emptiness of my mind, but I'm having difficulty making sense of it.

"Again! Clear!"

A continuous *beep* rings in my ear, followed by a long, flat tone. Am I dead? Where am I? My eyes groggily creep open, but a bright light blinds me, compelling me to slam them shut.

The excitement resumes to my side, but I'm far too weak to move, too weak to care. If this is my time, so be it. Just let me be.

My head pounds, and the piercing racket continues to soar. I force my eyes open and struggle to adjust them to the glaring light. The liquid in my chamber descends, and I hear it swirl down like a draining bath. I squeeze my aching head and realize it is shaved. Wires attach to my skull, draped where my hair used to fall.

"Clear!" I hear again, with more moxie than the last.

I release back into the cradle and glance to my left and watch deliriously as three lab coats huddle around my neighboring chamber, working tirelessly to revive someone.

I remember these chambers, in a room filled with hundreds of pods, lined up and filled with lifeless bodies, each living alternate lives in their mind's eye. Back in the Alter-life facility but returned with a newfound appreciation for life. I only pray Stella and the kids will forgive me for all the pain I must have caused them.

One of the lab coats places his hand to his head, wipes his brow, and steps aside. My heart races, and raw power is transmitted through my body, and my limbs suddenly move in desperation, fighting the twitch of the Aqua-tens.

Her body lies in a pod, departed, arm slung over the side while physicians work tirelessly to revive her. With every shock of the defibrillator, she arches and flops lifelessly back into the cradle, and I watch helplessly as she lay, exposed and inert.

Stella was there with me? How did she? How could she? I watch in horror as my heart sinks into the pit of my stomach.

"OK, let's try one more time. Ready? Clear!"

*Beeeeeeeeep*———————-

They stand in silence and simultaneously release the same defeated sigh.

"OK, folks, there's nothing more we can do. We lost her. Let's pack it up," the one in charge says.

He turns around to face me, and I'm met with overwhelming familiarity, and my two worlds collide. Doctor Chowdry?

I suddenly gag and violently vomit gallons of the mysterious liquid that gave me breath all over myself.

"No!" I attempt to yell, but my voice is lost. I push, bang, and kick on my chamber, attempting to jar it open. I must get to her!

"Aaaaaaahhh," I manage to push out a hoarse scream.

Alerted to my awakening, they rush to my chamber and hastily punch in the code to unlock my pod. During all the commotion, they hadn't realized my pod's alarm had sounded. Perhaps they thought it was hers.

The chamber lifts open like a space capsule, and I immediately grab its side, fighting to pull myself up. The lab coats struggle to hold me down, but I fight with every ounce of strength I have.

"Stella! Don't go!" I shout.

"I'm sorry, Mr. Grady, we couldn't save her. She's gone," Dr. Chowdry says.

I reach out for Stella, but I come up inches shy of her arm.

"Bring me to her!" I demand. "Now!"

"OK, Mr. Grady, but—"

"Please?" I groan.

They roll my chamber closer to her, and the EKG leads rip from my body, and the distress alarms sound throughout the unit.

Weak and frail, with their assistance, I hover on top of her, trembling, hardly able to hold myself up. I grip her shoulders and shake her with all my might.

"Wake up! Don't you leave me, dammit!"

A tear releases from the corner of my eye, rolls down my cheek, and outlines the road paved by my choices. It winds through the rhytids and halts at a crossroad. Where do we go from here? We make our own path. It skips off my cheekbone and falls, glistening in the light and splashes, forming a miniature pool in the crease of her lips.

"She's gone, Mr. Grady, please come back to your pod. There isn't anything else we can do."

"Leave me!" I shout.

They struggle to restrain me, but my love for her gives me overwhelming strength, and I punch and kick as they try to pull me away.

"Give him a dose of Lorazepam! Stat!"

Before they can inject me, I lean in and kiss her still warm, seasoned lips. "Please, Stella, I'm so sorry, my love…don't leave me."

I've returned to the world I once abandoned in grief. Someone very dear to me once told me life is all about choices. The choices you make bring you closer or further away from things. All you have in life are your choices, and a single choice is all that stands between you and a new life. These are the choices I have made.

I choose to live in a world where they existed rather than in one of emptiness. I prefer to have loved and lost rather than never to have loved at all.

The Lorazepam kicks in, and my eyes close to the sound of *beep…beep…*

*beep...beep...* We are alive. We are free. We have been resurrected.

I don't believe in happily ever after, but I do believe that it is a choice, and one choice is all that it takes to change your life.

The End

# ACKNOWLEDGEMENTS

First and foremost, I would like to thank my beautiful wife, Elektra Seaton. Without her support and encouragement, this book would not have been possible. At times, I wonder if, perhaps, she may believe in me more than I believe in myself. Her ever-loving strength motivates me through everything I do. I love you.

I would also like to thank my editor, Tim Marquitz, whose guidance and knowledge has truly helped me become a better writer.

Lastly, I would like to acknowledge my cover and interior designer, Mark Thomas (coverness.com), who made my vison come to life and pop off the page.

# ABOUT THE AUTHOR

Matthew J. Seaton is an American fiction novelist.

He particularly enjoys writing science fiction. Writing puts him into, what he describes as, a meditative trance; a stenographer detailing the action that unfolds in his mind. He enjoys creating memorable characters and placing them within unique worlds loaded with drama, adventure and intrigue.

Matthew lives in New Jersey, is married, and has two beautiful children with another on the way, along with two dogs that fill his life with joy.

To keep up to date with Matthew and his books, please visit his website:

**www.alterbooks.com**

Made in the USA
Columbia, SC
18 October 2020

23038820R00162